NINA'S
JUST DESSERTS

A novel by
Diana Krause Oliver

Edited by Melissa Sue Marks

Maurice & Omar, Elsie & Mike my traveling companions and the loves of my life! With you, the world is home.

Special thanks to my dearest friend and editor Melissa Sue Marks for her painstaking patience, dedication, energy, and time spent molding my words to tell a better story. To Amy Nelson, Kathi Kouguell, and Elsie Krause for your proofreading eyes.

To Tali & Sara S, Olga & Valentina S, Beth, Steven, Mark and Alice N, Liz W, Elise D, Michal S, Patti H, Makenna & Eric K, Carol M, Marie K., Mark R.

To L & A, and all the years of insane drama, without you there would be no story.

Diana Krause Oliver is a textile designer whose passion for documenting New York City began in the 1990's when she recorded the mosaic murals in the city's subway stations. The New York Transit Museum exhibited her collection of artwork and photography in a show, "The Lost Mosaics of New York's Underground Subways." Diana published her photography in, *New York, Wish You Were Here*, through Schiffer Publishing which documents the neighborhoods of Manhattan.

Diana studied Textile Design at The Fashion Institute of Technology and earned a B.F.A. in Fiber Arts from Parsons School of Design. Her textile career has allowed her to travel the world designing for the apparel, home furnishings and hospitality industries. Currently she lives in Chicago with her husband music producer Maurice Oliver and their son, Omar.

To Contact: http://dianakoliver.com/contact/

"The Gifts"

It took a long time for me to see,
        the gifts I have been given.
It took a crack in my memory,
        to remember it all.

Remember, remember when I was small,
        the playing and pretending,
        the art that led to mending ...
        all those spaces... and it did.

Cautiously welcoming back,
        all those years later,
        the music, the art, the dance,
        the flavors, the visions,
        the thoughts of elation...

As I whisper, so hopefully...
        "Come in, and thank you for returning,
          the gifts I have been given..."

        by:
        Melissa Sue Marks

NINA'S JUST DESSERTS

PRELUDE

As the sun set over the desert sands of Morocco, a caravan arrives at an oasis hotel high on top of the hill, La Maison des Olivier is written in mosaic tiles over the archway.

Aziz greets us with peace, as we enter the Riad, "As-salam alaykom."

"Alaykom salam," we reply as we bow to each other our hands in prayer.

Aziz in white robes and soft blue leather shoes quietly leads us along a brick pathway lit by candlelight from dozens of cut-metal lanterns. They glow orange in the twilight and lead the way across the courtyard. Their shadows playfully dance creating tiny geometric shapes on the building walls. The walls magically turn from white sand to lavender then a dusty grey blue; twilight darkens quickly as shadows lengthen.

"We shall have the full moon tonight, and many of her stars," says Aziz as we pass a stone fountain trickling cool water into a pond filled with koi. The water reflects the blue of the sky. Exotic architecture changes colors. Aziz feeds the fish from some crumbs in his pocket. He calls them as if using their names. They scurry to the top, their orange and gold scales glimmer and sparkle. They kiss his fingertips. It is a magical place.

The gatekeeper leads us down a path through an enchanted garden. On both sides of the path are bushes of roses waist high in a variety of colors. Their rich aroma is intoxicating. There are rows of geranium so heavy with flowers that they cascade onto the pathway. Beyond the garden are the orchards of olive and lime trees that line the outer walls of the riad.

The suites are circled around another courtyard; their scalloped archways and wooden balconies are draped with vines of fuchsia and white flowers. Their scent sugars the air like honeysuckle.

Through a royal blue archway we are led to a restaurant outdoor patio that overlooks the valley below. Our table is waiting under a white tent. Candles are lit and the tent becomes illuminated as the sun begins to set behind the mountains. We order wine and I wonder who the handsome stranger is across the table from me. Why is he familiar? He smiles with his eagle eyes and takes my hand in his. It is warm and safe.

Our waiter brings a bottle of Champagne and pours two glasses. We make a toast to our marriage. A bell rings in the distance as hundreds of little sparrows take flight weaving in and out and making figure eights over the landscape. The sun finally sets, as the wolves howl back and forth between the hills. The evening winds start to blow over the desert sands. In the distance, we can see the spotlights illuminate the ruins of the ancient city of Volubilis. It is our destination in the morning in order to photograph the recently excavated mosaics.

Behind us, the crescent moon climbs into the sky surrounded by hundreds of tiny twinkling stars. Magic fills the air as the distant bells begin to ring, a train whistle blows.

CHAPTER 1 – TRIBAL ART SCHOOL

I take the stairs up by twos flying faster then the crowd, up six flights of stairs that takes me from the underbelly of Penn Station to the crowded streets of Manhattan, where the pulse of the city vibrates.

New York, just as I pictured it...

"It's a jungle out there, little lady. They will eat you alive just as they would piss on ya..." says the preacher/homeless man standing on a milk crate outside of Penn Station. Crowds of people pass every which way but he points a long finger in my direction, "You, yes you, be careful of the animals, a tasty young thing like you will be eaten alive!" He laughs and breaks into song...

"If you can make it there, baby.
You can make it anywhere baby.
It's up to you New York, New York..."

The milk box preacher has wild hair, madness in his eyes and worn and torn clothes that you know he slept in. I get close enough to give him a quarter. He smells like old beer and piss. I thank him for his advice, sense of humor and because he can carry a tune.

I love street performers and have a soft spot for the homeless. I repeat to myself - "There for an act of God go I."

When I first walked to art school, I took 8th Avenue, walking downtown from 32nd to 27th Street. Even at 8 a.m. in the morning, the bars were still emptying out spilling their debris onto the morning streets. Some men were wasted drunk, fast asleep, lying unconscious against the garbage cans. Last nights trash yet to be removed.

Prostitutes of both sexes were finishing up the night shift hobbling home with high heels in hand, heading to the meatpacking district or to some closet of an apartment in the village to sleep it off. On 8th Avenue, at 8:30 in the morning, people didn't walk they staggered.

I wanted to experience New York and all its culture but this was a bit of the creepy side of the jungle, at any time of day. Today, I switch my route to 7th Ave., for different beasties.

7th Avenue

Today, the streets are wet from a quick downpour. I had worked the morning shift at the bakery and was heading to my afternoon classes. The rain washed away the dust but left the city streets hot and steamy. Lunchtime in the garment center brings everyone out of stuffy factories and showrooms onto the street. Fur merchants and textile manufacturers haggled in Yiddish. 'Garmentos' and 'shleppers' are all out hacking on their cigarettes & cigars as they check out the young girls and gay boys heading to the Fashion Institute of Technology. The street is a cloud of steam, stale smoke, summer sweat and what passed as witty banter.

"Oh pretty lady, come on, lady, wanna see my fur vault?"

"I have the keys, wanna try one on?" They laugh and poke each other.

"I'll let you pet my fur? I know you're gonna like it!" They laugh hysterically jabbing each other.

"The best on the street you know, pretty lady!"

"Don't believe him, he imports Yak hair."

4

"Yak hair black and permed right Marty the way you like it." They all laugh.

"Your mother's yak hair," they are rolling in laughter. Nice Jewish men in yarmulkes, old enough to be someone's sweet grandpa, each trying to top the other with something repulsively disgusting to say? I pass the drooling Jewish men and come to the Puerto Rican section of the street.

"Hey mamacita, you looking good! Mmmmmmmm, pay no attention to the old men they fart dust. I have what ya really want sexy young thing. Right here…!" He points to his pants, jerking his hips in a sexual manner, very classy. He stands behind a flat bed of rolls of brightly colored fabric. I can't help but check out the fabrics, rayon soft and drapeable in rusts, olives, burgundy, camel, sky blue and black the colors of the new season.

"Ah… I do have what the lady wants!" I quickly look away.

"Come on, mamacita, touching is free!" I walk faster. "You're breaking my heart!" The Spanish men make kissing sounds and wolf calls, obscene gestures with their hands on their crotch.

"Wanna touch, nice and smooooooth," they hiss, holler and slurp.

I touch the beautiful satin rayon fabrics, cool and slippery like silk.

Licking their fingers as if they were covered in frosting that they can actually taste, they switch to Spanish and laugh.

"You're all pathetic." I swing my bag over my shoulder, hold my head up high and just keep walking. Everyday this walk is a part of going to school in Manhattan. Beautiful fabrics rush by on carts pushed by sweaty factory workers being let out of their dark caves. In New York, you walk fast, hold yourself strong and forge ahead.

Cafeteria Jungle

Lunchtime in the cafeteria, each major clings together and forms a tribe. Like animals in the wild we group in according to our likeness. As we work, eat, live and sleep together we start to look alike. We speak a dialect that only our own can understand. We dress alike, act alike, carry the same art supplies that warp our bodies and alter our gait as we mold into our craft and who we want to be. At lunchtime the animals, each in a designated zone merged together to gaze and graze.

The Fashion Design students are by far the most flamboyant. They strut in like plumaged peacocks (bouncing to the beat of Madonna's *Dress You Up)*. They are punked out with blue hair, arms full of bangle bracelets, cropped striped tops held together with safety pins, spandex leggings and high-top sneakers. They are gay and proud and wild. Seekers of attention, they are the loudest, jumping up and down from seats that overlook uptown 8th Avenue; the direction they all wanted to be some day to make their mark on the fashion industry. They are stars if only in their own mind and in their mind it was only a matter of time before they too would be the next Calvin Klein, an icon, an alumni, their dream come true.

Merchandising girls in their power suits walk in a military formation swinging their brief cases (to the sound of Hall and Oats *Man Eater)*. They flip their big teased hair to the beat. They adjust their suits; dressed in power red, ambitious blue or kill 'em black with big shoulder pads, synch belts and go get 'em pumps. They wear tons of make up to hide their bad skin and wasp nose jobs. They believe that you dressed for success and for the job you want. They all wanted to be buyers at Macy's or marry men who could afford their desire to buy clothes at Macy's. Seated in a row, their power suits adjusted, they snap open leather briefcases as if on cue. With man killer manicured fingers they sip diet Tabs, eat their lean salads and squawk like geese over the latest fashion magazines.

The architect students with angular haircuts take forever to eat their lunch. Before they can begin, all lunch items must line up perpendicular to the edge of the table (their horizon point). Cutting their food or adding condiments to a sandwich was done with precise calculation in relationship to what else was on the plate. For fun they built structures out of cups and boxes, stirrers and cards, what ever was available. Today they stacked sugar cubes, each adding another piece until the structure collapsed. (Talking Heads *Burning Down the House* aids their construction).

Next to them the advertising students set down their trays. They are living commercials with colorful advertising slogans on their t-shirts. Their uniform is to wear designer logos on their chest announcing their alliance to a tribe of polo ponies and crocodiles. They love madras plaids and often dress like they are ready for a round of golf. (*Everyone Wants To Rule the World,* by Tears for Fears is their sound track.) They are a hyper bunch, nervous, fidgety looking for the newest stimulant; they all talk at once, hardly eat and down a lot of coffee.

The Fine Arts majors dominate the table by the windows, (to a beat from Robert Palmer's *Addicted to Love*). They wear paint stains like war paint, dressed in denim overalls and button down plaid shirts. As the year goes on, the smudges and layers of color increase, buttons go missing, knees gain holes but the uniform stays the same. They argue loudly on who understood color and texture better, Jackson Pollock or Van Gogh? And what if anything is left of the New York art scene. I would have liked to be at that table but to be a fine artist you better have some family money to back you up. These were some of the trust fund babies slumming it on daddy's dime.

I pay a quarter for a cup of hot water and bring tea bags from home. I take my place at the textile design table after saying hi to some friends at the fine arts table. My lunch is bread, cut up cheese and an apple. At our table, we all have large portfolios and art bins that we shift around to make room. There is little intermingling in the cafeteria. One stays with one's own tribe. It is safer that way. Our group had certainly gotten smaller. By second year, so many had dropped out we were less than half of what we started with the year before. Deadlines and pressure were a constant; only members of your own tribe understood the struggle. (*Another One Bites the Dust* by Queen.)

The Textile Design students were wan-a-bees, somewhere between business-minded mathematical nerds and artistic painters. We needed to know the science behind our materials and work within the limitation of our industry. There were rules to follow when composing a repeating pattern to be able to print on industrial equipment. We balanced colorings on a color wheel based on a mathematic formula. Yes even color was taught mathematically. We learned to work within the boundaries of our industry but occasionally with the right teacher, there was room for creativity.

Our next class was Surface Design. Our current assignment was to create an impressionist painting and coordinate a printed textile that would act as wallpaper. We argued on the meaning of abstract impressionism, and what we thought the teacher really wanted from us. I had something already in mind, a close-up of geraniums done in a pointillist style with layers of brushstrokes. I ate my lunch from home, knowing I wanted to buy a huge canvas and I needed a lot of paint to create my impression of flowers and leaves. I could see it finished in my head. As the table talked I sketched out my design in my notebook.

Design school was highly competitive. As much as we were friends and classmates bonding together to get through this experience, we were all sizing up our competition. We were dedicated to our vision, passionate about our struggles, in search of our style, hoping to make a mark in the art world of Manhattan. It was exciting to be part of this jungle of creative people! When they didn't bite...

For the first time in my life I loved school and was good at it. I could take what classes I found interesting and even the classes I was required to take I found interesting. I had always hated school; I was a terrible student. I was unable to read well, did poorly on all tests, couldn't remember facts or names and definitely could not spell. In my head I switched letters and numbers and had trouble pronouncing words. In Catholic school the nuns just made you feel stupid. I remember the nun in 2nd grade; she said I was worse than her worst boy. I couldn't read. She moved my desk right near hers and started a line of desks and students. She referred to us as the dumbbell alley. I seemed to have a permanent seat. Nuns were mean and scary. Legend had it that they used to whack your knuckles with rulers if you got out of hand. I think the Pope made them stop. They wore white robes with rosary beads dangling down in case they had a need for a quick round of Hail Mary. Notes and snot rags were stuffed up their sleeves, a truly gross combination. Nuns like clowns haunted my nightmares.

High school got better but I fought to keep a C average. I liked to write but I didn't think I was very good at it. I excelled at art and photography and was lucky to have an art teacher who encouraged me to go to art school and learn a trade. The Fashion Institute of Technology was a state school that was somewhat affordable. I thought about going into photography but liked the idea of painting textiles even more. I loved to sew and pick out fabrics. I wrote a good cover letter with my application and talked about growing up just mom and me, how she always told me that school would be my way out and that with an education I could go anywhere and be anyone. I won a local scholarship, which gave me a year's tuition. When the letter of acceptance came, my mom and I jumped up and down and celebrated with Chinese takeout.

Two Chinese boys walked by in short plaid skirts, crisp white button-down shirts, saddle shoes and spiked hair. Around their necks were large crosses swinging off heavy chains. The Catholic schoolgirl look was in; it still sent shivers up my spine.

After Catholic school I swore I would never wear a uniform again not even a plaid skirt for that matter.

CHAPTER 2 –DREAMS OF A TRAVELING BAKERY GIRL

The Morning Train

The morning train bells end my traveling dreams, as they always do.

In the morning, there is no need for alarm clocks as the train keeps perfect time. In my small town, the railroad station doubles as a town square and memorial park. In the center is a gazebo where all-important events take place year after year.

Every Christmas eve the Catholic girls' choir would sing *Silent Night* in three part harmony, around the plastic nativity scene. The choirmaster was dressed in a red cape, the choir in matching red wooly hats and mittens. They were choreographed to sway back and forth at the most appropriate notes, every year the same six songs the same red mitten movements and happy parents taking pictures. When the snow fell it was perfect, like a Norman Rockwell painting comes to life. Through it all, the train would roll through town.

Every February the Mayor and his cronies dress-up in tux, top hats and tails for their photo op with a petrified groundhog. If he sees his shadow there will be six more weeks of winter. If he doesn't, spring will come early. It was pretty stupid but it meant a lot to the mayor and the local news people who year after year made this non-event front-page news

On Easter there was a plastic egg hunt for the preschoolers and some poor soul in a bunny suit gave out chocolate to the little ones as their anxious moms took pictures at $5- a pop proceeds going to the ladies club.

On the 4th of July, the boy scouts would march around town sticking little flags in front of every building in every flowerpot in town. The girl scouts would make a wreath to place at the monument to those who have served in the military. Both would march down Main Street proudly along with the volunteer fire department, the high school marching band, the rotary club and lady's club. The police would follow in the rear with their sirens whirling and wailing. The parade would end at the fire station where a BBQ of hot dogs and hamburgers could be enjoyed. On hot days they used to open up a hydrant to soak all the kids. It was such fun, but one year someone broke an arm and the lady's club put a stop to it.

In the summer the lady's club would hold their garden bazaar followed by their gala evening under the stars. Tents would be set up for the Saturday flea market where vendors could swap or sell their old and used crap. The next day the wealthy in town would be seated at white linen tables in their finest. A band set up on the gazebo would play some nostalgic oldies and the Italian Kitchen restaurant would cater dinner. After way too many drinks dancing would commence to a playlist from Doo-Wop days gone by.

Halloween would mark the fall festival to raise money for new Christmas decorations. The fair was my favorite. There would be a pumpkin patch, cakewalk, carnival games and a hayride. Year after year, it was always the same. Very little changed in our small town. Once, the ground hog bit the mayor, the band led the parade in the wrong direction, and someone got dizzy and knocked over the table of cakes at the cakewalk. Oh and one year, the baby Jesus was painted black.

My mom and I watched from the living room window of our 2nd floor walk-up as our tiny park transformed with the seasons. Mom raised me by herself for the past ten years. Our railroad flat was above Guy and Diane's Greek Luncheonette. Guy and Diane have also helped raise me and through the years fattened me up.

Every morning at 5:30 the Long Island Railroad heads east to start the day. As it rushes down the one track it whistles three warnings as it passes through the station. The traffic gates clang and bang as their long arms block the road and warn the cars to stop. At that time of day, there was rarely any traffic as most of the town is still fast asleep. Not me, I wake like clockwork. I can hear the train coming from miles away. I keep my eyes closed to hold onto my last dream and just listen until the train leaves the station. Then I open my eyes and begin my day. On weekends the morning train comes later so the town could sleep a little later.

From the east the sun comes up along the tracks. In summer months, the tracks glow a fire orange. In winter months, the tracks reflect an icy-silver blue.

With the sun above the trees, daylight creeps across town lifting a sleeping blanket. I love the mornings from my window. I watch the ritual of our small town come to life. Animals scurry, commuters hurry heading in all directions. The animals have their nuts and berries; the commuters their donuts and take out coffee. It was a mechanical dance of sameness.

The commuters arrive in a line of station wagons. Overwhelmed housewives, sometimes still in curlers, drop off their relieved husbands. The men kiss their women, kiss the babies, they kiss the dogs, and the station wagons drive away. Then the men do the meet and greet their friends along the way as they take their pre-designated spots on the platform. They dressed the same in their two-piece suits and leather briefcases. On rainy days they huddle in the station until the train platforms then they rush and en masse crowd the doors to get their good seats. This always made me laugh until the train doors closed. Then off they would go into the city for their adventure, leaving their families to the small town sameness and their evening return, when once again the station wagons would line up to pick up the men.

For years, from my window I would make sketches of the men running for the trains as the women drove away with the screaming kids. I wished I were a man so I could have a career in the city and leave someone else to be the housewife and care for the children. By the 1980s I realized I was sketching more and more women in power suits and heels vying for that opening train door. Maybe there was a place for me?

Currently, my brilliant career isn't as glamorous; I work at Roberti's Pastry Shoppe to pay for transportation, books, and art supplies. Dressed in my white uniform I quietly lock the apartment door behind me not wanting to wake mom who has another hour to sleep. I skip down the stairs and out the door. Diane and her sister Dolores are serving up coffee to the commuters. They wave me to come in. From the smell of garlic, I know that Guy is cooking chicken cutlets. He waves me into the kitchen and wraps up a sizzling hot cutlet on a roll, slathers it with mayo and adds a pickle on the side. I kiss him in thanks on the top of his head. He kisses me back, "Knock 'em dead kid." Guy has been like an uncle to me and his family has always fed mom and me with the leftovers from the diner. He knows chicken cutlet day is my favorite.

"Thanks, I plan to." I stuff the sandwich into my backpack.

My commute is half a block away. I run all the way just because I can. At 6 a.m. the doors of the bakery open to the public. The bakers hate to serve customers if the girls are late. So I am always early. By 6:30 I have made fresh coffee and set up the window with today's specialties. I say hello to the deli guy Ryan as we both unroll our striped awnings to block the sun from our display windows. Ryan has always had a crush on me, so I have been told.

"Wait here, I have something for you." He quickly returns and hands me a cup of lentil soup. "Itttt is Wednesday, lenttttil soup day, betttter tttthan oatmeal," he stammers and smiles.

I return the favor and bring him a broken black and white cookie. "Tastier than oatmeal!" It is our inside joke that anything is better then oatmeal. Ryan eats his cookie and I drink the soup for breakfast. We have known each other for years.

Being the town bakery girl, I know everyone and everyone knows me. No matter where I go someone points me out and says, "I know you; you're one of the Roberti's pastry girls."

I smile politely as I cringe with my celebrity status. As a 'pastry girl', everyone seemed to know my business. I long for mystery, I dream of adventures in a world beyond the train tracks far away from the sameness, the station wagons, the women's club and the Pastry Shoppe.

So, I enrolled in art school in Manhattan.

The morning shift passes quickly as there is so much to do. Hot steaming rolls line the wall in metal baskets. Hot rye, wheat, and white breads once cooled are sliced in a cutting machine, balanced in one hand and bagged in plastic and tied with a twisty.

I like filling the window and make room for the fruit pies oozing with berries that drip out of a lattice of sugary dough. I place them on a center shelf in the window, their sticky goodness shimmers in the morning light. There are deliveries to prepare, custom orders to box up and customers to serve.

By 8:00 the bakers, exhausted, bag a snack and leave for the day. At 8:10am Lannie Johnson, the crossing guard comes in for the usual lemon poppy seed muffin and black coffee with three sweet and lows. She buys a copy of the local papers and the New York Post. Lannie has bright orange hair that she tucks into her crossing guard cap. But at the bakery, while she eats her breakfast, her hair is set free. As I wait on other customers she reads her papers from on top of the ice cream cooler. Lannie always checks the obituaries first.

She shakes her red hair from side to side muttering to herself.

"What a shame, what a shame." It seemed she personally knew everyone that had passed away. Lannie switches to the N.Y. Post and laughs as she reads the headlines. "Homeless man sues city over alligator attack in the subway! Ha…" she announced as she picked poppy seeds out of her teeth. "It serves him right for living in the subways!" She laughs at her own jokes as seeds fly to the floor. Lannie is a dreadful sight but very funny.

I listen but never look up from my task. There is an art to stacking little chocolate dipped cookies all in a row into a perfect pyramid it takes great concentration. One wrong move and the pyramid collapses, than you have to start all over again. With my pyramid complete I pop the broken pieces into my mouth. Which explains the weight I have put on since working here.

Lannie stuffs her hair under her cap and secures it with metal bobby pins. She checks her teeth in the soda machines' reflection. At 8:25 she is out the door ready to meet and greet the Catholic school kids in their plaid uniforms, as they cross the street heading to Our Lady of Perpetual Help grammar school.

Like clockwork, Melvin is next. Melvin is a middle-aged man who every day greets the commuters as they wait for their train, rain or shine. He would advise the people of the day's weather and the headlines from the news. Melvin lived with his mother Sadie in their victorian house on the hill. Sadie's family dated back to when the whole town was a farm. The farm was sold at the height of the building boom of the 1920s. It was said that Sadie was quite rich but a recluse and never seen in town. It was town speculation that she was dead, stuffed, and sitting on a rocking chair in the attic of that old house.

Melvin on the other hand is out everyday by 8 a.m. to make his rounds dressed appropriately for the day's weather. Melvin talked to anyone who would stand still and listen. By 8:30 he hit the bakery. Today dressed in a colorful striped polo shirt and khaki pants carrying an umbrella.

"Looks like rain, don't ya think? You should have taken an umbrella! How about those Knicks last night? The Post says they dropped the ball? Yes the weatherman says it should rain, maybe by noon." He was hard of hearing and shouted as he rocked back and forth on his feet. "Sure if that weatherman isn't right, it sure looks like rain today." He had a nervous chuckle as if it were a great joke. It made strangers nervous. Sometimes he would wait for your answer, other times he just went on to the next victim and said the same thing. New people were his favorite. He'd sneak up and catch them off guard.

"Looks like rain, don't ya think? Gonna be a hot one? Weatherman says 86 degrees this afternoon, gonna feel more like 92. Yes it's gonna be a hot one! You'd think the rain would cool things down? But it never does. Nope, it never does..." he shouts. Everyone knew Melvin. He was the unofficial Mayor.

Day after day Honorary Mayor Melvin would hit the shops and stand around the platform tormenting the morning commuters. His routine went from the bakery, to the deli, the candy store, the delicatessen, the supermarket, post-office, bank and the public library. By 3 p.m. every day he would head home and prepare his weather and sports knowledge and outfit for the next day.

"Good morning Melvin, will it be a nice day?" I shout from behind the counter.

"Nice day! Yes, gonna be a hot one, don't you think? Maybe it will rain? Might cool things down? Might not?" He says as he examines the goodies in the glass cases.

"Cinnamon cruller?" I ask, knowing that is his standard order.

"Why yes," he says surprised that I know what he wants. He eats it at a side table; swallowing in one bite while powdered sugar covers his chin. I hand him a napkin. "Sure hope it rains may cool things down...!" He yells to Officer Nyburg who is collecting his free bag of donuts for the police department. It is an exchange the owner permits once a week, protection for a dozen jelly donuts, seemed like a fair trade. The local cops had this deal with many of the town vendors and were starting to get a bit round around the middle and having trouble fitting in their cop cars.

From the window we all spot a canary yellow Cadillac pull up in front of the store. All conversation stops as we watch Flo hoist herself out of the car. Officer Nyburg grabs his bag crushing the donuts and rushes out the door. Melvin has his back to the door and doesn't see what is coming. The other bakery girls quickly grab the empty pans and run to the back of the store, leaving Melvin and me alone to face...

Florence Petite. Flo, as we all call her, loved her bakery goods a little too much you could say. She is a delicate woman in some ways with oversized hips and a humongous butt. Flo wants what she wants, when she wants and can be a bit pushy at times. She is not very well liked in the community. With a determined look on her face, she walks her perfectly quaffed poodle down the street and into the shop. They both have a similar overbite and bounce in their step. Flo turns sideways to get through the front door. But she does it with such grace and ease like her mass weighs nothing. She is like a ballerina on point. There is a sign about dogs not allowed in the store, but that never stops her. She does as she pleases and most people let her. No one wanted to get in her way.

Flo's body is so unique that she has all her clothes tailor-made. Today, she is a vision in a purple and white polka-dot swing dress. Her dog, Tiffany the 3rd, has a matching polka-dot bow. Purple is their favorite color and like royalty she and the dog wear it proudly. I try not to laugh, as they do look ridiculous.

Melvin turns in horror to see Flo and stands frozen in fear.

"How is your mother getting on Melvin? Don't see much of her about? I do hope she is well. Do send my regards." She gives Melvin a discouraging snarl; "you have sugar all over your chin Melvin. You may want to clean yourself up?"

Melvin quickly backs out of the store wiping his chin on his sleeve. Left alone to serve the front of the store, Florence is all mine.

Unlike the other girls, I can't avoid her. She went to high school with my mother.

"Good morning, Mrs. Petite, how are you and Tiffany today?" I say with my best bakery smile. She taps a purple fingernail onto the display case pointing to the little chocolate dream cupcakes. "Are those the ones with raspberry cream filling? You know I tried the apricot ones and didn't like them as much, threw most of them away. Though Tiffany Diamond here likes the jelly." She snuggles the little dog to her face. "Don't you baby cakes?"

She suddenly returns her attention back to her pastry mission and leans in to whisper, "These are today's? Are they not?"

"Yes Mrs. Petite," I whisper back,"everything in the window…" I look around in case someone may be listening, "…is today's." It is our little secret. "I would suggest one of the pies."

"Yes indeed, blueberry." I grab a box and slide in a paper doily and a pie.

"Dream cupcakes, give me 6 in a box, no, make it a dozen!" she purred as she dances up and down along the counter checking out the 'treaties' as she likes to call them.

Tap, tap, tap goes the purple fingernail down the counter, as if to say hello to all her pretty little cake friends who smile back at her. I continue to box up the items and ring them up.

Mrs. Petite asked lots of questions in order to get 'her treaties' exactly as she wants them. Next to talking food, gossip is her favorite passion.

"How is your boyfriend, away at college again this year? I understand from his mother that the two of you broke up? Oh poor thing, I feel for you, you made a cute couple."

I tried to hide my inner pain as I tied another box.

"I guess its time to move on dear, clearly he has. My mother always said, it is just as easy to marry a rich man as a poor one. Find a nice man with family money I always say to my girls." Like Melvin she never waits for an answer. They just like to hear the sound of their own voice.

"Give me one dozen marble cookies in a box with paper in between. Make half with nuts and half plain. (Tap, tap, tap) Poor Mr. Petite cannot tolerate nuts. I could put nuts on everything! Everything I tell you…and are you still going to that dressmaking school? What was it called The Academy of …something or another? You know my girl does quite well for herself making my clothes. I guess we all need clothes."

I always did my best to divert her questions but the 'little dress making school' thing bothered me. We have had this conversation before. I tie the knots tighter on her boxes as we go along. I correct her yet once again, "It's the Fashion Institute of Technology," - she ignores me.

"Brownies and the éclairs are Mr. Petite's favorite." Florence eyes the brownies and licks her lips, "I'll take four of each. I just don't understand why a young girl needs an education? Why would anyone want to head into the city when we have community colleges right here on Long Island? I hate the city, too much commotion; people are rude and way too pushy. And what were you looking to do again, costume design, something like that? I was thinking about ideas for my dog the other day."

"No, I don't do costumes I do more graphic surface design" I say as I glanced up at the clock; it is 11:45, my shift ends in 15 minutes and the clock can not move fast enough. I tie up the boxes and count the cash into the drawer as I ring up the sale.

"...Well that's very nice dear, at least at Halloween, you will be able to make your kids' costumes." She counted her boxes quite pleased with herself.

Yes I was going to college to learn to make my future kids and her dog Halloween costumes. Seems she always knows how to say things that make you hot under the collar. It is her gift. I wonder if she is being condescending but I remind myself it is just her way. I bite my tongue to not say anything I may regret. I force a smile.

"Now speaking of Halloween I need to order a buttercream sheet cake."

At 11:55 the train bells start to ring. "I would love to but I have to catch that train." I motion to Lisa in the back, "Lisa would be glad to help you with your cake order and Mary can help walk your packages to the car Mrs. Petite, got to run" I say loud enough so the girls in back can hear. From behind the cases they snarl in my direction then switch to happy bakery girl smiles as they walk in to help Mrs. Petite place her order. In the bakery you learn to smile even if at the same time you are squashing cockroaches with your foot. I guess that was why everyone liked the bakery girls, as it was always our pleasure to serve you.

"Have a nice day," I yell as I run out the door grabbing two cupcakes.

"Regards to your mother," Ms. Petite calls out as she examines pictures of decorated holiday cakes as she and her dog lick their lips.

The noon bells rings in the town square, the traffic gates clang and bang, I have ten rings left to make the train. I stuff my white smock into my backpack, check out on the time clock and run to catch the train.

"All aboard!" yells the conductor as I fly up the stairs and onto the train. I collapse in the group seats facing each other.

18

After Billy the conductor punches my ticket, I hand him a cupcake. "Thanks, close one today. Must be Mrs. Petite's day to stock up." We laugh.

"How's Tommy?" I went to school with his younger brother. Tommy dropped out early from high school and had yet to find his way. He was a regular at the Bucket of Suds, a local dive bar on the far end of town. Nothing ever good came out of the Bucket of Suds. Tommy was a straight-A student but let it all slide for suds.

"Same old, same old." He hands me back my ticket. "What's Melvin say for today?" Billy stuffs the cupcake in his mouth and swallows in two bites.

"Rain, by noon, but it probably won't cool anything down." I roll my eyes and smile.

"Well, he should know." Billy makes his way down the aisle to collect a few other tickets. "Have a good one."

The train begins to roll. It rolls past the traffic gates that cling and clang metal on metal, holding back the noonday traffic. There are a total of six cars waiting. As the train picks up speed, we pass Lannie already in position for the lunchtime crossing. We pass the striped awnings of the bakery and deli faded in the noonday sun. Past Main Street where Melvin takes his position for the lunch crowd in front of the Chinese Restaurant. I reach into my bag for my cold chicken cutlet sandwich that still reeks of garlic and oozes with mayo. I take a bite as I watch suburbia pass me by. The cupcake, a little squashed, I always save for my 3 o'clock break. After a few more local stops, the train picks up speed and heads through Long Island. By the time we reach Queens the rain begins to streak the windows. At Jamaica we pick up more passengers before we rush to the island of Manhattan. As we descend into the tunnel under the East River it starts to pour.

Melvin as always, is on top of the weather.

At Home in the Land of Misfits

In the first year, everything was exciting and new. I now looked like an art student with my large black portfolio and backpack filled with art supplies and books. As the two years passed, my jeans gained paint stains and my hair grew longer I tie it to the side very French. For the first time I liked who I was and was excited at what I could become.

I couldn't get enough of school, I was in the land of misfits and fit right in. On the train, I could catch up with academic classes and study up on art history. Or plan out my art assignments in my sketchbook. Or just take a break and daydream out the window. I imagined having my own loft in one of the warehouses along the tracks. I promised myself that before I settled down with any man I would have my own studio apartment. I didn't want to have children I wanted to continue my education. I wanted to travel to all ancient civilizations that I was learning about in art history, and take pictures and write stories. There was a whole world out there with so much to offer.

In my Surface Design classes, I could use my imagination to solve problems and see beyond the norm. All over the city I was inspired by textures and patterns. It was like I had been blind and now I could see a whole new world. I experimented with charcoal and pencils, with gouache and dyes, with wax and clay. There were classes in nature studies, in the composition of still-lives and in the positive and negative lines of a human form. Art History I and II, literature, advertising, economics, and science filled my days.

The Fashion Institute of Technology was world-renowned. Students didn't just come from other states; they came from other parts of the world. They brought a perspective, influenced by their culture. I came from 25 miles away and brought as they put it 'local color.' They had apartments and roommates, hung out in cafes in the village where they met each other over espressos and cheesecake. I served coffee and cheesecake on the morning shift three days a week and always-on holidays when the pay was time and a half. They had money to buy antique rugs and vintage furniture at the 6th Ave. antique market. I bought only the necessities.

At the end of my day, I would rush out after my last class and fight the commuters who were returning to Penn Station. If I missed the last express train for home, my commute would take two hours. So as soon as a class was over I ran to catch a train. I could read and study on the train, or plan out my assignments. I'd paint way into the night. My desk looked out my bedroom window where I watched as the midnight train passed through the dark and sleepy town. I would then shut off my light and call it a day.

Friends Along The Way

My best friend was Clair, she was French and always dark and brooding. She could be the life of the party or fall deep into a depth of a dark depression. She had a sense of humor that at times could knock you on the floor in hysterics or cut you like a knife. Clair was the oldest and had been to art school in Paris. As she put it, she was trying New York on for fun. Her boyfriend Nikolas was going to school in America to escape the Greek draft. Nikolas liked to tell us that his name meant 'victor of the people'. As one of the few straight men, he had his pick of the ladies and was well 'victorious'. Students and or teachers, he flirted with them all and they all went to bed with him.

Clair prided herself on being very French. She smoked clove cigarettes that had a strange smell. She cut her hair like Cleopatra with long bangs that she flirtatiously flicked back, to show off her green cat eyes that she lined with black eyeliner. She was unique and I loved her style. By second year, Clair claimed she was bisexual. She liked keeping Nicki around as it allowed her to flirt with the ladies. And sometimes there were threesomes.

Over winter break, while I packed tins of cookies for the holiday crowd and worked double shifts, they had a threesome with a girl from the fine arts department. Clair told me all about it over the phone the next evening. As she explained the sordid details of how they painted each other with finger paint I ate an entire bag of broken cookies. - An entire bag.

Saturday nights we all gathered in the village and met up on 8th Street. Sometimes we'd go to see the Rocky Horror picture show. Clair would dress up like one of the lead characters and mimic the movie on stage. She was very good. We all dressed up as punks and cheered her on. Inspired by the dialogue we spray water, throw toast, and hide under newspaper. I liked the character of the butler Rift-Raft. I thought he was sexy in a ghoulish sort of way. She offered to fix me up with the guy who played the part on stage, but I was way too bashful and ate an entire bag of popcorn.

Tizzy was from Yonkers and frankly was out of her mind. She had found transcendental meditation, green tea and the teachings of Buddha. One semester she got us all to take yoga as a gym elective. She loved paisleys, fairies and guardians who looked out for you. She wore Indian dresses and braided her hair. She was born a little too late to have been a hippie. Her unique strangeness made her seem like she was from another planet. She dropped out before the end of second semester. She had a nervous breakdown after the class critiqued her work. Part of every assignment was the review where you had to go in front of your peers and present your concept. Good practice for the future I thought. But critiques became very clickish, as did the teachers; you needed a tough skin to not let it get the best of you. It got the best of many and only the strong survived. Art school in Manhattan was survival of the fittest.

Valerie had great talent and was one of the best. She wrote poetry and always included messages in her paintings. When she presented her work she took you into a dark place where she could see things so surreal. She took uppers to stay awake and downers to get some sleep. She painted her hallucinations. It had nothing to do with the assignment, but the teachers allowed it. She lived on coffee and cigarettes and weighed about 90 pounds when they found her dead. She died of an overdose, in her dorm room with a note. Her parents let it be printed in the school newspaper. I kept a copy in my datebook to inspire me to keep going when times got hard.

> *Days, I count these days by one,*
> *One, two, three,*
> *Stop.*
> *Tomorrow I say not days to weeks to months,*
> *Stop.*
> *Tomorrow I say with a smile.*
> *The end of a long awaited countdown,*
> *is here, is at my door,*
> *Stop.*

There were the debutants (both male and female) who just wanted to play at art and not be assigned to create art. There was Jill from Chicago. Her grandfather peddled art supplies from the back of a pick-up truck all around the Midwest in the 1930's. Her family now ran one of the largest art supply retailers in the country. The first day of school, she came to class with a deluxe art bin, more like a tackle box with six layers of drawers all stuffed with every art supply one could imagine. She had no sense for color or design and could never finish a repeat or complete an assignment. Jill left after first year. She realized she didn't have the drive to be an artist and left to work at the family business.

While she was in New York, Jill had a fabulous apartment on the Upper West Side. Her mother had an interior decorator design it as the perfect student pad. She threw dinner parties, with takeout food and wine and a score of cocaine that she shared with a select few on Friday nights. She had a maid who came in on Mondays and would clean the place before Jill got back from school. Jill slipped her an extra $50 once a week to not tell her parents about the state of the apartment on Mondays. Jill and I really didn't have a lot in common but she let me stay on the pull out couch some nights when I had early morning classes or if there was a transit strike. I often missed the Friday night parties as I worked the am shift at the bakery on Saturdays.

Jill had quite a cocaine habit by the end of her first year and was no longer showing up at school. Daddy cut off her ATM card and Jill fell apart. Her mother came to get her. She spent 3 months in some detox clinic under the palm trees in California. After that her family moved her to San Diego to manage one of the family stores. We never heard from her again.

Heidi Benz was from a wealthy family in Bielefeld, Germany, who were in the automobile business. Her whole family was in the business and it was expected of her to also play a role. She liked to draw so her father insisted that she learn a craft and sent her away to school in America. He figured if she learned about textiles she could be an asset to the company and be responsible for the interiors. She was not the brightest or most talented and really didn't care a lot about the 'auto mobile business" which she said with a heavy German accent. Rumor had it her father funded the new gallery renovations in the design library to get Heidi accepted. Heidi's real desire was to marry her childhood sweetheart Herman and return to Berlin where he was studying engineering. He would send pictures of the dream house they would one day build. He would go into the family business and they would get married. They each wanted three cherubic children and already had names picked out. Heidi was 22 and had her whole life figured out. It kind of made us sick, as married with children was not the prize.

Art Appreciation

In my second year, I had an in school boyfriend, named John Wayne.

John was from the land down under. He was awkwardly shy, tall and handsome with a great accent. John liked to keep our relationship a secret, not wanting people to talk. But everyone knew we were together and talked anyway.

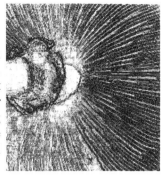

I had gone steady for three years in high school. We kept our relationship a secret. When my sweetheart Ben went away to school we agreed to see other people. When he left, I found out that he was seeing another girl while we were together. Rosemary earned the name Roamy for good reasons. By the first Christmas vacation we knew it was over. We slept together for one last time and broke up. At first I was pissed off, but then I felt relieved that I had no serious ties while I was in school. Going to art school was always a dream and I was now living it. Mama always said, "don't let some Joe stand in your way."

So keeping my relationship with John a secret wasn't so hard. He came in second year, missing all rules and formulas of the foundation classes. He was 32, a lot older than most of us. He was a bit shy, lost and confused. In my eyes, he was an adventure. He liked everything American about me. I loved to hear him talk and tell of his life in Australia. He would describe home with such love of the landscape and the traditions of the Aborigines. I could talk of Long Island… John was in the US on a student visa that would expire by graduation. Then he would return home and that was fine with me.

"Thus the perfect F- Buddy," as Clair liked to call it.

John was a straight man in an art school, a rarity where the desperately horny women outnumber the straight men one hundred to one, maybe more. On the outside John's persona was stoic but he was quite unsure of himself. He had come to America to follow his old girlfriend Sara Jane back to Brooklyn. They had met in Katmandu on a hiking trip and lived together for three years in Australia. She was still the love of his life but she grew tired of him and found herself another Australian man and moved back to the States.

She and John were still friends. We would all meet for Indian food on the lower east side. They had a strange relationship and I could tell he still cared for her deeply. She mothered him and bossed him around advising him on what to eat and what to do. He liked other people to make decisions for him, not wanting to be responsible or committed to much of anything. He had a difficult time making up his mind. Seemed her current boyfriend was very similar.

As a sometime boyfriend, John passed the time and served a purpose. Occasionally we would see an art film or get coffee down in the village. Neither of us had any extra money so we had to do things on the cheap. John sublet a room that was just blocks from school. He shared a flat with a gay actor above a discount clothing shop on 34th street. The place was decorated theatrically like a medieval Spanish inquisition with heavy wooden furniture, gargoyles, red velvet drapes and a giant wooden crucifix that hung from the ceiling over a platform bed. For all the red velvet, the place was cold and surreal. His roommate worked in the afternoons and I never saw him.

Between classes, John and I would rush to his place for an afternoon break. We would smoke a joint and get undressed. Surrounded by medieval furnishings I drifted into a trance, somewhere between religious experience and sacrificial offering. John didn't like intercourse, something about an abusive uncle, electric shock therapy, nothing he cared to ever really talk about. Unable to perform, his last girlfriend taught him how to properly orally service a woman. I was grateful to her as I clutched a red velvet cushion and tried not to scream out loud. If I did I don't know that anyone would have even heard me with the street noise below. John had learned this lesson well.

I liked having a secret lover; it was very Bohemian.

Flushed and weak in the knees, we would rush back to school in time for our 2 p.m. Nature Studies class. We would sit on opposite ends of the room and not acknowledge each other as we drew our impressions of flowers, bones or cut up vegetables. There was no commitment between us, it was just fun in the middle of the day. We met once a week and I was always more relaxed after my weekly orgasm. I grew to love nature studies.

"Helps to relieve my mind
Sexual healing baby, is good for me…"

Clair would sing in a deep voice like Marvin Gaye, as she'd pass my desk pumping and grinding to the music in her head, making me blush more.

"And when I get that feeling
I want sexual healing
Sexual healing, oh baby
Makes me feel so fine"

One rainy afternoon as we were rushing back to school John handed me a pill that read 714.

"Just try it, you'll see. It will make nature studies intense." He also handed me his Dr. Pepper soda as we dodged through the crowded streets of 8th Avenue. I only remember that we made it back to the school before it really started to pour.

Several hours later I realized I was still in the back of the classroom working on a pen and ink study. It was 9 p.m. and I had studied the under belly of a mushroom which I had reproduced in detail on an 18" x 24" scale. All those intensely beautiful lines one right after the other, filled the entire page. I remember at times, people had gathered around to see what I was working on. It certainly was an intense experience. When I realized it was so late, I shook myself and packed up my things running all the way to Penn Station. I barely made the 10 p.m. train as I craved mushroom pizza. As I ate my pizza on the train I tried to think of what had happened to the hours of the day? I did not remember anything, which scared me.

John became the dealer of these little white pills marked 714, until the school guards caught him with a locker full. He was expelled and deported back to Australia. Gone too were my afternoon orgasms. I appreciated him most when he was gone.

Packed Bags

One day at break the subject turned to summer vacation. Nikolas said we could all come to Mykonos for the summer and earn a living picking olives. He had an uncle that could fix us up. We didn't need much money and could live on the beach with the gypsies. The way Nikolas described it, life in Greece was carefree and clothing was optional. I tried to imagine myself standing in the wind on the top of Mt Olympus, among the ruins dressed as a gypsy with my boobs exposed, selling olives to the tourists.

Graduation was not far off and everyone was heading someplace exotic, except me. Clair would need to travel with

Mums back to France to attend the family reunion at the vineyard. After the freedom she had in America she was not looking forward to going back. She was considering coming back for two more years of study. Those with money were coming back; those without needed to find work. Clair was always recruiting and teasing me. "Come back to school next year and we could be roommates. I could teach you to come over to the dark side my dear. You won't ever go back!" Clair always made me blush.

As everyone at the table talked about his or her future travels and plans, I realized I had none. John and I had talked about going to Australia before the little white pills took him away. He never said good-bye, just disappeared and in spite of myself I missed him. Men in my life always did that.

Heidi was getting married at the end of summer in a castle on the Rhine and all she could think about was the wedding, the dresses for her sisters, and her honeymoon along the Mediterranean. Her mother had recently flown in to NY to shop for a wedding dress and now she was busy planning her fairytale wedding and dieting. Her heart was elsewhere and not in her work. She gave everyone a beautifully embossed wedding invitation of a castle in the clouds. I thought her head was in the clouds, but she was happy.

I was happy to be finished with school, but wasn't quite sure what was next. Home for the summer, most likely my adventures would be stacking cookies in pyramid shapes and tying up boxes. I needed a job and started to hunt the job boards. I ate my bagged lunch quietly as I listened to the table talk.

One of my electives was clear across the school in the fine arts building. It was a hike so I was always late. I grabbed my knapsack to make the run to my next class. I pushed my bakery uniform deeper into my bag. As I ran from the A building through the B & C buildings to reach the D building, the halls were abuzz with the panic of finals. Everyone was on edge trying to finish up the school year. I loved the D building for it always smelled of oil paint and there were large canvases thick with paint drying in the hallways and by the windows. Deep down I longed to be a painter.

I was taking a printmaking workshop, which I was really enjoying. The teacher Ian Silverman had been teaching the class for years. He was like one of the students, relaxed and fun in overalls and a white T-shirt. It was an easy two-credit course. Students from different majors were together creating art and it was most interesting given the same assignment to see what everyone came up with. We worked in different mediums while Ian went around mentoring.

I began to notice he was spending a lot of time with me in each class, asking me lots of questions about myself. A month earlier, as I dipped a metal plate into an acid bath he rushed to do it for me, not wanting me to upset my beautiful hands. It was an awkward moment but I knew he was clearly attracted to me. One day as the hecklers barked me down 7th Ave. I ducked into a coffee shop to get some coffee. Ian was with a few other teachers paying his tab; he paid mine as well and bought me a muffin. He lingered to talk to me and as we headed across the street, he invited me to join him on Friday for an art opening downtown. I said yes. The art show turned into Mexican food and a walk through Washington Park. He was easy to talk to and very nice. I liked that he wasn't like the 'boys' I had been involved with.

Our final assignment was based on dreams and summer plans. I had carved a woodcut of suitcases stacked on top of one another branching up to the sky like a tree. As he was helping me position the woodcut on the press machine he asked what it meant. I told him how I longed to travel, that in my mind, my bags were always packed. But like a tree, I am firmly rooted to the ground unable to move so the bags went nowhere.

He told me of his summer plans to fly to Paris, travel by train to Italy where he was renting a farmhouse in Tuscany for a month with two other teachers. The trip was planned around four artists who were each paying their own way. I thought looking at my print that he was cruel to tell me all of this until he asked if I would be interested in joining them.

"The trip is planned for four people. My friend needed to drop out at the last minute and we are looking for a fourth. The other two people are female. They teach in the fine arts department. The trip is based on art and painting. We are leaving two weeks after graduation. Wanna come along?" Just like that 'wanna come along' he said as if I was joining them at the diner across the street.

On the train home that night I stared out the window as we traveled through the stations and neighborhoods of Queens. There were just two weeks more of deadlines, projects and finals. I reviewed the list of things still needing to be done before the end of school. I sank down deep in my seat. It seemed impossible to get all of this done. I can count down the days in my date book again and again trying to see how to fit it all in. I take out Valerie's poem and wonder why she couldn't make it to the end. Why so many had dropped out? It had been a test in endurance.

Finally after two years I will be finished with school, but then what? My mom wanted me to go to business school; get my bachelors at Nassau Community. I thought of getting a job in the garment industry and start making money to pay back these student loans. There was so much to do, so much to think about; I closed my eyes, exhausted with my brain.

I imagined myself sewing in a tower with long swatches of fabric floating out the window. It was a race to keep making more. There were half a dozen fat kids scratching at the window screaming at me for cookies.

"No," I told them, "I have no more cookies to give. I have to make dresses now. Come back tomorrow, we will bake more."

Mrs. Petite with purple lipstick sits on top of a mushroom. She points a finger at me, "I told you so dear, you should have married a rich man. Now you are stuck in the tower, making costumes, when you could have been making me cookies and cakes." She shrieks wickedly and turns into an octopus reaching up to my window.

Suddenly, the train jolts me back to reality as the crackled announcement rings out over the speakers, "Jamaica, next stop Jamaica."

I have a little money left from my grandmother. I am graduating. I had worked hard. Why shouldn't I see the world? What was keeping me here? It was certainly not my small town life, or my dead-end bakery job, or a relationship that was keeping me put. When would I have such an opportunity like this again?

The train lulls me back to sleep…

...I imagined the morning sun of Tuscany, rising over the fields in the morning with the towers casting long shadows. Small town coming to life, birds signing, bells ringing, merchants taking down their striped awnings as the sun climbs orange in the eastern sky.

Monsignor Melvin dressed in a fine Italian robes tips his head and greets his parishioners as they enter his Church.

"Buongiorno, Buongiorno!" they greeted one another with big smiles.

I am at a table alone sipping cappuccino and eating sugared pastries that stick to my fingers like frosted glue.

"Buongiorno, per me si mette a piovere?" he rocks back and forth.

The bell tower chimes a morning song; nuns hurry up the church stairs late for mass.   Children with book bags sing an Italian song as they chase a ball with sticks down winding cobblestone streets. The baker gives them treats.

Monsignor Melvin rocks back and forth laughing, they all wave...

CHAPTER 3
– THE EUROSTAR

I am jolted awake and find myself on the Eurostar.

The conductor announces in French, Italian and then in English - "Ladies and gentlemen, our next stop will be Milan."

In France we pass stone villages, winding waterways filled with boats and barges along long interlocking canals. Farmers are still using horses to pull their carts. There are farms with sheep and chickens and fields filled with sunflowers. We are headed to Florence and it is early in the morning. The sunflowers are just waking up and turning their heads to greet the day. They are beautiful and I begin to appreciate Van Gogh's love affair with the flowers and why he painted so many of them.

I am spending the summer with three fine art painters. I will need to paint some sunflowers this summer. In two days we will meet up with the other professors in Italy.

Ian has been a gentleman. He took me to a three star restaurant while we were in Paris and we saw the Mona Lisa while at the Louvre. I bought a polyester red Chinese robe with an embroidered dragon on the back from a vendor in the metro station. Ian bought me perfume in the Galleries Lafayette, where we marveled at the Art Nouveau architecture and the stunning glass domed atrium. Paris is a romantic city at night with everything lit up and reflecting in the River Seine. Stuffed from many courses, we walk along the river back to our hotel. We were drunk from the wine and the beauty of the city at night.

At the hotel I take a bath and change into my oriental robe and spray my hair with perfume. I had hoped we might go to bed together but Ian spent two hours plotting out our itinerary. I fell asleep. The alarm woke us early and we were off to catch a train. I wondered if Ian would miss half the trip just in planning the itinerary of the next day. He was compulsively organized, lost from living in the moment. But then I did meet his mother.

Three Martini Lunch

Once a month, Ian meets his mother at the Plaza Hotel for lunch in the Palm Court. It was an opulent setting familiar to them, all new to me. It was time for Mama and I to meet. We were led to their usual table. Ayn said hello to the many people she knew, clearly this was her turf. She was gracious, a presence that demanded attention. What did I know about this woman?

Ayn divorced Ian's father when he was in his late teens. She married her second husband shortly after that. Ian said, his father was the love of her life, but he had a history of mistresses. The second time around she married purely for money. She lived on Central Park South with Mort Solomon who made his fortune in real estate. While stationed in Europe he bought art from the French salons. Ian said that Mort acquired most of his collection suspiciously during the war. He picked up impressionist art for a song when no one wanted them. There were walls throughout the duplex dedicated to Monet, Renoir, Cezanne, Picasso and Matisse. Their apartment had so many paintings that the once servants quarters were now used as storage rooms. Most museums couldn't come close to Mort's collection.

It was Ayn's mission to make the most of all of this. She was fixated on converting a mansion on the Upper East Side to house the collection known as the Mort and Ayn Solomon Museum. The city had its own plans for the mansion and wanted her to consider converting a factory warehouse in Soho. She was not interested in urban renewal on her dime. She felt it was a terrible idea to build her museum in a desolate area like SoHo. Ian tried to convince her of the merit of building in the heart of the art community.

"Well you may enjoy being around these abandoned neighborhoods but it is not my mission to revitalize the bums and homeless."

Married to Mort had given his mother great wealth and great power. She waved these around as easily as her Hermes silk scarf. Ayn had changed her name from Ann Lynn and lost her South Carolina accent when she moved to New York. After divorcing her first husband, she worked as a secretary for Mort's firm and worked her way up. Now she was his wife and partner in real estate developments. The press often described Mort as a tight-fisted penny-pincher. They described her as the Queen. Mort was a simple man and as much as 'The Queen' tried to spread her airs, Mort grounded the operation. It was a battle of personal humiliation but she wore it well and used it always to her advantage.

Ian said he heard from the maid that Mort traveled to Harlem to buy dented cans of food at a discounted price. He shopped at the Salvation Army while his wife ran up her accounts on 5th Avenue. Ayn splashed their wealth with fabulous designer fashions she wore to charitable lunches. She dropped names, only the best.

"Have you heard...? ...Jackie and the Landmarks Preservation Committee... such a noble cause to preserve buildings like the Grand Central Terminal. It was such a loss when the original Pennsylvania Station came down."

"Diane's new line is simply divine... Why, what that woman can do with a swatch of polyester and turn it into the cutest little wrap around dress... genius, simple genius, I have several." She picked up her fork and pushed her food around her plate, she kept on talking.

"**The Donald's** buying the Plaza, have you heard? His wife Ivana has done wonders with the Taj Mahal in Atlantic City. She's an ambitious cookie! Still, all that glitters is not gold. It is said he keeps a mistress in Atlantic City, some Georgia Peach, which is why he needs a project for Ivana back in New York City. The Donald is an arrogant, obnoxious man; his drug is attention. One day he will have his name in big letters over every city, in the country - mark my words! He has the leverage and chutzpah to pull it off."

Ian muttered under his breath, "Maybe one day he will run for President?"

"Don't be absurd… maybe, if he can't be King! I do so admire a man with ego," Ayn said laughing as someone came to the table to take a photo. It was just another opportunity for her picture to appear on the society pages. Ian and I were asked to lean out of the picture frame.

Half way through lunch and on to her second martini she stopped talking about herself and her fabulous friends and switched the subject to Ian.

She had definite opinions of what Ian could and should do with his life. Clearly he was not living up to his capabilities, unlike his brother the doctor who was expanding his practice.

"Why an artist?" she asked the sky, as if it were some new decision that he had just made. "He could have been so much more…he has a brilliant IQ. All the men in his family were brilliant successful doctors. None chose academia; you can't make a fortune teaching." She said to the empty chair across the table.

"I love teaching, Mother," Ian must have been defending this career for quite some time. I could hear it in his voice.

"You should seek more commissions. I have a great PR person who could get you some recognition. You need to get out more. There is a party on Friday at the MET you should attend with me, and Mort will be out of town and…"

"No Mother, I have plans for Friday night."

"Plans… whatever happened to your book? He wrote a brilliant thesis on mobile sculptures or something like that. You were going to turn that into a book. What ever happened to that?" The Southern drawl came out as the martinis went in.

Ian stared nervously shaking his leg under the table. "My thesis was on kinetic art and Alexander Calder. And no it is not in my plans right now to turn that into a book. I am working on some new pieces."

"Pieces? Those hanging things you call art, I just don't understand that. Pieces? I liked it better when you sculpted those shapes. I just wish you would work on a bigger scale. I declare make a statement! It is all well and good but you need to make a mark, Darling, before you run out of time. You know you are not getting any younger," she took a breath.

There was silence.

"Mother, you are the executor of such a massive collection of art and yet you know so little of the lives of those who dedicate themselves to be an artist. Would Gauguin have been such a prolific artist if he did not give up his business and family to paint? And Van Gogh, he lived a hermit's life in the south of France in order to create a body of work. Artists are dedicated to their work. They would gladly starve to continue to work. I have a job, a nice apartment. I enjoy working on my 'PIECES' in my studio! I do not seek publicity to do what I do." Ian pushed his plate away, clearly no longer hungry.

I continued to eat my grilled shrimp salad as the food was expensive and I was not going to waste such a good meal. Their banter was entertaining in a sick way.

Ian's anger calmed her down, but she continued, "What about that gallery in New Jersey that Mort suggested last fall? These mobiles are simply clutter that hangs from wire waiting for the wind to blow. I just don't get it? Not everyone understands the art of your mobiles, Darling."

"I don't care what others think, Mother and I am not interested in showing my work in New Jersey, Mother. Can we change the subject?"

"Really, you need to work the art scene, not just the student registrar." She looked at me. "No offense dear," she said as Ian rolled his eyes. After a while, I excused myself and hid out in the bathroom talking at length to the attendant and sampling the perfume displayed on a gold leaf vanity. It smelled musky like old ladies and for this she wanted a tip. I told her I'd be back.

Eventually, Ayn and Ian tired each other out. She was finished for the day and had scheduled a massage after lunch. She ordered another martini. Ian and I also had another drink as well. In truth, she barely acknowledged that I was there. When I tried to speak she just cut me off with a wave of her hand. So I sat quietly and ate my ridiculously priced but very delicious meal. Clearly I was just another student of interest, just another summer vacation in a long line of students and summer vacations. If she could have, she would have waved over the waiter to remove me like the uneaten food on her plate.

"Take her away and bring me another dry martini." I thought I heard her say.

"Mother that would make this a three martini lunch." Ian noted.

"Since when do we count Darling?" Ian ordered another drink as well.

She reapplied her red lipstick and powdered her nose. At the end of lunch she slipped Ian a check under the table. "Here's a little something Darling, tell me about your trip." He thanked her and stuck the check into his vest pocket and told her of his plans. She loved Venice when she and his father traveled there in the 40s you could tell she was melancholy remembering her first husband with a tear in her eye. But she shook off her memory as she pushed herself away from the table. Just like that the lunch was over.

Ian kisses both her cheeks. She made kiss noises in the air with those red lips. He hurried us out the door. He hailed her a cab sending her on her way. After he waved goodbye, his body slouched over as if in pain. We walked to Penn Station where I caught a train. Ian caught a cab to his therapist before going home to get drunk. It was part of the ritual.

By 9 p.m. when I called him up, he was intoxicated, as he detoxed from his mother.

"So why do you agree to meet for lunch once a month if it upsets you so? I understand now why you have been in therapy. "That was brutal. Was the money really worth it?" I asked.

Ian had spent a decade in therapy and simply says as if memorized from rote, "Allow me to accept the things I cannot change, the courage to change the things I can and the wisdom to know the difference. This is my mother. I cannot change her I can only change how I let her make me feel." I can hear the ice clink in his glass. "My mother is disappointed at her choices in life, in the men she has married. She loves me in her own bitter way. Besides, what point would there be in not taking her money? They have more than they know what to do with. Mort has no children so someday I will inherit a fortune that I don't even want. My therapist says it takes away from my motivation but at least I get paid for taking the abuse. If all mothers paid you for their abuse it would be less painful."

Somehow I didn't think so. As much as his mother hated his summer vacations she paid him to take them. So with money in hand he headed to Europe, she headed to the Connecticut estate. In the fall they would return to resume their ritual lunch dates.

The Art of Mobiles

My mother worked as a secretary for the school board. She worked her way up to administrator. She ran the place after 14 years. On weekends she sold Mary Kay cosmetics and took business classes at the community college until she received her degree. She will tell you that Mary Kay saved her life, or at least gave her back a life. She loved how makeup and a positive attitude could bring out the beauty in people. Much to her disappointment, I hardly wore makeup.

She raised me on her own and managed remarkably well. My father died when I was still in grammar school. He was a roofer and had his own business. Mom had to sell the house, her fancy car, furs and most of the furniture. We moved to this 3rd floor apartment a few years later. Mom had a boyfriend for years but wouldn't think about marrying until I was finished with school. There are so many things she had missed out on being a responsible mom.

I brought her to Ian's to meet him. He made dinner. She enjoyed Ian who is closer in age to her than to me. He made a Greek dish and they talked about marinades and the dishes they liked with eggplant. I hated eggplant and just picked at my food. After dinner, Ian played the piano, a medley of show tunes. My mother turned the pages and sang along as I did the dishes and thawed the ice cream.

Ian's mobiles hung all over the apartment. Each had a theme. Over the piano the mobile had tiny instruments hung from fine wires. The effect looked like a chandelier. Ian explained that it was divided between brass, wind, and percussion instruments. In the kitchen over the table that looked out into the street was a mobile of twisted forks and spoons that flickered and clanged like a wind chime when the wind blew from the open window. In the bathroom there was a mobile of little yellow squeaky ducks. He had walls of books, walls of records, a wall of photo albums from every past trip dating back to when he was nine. An organized pack rat, everything was alphabetized and in order, including his spices.

Ian was married once, briefly. He had a string of short affairs and a number of female roommates. His father was a doctor and taught Ian how to be organized. His brother followed in his father's footsteps. Much to his parents' chagrin, Ian wanted to go to school to paint. They sent him to Harvard insisting that he would like law. After college, against his family's advice, he had spent two years in the Peace Corps and traveled through India. When he returned to New York he started teaching. Now he had tenure. Twelve years ago, his father paid for the key money to get him into a rent-stabilized two-bedroom apartment in the heart of Greenwich Village.

At 39 he was completely grey and completely settled in his ways. He talked about wanting to get married and starting a family but he always chose bohemian women who were too young, too adventurous to be ready to settle down. He had a comfortable lifestyle and didn't have much motivation because he didn't need much more then he already had. On some level this really upset him and so he spent years analyzing all of this in therapy.

One Saturday afternoon I met Ian in the city and he took me to see his work. Ian shared a loft studio with a college friend Marco in an old factory building on the Bowery. His space looked out over the street. On benches, there were drunks and junkies fast asleep leaning on garbage bags filled with their belongings. There was a grimy looking tattoo parlor, an Irish pub with black windows that smelled of stale beer and piss, prostitutes on the far corner and graffiti covered everything. Ian felt creative here.

By morning the sun shone through the large windows making his artwork come to life. He worked in aluminum mostly and cut up shapes, which he painted with metallic colors. He collected miniature objects that were stored along a floor to ceiling wall of plastic bins. Each was labeled accordingly A for animals: domestic and wild, automotive, aviation, balls, bodies, bolts, candy, coins, dolls, doorknobs. The wall went on and on endlessly to the back of the hallway. He showed me how he would tie these tiny objects to fine wire and secure it to a base allowing the objects to float in air. I spent the day on his futon watching as he worked on a piece of colored plastic triangles we had bought earlier on Canal Street. He drilled small holes through the plastic and tied the pieces to long strands of wire. Once assembled, the light reflected off of the colored triangles and like a prism refracted a rainbow that shimmered against the white walls. It was truly magical.

He was a series of contradictions ridged yet wanting to be a Bohemian. He needed great order and logic, a steady job, a secure apartment, and a live-in girlfriend. He longed to be respected as a real artist but didn't like to play the art scene game. He divided his friends amongst the teachers with whom he worked and the members of his therapy group who had been together meeting once a week for the past fifteen years. He talked about his therapist as if he were a best friend and the members of his group as if they were family.

After working for a few hours drilling holes into plastic he got horny. I both admired him and felt sorry for him. Although he was my teacher, we had sex on the futon, awkwardly. It was all over quickly and he seemed satisfied. I dressed feeling a bit confused wondering if this was legitimately an encounter or just a drive by? The only thing fun was watching the mobiles float in the breeze above our heads throwing colored lights around the studio. On a vintage Victrola a record playing crackled.

My thoughts return to finishing washing the dishes. I join Ian and my mom by the piano; the music had shifted to Beatle tunes. My mom knew all the words and they both sang along. I drank wine and soaked in the bizarreness of the situation. Ian was 19 years my senior, the same age as my mother. I wondered why they weren't dating? He had his charms and my mom seemed to enjoy his company. After the sing along, he took out his maps and showed my mom our itinerary, pictures of the farmhouse we were staying at and talked about the background of the other two women who would be joining us. How we each would have separate bedrooms and dedicate our time to visiting museums and making art.

On the way back home mom took the Battery Tunnel and drove along the Belt Parkway through Brooklyn. It had become a beautiful night the lights of the Verrazzano Bridge reflecting on the water like a diamond necklace. Barges heavy with cargo lined up waiting to enter the harbor. Driving further we pass the train yards and the tall attractions of Coney Island glowed in their neon lights.

"It is an opportunity of a lifetime," I plead my case. "Good jobs will be there when I return." She agreed. I had a small inheritance from my Grandmother that was mine upon graduation. We agreed that I could take half of it and spend the summer in Europe. My mom's advice was to enjoy the summer and make sure I had set something aside if I needed to come home.

"And Nina," my mother said very seriously as we stopped for traffic, "if things don't work out, you can always come home.

Saturday Night Live

There was much to plan and organize. The following week I caught up with some old friends.

Saturday Night Live! The TV flashes pictures of New York, the Statue of Liberty under renovation surrounded by scaffolding. The camera pans uptown, to 30 Rockefeller Plaza, Studio 8H and the SNL opening credits. The guys laugh hysterically as they light up another joint and pass it around the living room.

It's like the old days and my friends have gathered to make food, get high and watch SNL. It had been almost a year since we all got together. Most of the guys were older and had been away at school. Everyone was around this weekend. It was 'make your own pizza night'. Since high school Saturday night was open house at Cori's house. Cori's parents were divorced. His father spent the weekends with a girlfriend on Fire Island, so the house was ours.

He called our little group the 'cook and fry club' or the 'cook and get high club'. When we were all in high school we would meet on Saturday nights. Cori was an honor student, went to Yale for chemical engineering, but had dropped out his first semester. He wanted to be a chef and open his own restaurant. He was working in midtown as a busboy and looking into culinary school.

Cori chose the menus and took the money his father left him to buy supplies. 'Make your own pizza', was a crowd favorite.

Everyone brought something. Either you cooked, or you brought beer and smokes. We piled our goodies on the kitchen table as he took inventory; cheeses, pepperoni and ham, onions and peppers, pear and pineapple, wine and a seven layer cake that got smashed on one side from the bakery. The joint was passed around as we tuned in to watch *Saturday Night Live*. From the first show we were hooked and tried not to miss a weekend of getting together but that was when we were all back in high school.

Like the show, it was another new season for all of us. A cast change seemed to have changed the show and we weren't sure it was for the best. We were a bit awkward, getting to know each other again after time apart. After the first joint circled the crowd, it was like old times. Seemed everyone had a story of where he or she had been and what he or she had done. A few of us wintered in town, got jobs, went to community colleges. Our stories were short and not so adventurous. For those who had gotten away, small town USA was now dreadfully boring. On that we all agreed.

In high school we all had big dreams of what our lives would be. The guys were a year or two older and left first. They were off to become doctors, biochemists, environmentalists and acclaimed lawyers. They left with strong determination for a future of riches and fame. They were masters of their universe, with a million opportunities within reach to change the world, but college wasn't what they had thought. Some failed out. Others just dropped out pursuing careers in sex, drugs and rock and roll. Middle class suburbanites, they were pampered and spoiled; now they had to maintain jobs and make grades. I looked around the room; all but a few were still in school.

"Yeah we're freaken funnier than the guys on this season! We could write better comedy then this crap! We should become writers, go to Hollywood and make millions!" Jimmy said as he tried to not cough the last hit he had just taken.

"Yeah, a mill for you, a mill for you and one for me," Don passes out tissues as if they are cash. We all laugh.

Jimmy grabbed the remote control as if it were a microphone, "I would like to thank the little people of the 'Cook and Fry Club', who gave me my inspiration. Without them I would be nothing!"

"Jimmy, you are one job short of working at the 7/11, you are nothing!" we laugh some more.

My old boyfriend Ben shows up late with Romey on his arm. I knew Romey had always had a crush on Ben. Even while we were dating she flirted openly with Ben. I was jealous but Ben said I was imagining things. Here years later they are still together. She sat on Ben's lap as if there were no other seats. Her short skirt up to her ass, even he yanks it down.

"Such a lady…" Jackie says in my ear as we head into the kitchen to see what the real girls were doing.

"She'll drop a litter before he knows what hit him." We head to the kitchen. "He wont even know what hit him." We laughed.

"Yus would think that college didn't smarten up any of them's assholes." Jackie grew up on Long Island but talked like she worked on a loading dock in Brooklyn.

"Yeah, jerks will be jerks…" The girls laughed.

"Soooooo, have you made up your mind? Are you going to Europe?" asked Ann.

"Europe?" the girls ask.

"…With the older art professor?" Ann tells all.

"Yeah, I have my passport and plane tickets. We leave in less then a week. There are two other women painters as well. We will share a farmhouse in Tuscany for a month. I can't believe it." I said and passed the Blue Nun wine.

Jackie ate another slice of pizza; all that was left was ham, pear and pineapple.

"You know, this is really good." Jackie said with her mouth full. "Do it man, I would! Whad'ya gonna do hang out with these stoners and work at the bakery? No man, run like the wind. Run like hell!"

"Just don't fall for some hot Italian lover and never come back!" Cori said as he entered the kitchen. He knew me the best.

"I promise nothing." We laugh.

CHAPTER 4 – A TUSCAN FARMHOUSE

Ian, fluent in Italian, ushers our bags and me through the majestic Milan train station. We peek inside the Orient Express on our way to board our next train.

"A journey into another world," he reads in English as we settle into the compartment on our train. We can still see the Orient Express across the platform. "Romance, excitement and pure pleasure are all bound up in journeys that link the great European cities like Paris, Innsbruck, Istanbul and Venice. The adventures of celebrated historic personalities are still palpable today, original 1920s carriages with Lalique glass panels, wood burning stoves and magnificent Art Deco details."

"It is beautiful," I say as I try to snap a few pictures, I love trains."

"Venice... Yes, Venice! It wouldn't be but a day trip by car", Ian dives deep into his traveling bag getting upset with himself when he can't find what he is looking for. He pulls out his notebook and calculator and within an hour he has plotted miles, cost of gas and found where the Michelin guidebook said was best to eat and where to stay. I look out the window at the beautiful farmlands filled with sunflowers. He unfolds a map, blocking out the view.

Driving down a bumpy dirt road, we put down the map as we are faced with a fork in the road. We take the left and follow the road down to a makeshift wired gate. A small ceramic sign reads Casa Solo. Ian gets out of the car following his written instructions. He pulls out one of three keys, and tries it in the lock. It opens.

He runs back to the car all excited, "This is like a treasure hunt!" he declares. It is.

Casa Solo is a farmhouse built in the late 1700s. The building is ochre and blends in with the colors of the ground. It sits on a small site next to an old tree and is nestled between the grape and olive vineyards. It is tranquil and serene, picture perfect in every way. Another skeleton key opens the heavy wooden door with a creak as we enter the main room. It is musky and old. We move the white curtains and unlatch the windows for some fresh air. There are two couches and side chairs covered in white sheets. There is a potbelly stove and a small library filled with English books and magazines. Around the room there is a cement trough.

"Look a trough to feed the animals! This had to have originally been the barn and the family must have slept upstairs." We agreed that seemed a bit 'icky' but everything was clean and remodeled. The building belonged to a teacher from England who rented it out in the summer months. Ian had found it on a teacher's exchange. It was this same exchange that he used to find other teachers to sublet his apartment in N.Y. while he traveled.

The kitchen had a real fireplace and a long wooden table with six neatly arranged chairs. It was charming. The second floor had three separate bedrooms.

"The one with the double bed can be our room" Ian smiled, as he passed me on the stairs, off to unpack the car.

The bathroom down the hall was a work of art. The walls and floors were covered with lapis blue tiles. The bathtub, white porcelain on lion claws, stood positioned so that while you took a bath you could look out the window. I open the window to breathe in the fresh air; it smelled of pinesap baking in the afternoon sun.

As far as I can see, there are vineyards and olive groves in perfectly spaced rows reaching out to the horizon. A bird sitting on the tree, sings to me a little song, I smile. This is amazing I am really in Tuscany. It is all so romantic.

We meet up with the other women the next day at the train station in Florence and head to the town of San Gimignano to shop in the little specialty stores. Ian flaunts his Italian skills and soon we have our arms full of packages tied in white paper and string. We bring back a feast of cured meats and cheeses, crunchy breads, olives, figs, fresh coffee, and a huge flat cake filled with chestnut cream. Living in a town surrounded by vineyards, wine is a dollar a bottle after the exchange rate. We buy a case of red and a case of white. Ian and I set up lunch as the ladies settled into their rooms.

Joan is an Adjunct Professor, she teaches life drawing and perspective. A big stocky woman, she is fiercely independent and opinionated. She lives alone in a factory loft in the garment center, which she has had for twenty years. In the summer she travels and paints. She sells her still life and landscape paintings in a gallery in SoHo. She hates the politics of teaching but has been working towards her tenure. She hates the students, their arrogance, their disrespect, and their daddy's allowances. She hates the politics of the art scene but attends every opening and event; at least there is free wine and snacks! She hates men for the most part and seems to always fall in love with the wrong ones. I like Joan. She has an intimidating New York toughness, with a 'take no prisoners' attitude. She shows off her tattoos that mark the men and bad relationships of the past as if she were a totem pole.

Alice on the other hand is as opposite to Joan as you can get. She is timid and mousy. She teaches color and theory. She lived with her aunt for many years when she first came to New York from Pennsylvania. I think maybe she was Amish? She has seven cats each named after a different dwarf from the Disney movie, *Snow White*. They are her family. When Sleepy died she replaced him with Sleepy #3 or #4. It seemed that Sleepy wasn't a lucky name for a cat. She tells of the passing of Sleepy #4 as she hides behind long bangs and dark rimmed nerdy glasses, which are always slipping down her nose. She is cute in an awkward way, uncomfortable in her own skin. She wears layers of prints that do not match. It is summer and still she hides behind a bulky sweater and a long skirt.

The table is a work of art, a feast to be had. Alice takes a picture from every angle before we can eat. Every bite is better than the last. Crunchy bread, salty meats, cheeses that are so fresh and creamy they melt on your tongue, we lick out fingers with every bite. Joan hums in happiness sucking on grapes. Ian slices a ricotta cheesecake covered in wild berries that ooze down the sides. Bottles of wines from Vernocia are opened one after another. Their sweet fruity liquid goes down way to easy. By the fourth bottle we are feeling no pain.

Alice clings to Ian's every word while Joan likes to argue and get the last word. Alice has tenure and finds comfort in the day after day sameness of teaching. She struggles with understanding her own art. As the afternoon grows long in shadows and the empty bottles start to line the windowsill, I can sense that there is tension between Alice and Ian, and I am aware there must be a story behind this.

Ménage à Trois

Ian brings out his guidebooks and maps. He has created three different calendars filled with itineraries, day trips to museums in Florence, churches with frescos that we simply must see, excursions to Pisa and Siena and plans for a weekend in Venice. By the time he is through we sit back to take it all in.

"Ian is truly the best tour guide. I love to travel with him. Not only does he get you places you didn't think you could manage but he will do it all on budget. Yes, you missed your calling; you should be an international tour guide!" Joan declares and Alice nods in agreement as we all toast to Ian.

Joan pushes back her chair. "I almost cancelled this year. Did Ian tell you what happened last summer? Did he mention the night on the beach? The affair…?"

"I wouldn't call it an affair," said Ian in his defense. Alice whose cheeks were already red from the wine hides behind her bangs.

"Whatever?" says Joan as she continues her story, "A group of us rented a house in the Yucatan in Mexico... after a night of many margaritas, Ian and Alice slept together! We found them the next morning passed out naked on the lawn chairs on the beach. Alice fell in love while Ian insists they are just friends." Alice and Ian are embarrassed but Joan keeps talking about that night.

"I wouldn't call it a love affair," says Alice meekly. "Tomlin says we have been and always will be good friends. We have worked this out."

"Yes, Tomlin says we have made excellent progress," says Ian as he peels away the label on the wine bottle with a pocketknife. He is making a collection for his trip scrapbook, and he is off to a good start with 4 labels.

"Yes, Tomlin says we are at a friendship phase and although there will never be a relationship between us it doesn't mean that we cannot still be good friends."

"Wait a second," I say woken up from my daze, "Tomlin? You both have the same therapist?"

"They do!" Joan reaches for the bottle, "Tomlin this and Tomlin that – welcome to my nightmare! I have been listening to this since last summer's vacation. Tomlin thinks that this trip will be an experiment. If they can handle living in the same house then their friendship can endure. Didn't know that you were part of this experiment...?" Joan turns to me. "Hmm, I didn't think so! I think with you here and well the current sleeping arrangements that may not be what Alice was hoping for."

Alice bites her lip. Ian starts to wash dishes turning his back to the conversation.

Joan is on a roll and just keeps going. "You two better not fuck this trip up for me, or I will never forgive you! And while we are on the subject, Ian, what you were you thinking bringing along another student? No offense," she turned at me again, "I like you already and feel you need to know what is going on here. How much of this saga did he let you in on before you agreed to come along?"

"This is all news to me. I just heard that a fourth person dropped out last minute and there was an opening to fill." it was my turn to reach for more wine though I already had my fill. "Ian and I are just friends," I add much to Alice's relief.

47

"There was nothing to tell, it was one time we were drunk! Alice and I have been friends for 10 years. We have a lot of history together and we will remain friends. Isn't that right, Alice?" Ian struggles.

"Yes, we are just friends, I am over you." Alice declares with a bit of a slur and not very much conviction.

"Well that seems like a lot of progress for one night" declared Joan. "It is time to move on. Let's kill the bottle and toast to these good friends new and old. Now as your Italian therapist for the next four weeks I say we call it a night." She turns to me, "maybe it is good you are here that should bring all of this to a head."

We kill the fourth bottle and stagger to our rooms. Joan snores loudly while everyone else tosses and turns all night.

In the Land of Michelangelo

At daybreak, an owl hoots outside the window I am alone in the bed. Ian is up first and has breakfast on the table. The smell of coffee fills the air. We are all a bit hung over from the night before. Strong coffee, sweet rolls, prosciutto and melon help our focus return.

Joan was the last to wake and quickly grabs some coffee on her way out the door. "It is important to catch the morning light. The shadows are best this time of day and at twilight." She is not hung over in the least. Alice and Joan head out the door with their portable easels, box of paints, big hats and sunglasses. Ian and I clean up before climbing the driveway out into the field to sketch the countryside.

It is a picture postcard with olives trees and grape vines all in rows like a patchwork quilt. In the background is the medieval city on top of a hill. The town of San Gimignano is famous for its stone towers. In the 15th Century, wealthy Tuscan families built towers to show their good fortune. Each family built a little higher to exceed the towers before, a lot like New York City with its skyscrapers competing for world's tallest.

"What would Freud say?" insisted Joan one morning.

There is something magical about the light and the earthy aged ochre colors of the buildings against the sage greens and red browns of the soil. The cypress trees all line up like soldiers along the roads dividing property lines. The vines glisten in the early light still wet with dew. There is an earthy smell as the day's sun quickly dries the morning mist. We walk awhile to the best spot and take out our sketchpads and colored pencils.

By noon it is hot and we all head back to the farmhouse for lunch. Joan has two paintings that are drying in the sun. They are beautiful landscapes, quite delicate for her brassy demeanor. Alice has one painting, kind-of childish and primitive. She plays with opposite colors so the landscapes look a bit surreal.

Ian's painting is abstract, with broken lines of sun and shadow forming diagonals across the objects. It is colorful and playful, reminding me of Cubists.

I have sketched the farmhouse, the winding road and the old tree that shades it from the noonday sun. I study a pinecone and sketch it in multiple repeats. I realize I don't have painting skills, just textile skills. Over the next two weeks our mini gallery fills up. Our work lines the trough.

In comparison to their work I am clearly frustrated. Joan's landscape watercolors are beautiful compositions. I admire her work one night and express my frustration and lack of true art education.

"You don't know about perspective, do you?" Joan can get brutally honest after a few glasses of wine and agrees to critique my work. "What did they teach you at school anyway?"

"We focused on nature studies and putting elements into half drop repeats. There is so much I don't know about being a real artist. Can you teach me perspective?"

"No," she pauses, "I like what you do better." She looks at a still life I sketched of the table and the windows with the landscape behind.

"The shutters confused me, they look like they are coming and going." I said a bit embarrassed.

"It is primitive and naïve. I like it just as it is. I teach perspective all year. I am on vacation. You'll just have to figure it out yourself. Ok?" She rethinks after a while. Perspective is overrated, one must learn it and then forget it. If you really want to know I'll show you tomorrow when we are in Florence.

The next day, Alice and Ian head off to mail a package so Joan and I walk the city of Florence. "Before we look at Early Renaissance painting, you will need to learn about the linear perspective. In the 1400s, Brunelleschi developed the principles for linear perspective. The ancient Greeks and Romans may have understood linear perspective too, but if so, all knowledge of it was lost during the Middle Ages. Linear perspective is a way of creating a convincing illusion of space on a flat or two-dimensional surface. Florentine painters and sculptors became obsessed with it." She reads from a guidebook, 'it structured all images of reality to address a single spectator who, unlike God, could only be in one place at a time.' "In other words, linear perspective eliminates the multiple viewpoints that we see in medieval art, and creates an illusion of space from a single, fixed viewpoint. This suggests a renewed focus on the individual viewer, and we know that individualism is an important part of the Humanism of the Renaissance.

There are two main elements in perspective drawing; linear perspective which deals with the organization of shapes in space and Aerial Perspective which deals with the atmospheric effects on tones and colors."

We head to the Academia Gallery before meeting up with our group later at the Uffizi Gallery. Joan wants me to see Michelangelo's statue of David. We walk through the gallery viewing one religious painting after another.

"We are almost there." Joan leads the way to a long room filled with white marble statues. En route she explains that these statues are of slaves trapped within the marble. "Michelangelo saw the struggle of man and shows it with these twisted muscular beings emerging from the confined state of solid marble."

"They are beautiful." I stand amazed.

"Some people feel that Michelangelo just didn't get around to finishing these. Maybe... but I think they say so much more unfinished, don't you?"

"Yes, they are beautiful," I say in awe.

We make our way through a crowd of people. "I think they express an inner struggle within Michelangelo. He was believed to be a homosexual." She says loud enough to turn heads. We walk on.

"Both Verrochio's and Donatello's version of David has David depicted standing over Goliath's severed head. Michelangelo has depicted David before the battle. David is tense, but not so much in a physical as in a mental sense. You can see this in his eyes, which are intensely focused ahead to the upcoming battle."

At the end of a long corridor, proudly stands David.

"The slingshot he carries over his shoulder is almost invisible, emphasizing that David's victory was one of cleverness, not sheer force. Look at that body, man what I wouldn't give for a hunk of that stone!" We giggle as we circle around the statue. I like Joan.

On another day, Alice shares with me the art of stained glass. How artisans used layers of colored glass to achieve such dramatic effects. Colors sparkle like water when the sun hits the glass just right. Like a prism they glitter color and warmth throughout the interior. I remembered the same effect in Ian's studio colors dancing in space. She shows me how pictures tell stories to the masses of people who could not read.

"These stories were often pagan in origin but the Catholic Church adapted these myths, legions, and symbols into their new religion. It made the people feel comfortable, it made the Catholicism familiar." She shows me the craftsmanship of mosaic patterns, how cut marble was used in different colors and shapes to create elaborate patterns and designs. The floors are covered in intricate geometrics. Patterned tiles make circular shapes intersect and interlock with each other. The interior walls are inlayed with smooth sanded marble that extend to the ceiling and are cool to the touch. Above the altar is the stained glass window of the Resurrection of Christ. It is meticulously inlayed with colored stones and gold that reflects the light. Every surface is decorated in a colored pattern. Italy is a show of light and pattern, color and design, and food. We stop for cappuccinos and creamed-filled pastries. We buy postcards.

"San Gimignano has some of the best examples of medieval religious painting." Ian continues my education in the techniques of fresco painting in hidden corners of San Gimignano.

"Artists used water-based pigments onto freshly applied plaster walls. They made colors by grinding dry-powder pigments in water. The pigment and the plaster dry together to become a permanent part of the wall, that was very durable." He teaches me about good composition and how an artist can keep your eye moving around a painting by the placement of angles, the position of Christ's hand or the drape of a fabric." Every church that had a fresco we visited. I grew tired of religious art.

An Unlucky Rose

One day while in Florence, Ian and I walk the Ponte Vecchio Bridge over the River Arno and look through the jewelry merchants' stalls. These represented families that had been in business for hundreds of years. Ian finds a tailor and we head inside to look at the textiles. He picks out a striped cotton fabric as soft as butter, with fine stripes of blues and greens. He orders a dress shirt for himself. As the tailor is measuring him, I head to a shop across the street that features lingerie in the window and is having a sale. An impeccably dressed sales woman speaks a little English; she directs me to a rack and picks out a silk gown in a soft rose color. I look at a few others but she shakes her head no. She leads me to a dressing room behind a heavy brocade fabric. There is an ornate vanity and little seat covered in the same brocade. In the corner is an ornate gold leaf full-length mirror. I try on her selection, the plunging neckline is very sexy, and the bias cut of the fabric flows to the floor. There is a long slit up one side. It is incredible flattering on my body. I have put on some weight but in this gown, I feel like a starlet from a 1930s silent film. The sales woman enters the dressing room and speaks to me in Italian with an all-knowing smile. The only thing I understand is 'Lauren Bacall'. It is the most expensive thing I have ever bought myself. She wraps my purchase in fine pink tissue paper. Even the tissue paper is the most beautiful thing I have ever bought.

At night alone with Ian I model my purchase.

"Bella," he says as I come to bed. He holds my breasts in his hands and jiggles them up and down. "Your breasts are like the domes of Florence, round and firm." He then rubs my belly like he was making a wish on a Buddha. He gives a little uncertain laugh and shuts the lights, rolls over and in no time is snoring. I can't believe he has gone to sleep. Sex with me is not something he has on his mind. Oh, he can be poetic and hold my hand in public but alone, we are like roommates.

I wondered what was wrong with my choice in men. It was the 80s and everyone is sleeping with everyone. Clearly something is wrong with me? Frustrated I put on a sweatshirt and head to the kitchen to drown my sorrow in what is left of the pignoli cookies. If sex is not my friend at least baked goods were.

Alice is still awake drinking at the table alone. She pours me a glass of lemon liquor and I offer her a cookie covered in nuts.

"You know these are not so difficult to make. You need pine nuts, sugar, almond paste, and vanilla; roll them into balls and press into whole pine nuts. Bake 20 minutes," she takes a big bite and chews awhile before continuing.

"You know, I don't want to like you," she takes another bite, "I have tried hard not to like you, but I do. I wish I didn't." She starts to cry. "I wish I didn't love Ian but I do. I can't just be his friend it hurts too much. I want so much more from him and he won't even give me a chance. I'm too old for him. He only likes young girls. I have cut my hair, changed to contacts and started wearing makeup. But how can I compete with a 20 year old? You wake up out of bed and look good!" She pours us each another shot and picks off the pine nuts of two cookies. "The two of you sleeping together night after night it is eating me alive. I can't take much more of this!" She pounds the table with her fist. We each grab another cookie.

"Alice, I am so sorry you feel this way." It was ironic that here she was so upset over our being together and night after night nothing was going on between us. "Ian and I are not serious in that way."

"Yes maybe, but while you are here, Ian and I won't be serious in any way! I had hoped we could come together on this trip, but then at the last minute he brought you. I can't compete. Tomlin was right. I am just not mature enough for this. I am thinking of leaving early and heading to Paris, I have a friend in Paris and I can stay with her." Alice says with determination.

"Alice, if the situation in the house is upsetting you so, then you shouldn't stay here. If I were you, I would head to Paris where you said you had a friend. It is not healthy to stay here feeling the way you do." We hugged and she headed off to bed, I slept on the couch. After talking it over with Ian the next morning, he drove her to the train station and gave her roses as a parting gift. Then he called his therapist long distance.

Hidden Treasures of Ravenna

It is our last weekend. We drive along cypress-lined roads and head to Venice. I drive the rental car as Ian reads about the next stop, to see the Byzantine mosaics of Ravenna.

"Superb Byzantine mosaics," he reads, "finest outside of Istanbul. It was once a thriving seaport in ancient times; it now sits five miles inland. Ravenna rose to power in the 1st century BC under the Emperor Augustus. The town converted to Christianity very early, in the 2nd century AD. As Rome's power declined,

Ravenna took over as the capital of the Western Empire (402 AD). The following century it came under the rule of Theodoric and the Arian Ostrogoth, and in 540 the city became part of the Byzantine Empire under Justinian. Ravenna's exquisite early Christian mosaics span the years of Roman and Byzantine rule. As an extra bonus, we need to taste the famously delicious food of the Emilia-Romagna region."

Ian cross-references the dining out on the cheap guidebook. I adjust the seat belt; four weeks in Italy and nothing I brought fits. There was no dieting in Italy for every dish of pasta, every piece of crunchy bread or buttery pastry were savored and devoured completely, with wine, lots and lots of wine. Nothing could be passed up. But I have grown uncomfortable in my new round body.

"We could skip lunch and hold out for dinner." I checked my rearview mirror to see a red sports car come up quickly behind me. In no time the car is passing us. A sexy Italian man in dark sunglasses smiles as he passes our car. I smile back. Italian men are beautiful creatures. With a rev of the engine, and in a gust of wind, in no time, he is far off in the distance.

Joan wakes up from the back seat startled. "What the hell was that?"

"Just a beautiful Italian on wheels." I say.

The red car was now a blur. "What color?" She strains to see.

"Red," I smile.

"Oh, I'm sorry I missed that." She rubs her eyes and turns to Ian. "This expedition better be good, Ian. This is taking us way out of our way. I have four more paintings to complete before we leave. I swear the air conditioner has stopped working back here." Joan opens the window and gasps as the hot air outside hits her face. She quickly closes the window back up.

"We're almost there, trust me, have I let you down yet?" Ian laughs.

"No you have never let **me** down." Joan stretches across the back seat.

Ian makes me stop at a farm stand. We unfold out of the car into the hot dry sun. We buy grapes, bread, mozzarella di buffalo cheese, vine ripe tomatoes, olive oil and fresh basil. We drive a little further on and stop by a lake to have a picnic under the shade of the trees. There are other cars parked along the lake with families and workers stopping for an hour or two to eat and nap. As I have learned from every museum we have gone to, the Italians stop everything for lunch and a nap. The heat alone can put you to sleep. We laid out our blanket, and set out our dishes and utensils. Ian cut the tomatoes and cheese on a cutting-board and made sandwiches with the basil and oil. Ian had packed everything we needed. We eat our fill and Joan and I want to nap a bit, but Ian has a schedule to keep. We drive on.

The sign reads Ravenna as we enter a small town. It looks like any other Italian city with old streets, a town square center by a church. Lots of hunched over little women wearing black and heavy stockings, carrying baskets with the day's produce. They look as if they could just fall over sideways in exhaustion but they carry on.

The mausoleum looks boring from the outside, Italian brick archways make it look heavy, and a tiled roof like a hundred buildings we have passed along the way. Joan and I are not impressed.

We pay our admission fee and enter through a dark passage. The air is deliciously cool. Inside when our eyes adjust, it is like walking into a dream. Every surface is decorated with pattern all made up of tiny colorful mosaic tiles. One's eyes rush in every which direction to take it all in. Vines and leaves intertwine. Ribbons of color float up to a star-filled lapis blue sky. Geometric borders pattern in a rainbow of colors decorating the inner arches, and 24K gold angels and stars flicker in what little light there is.

It is breathtaking. It is magnificent. It is spiritual. It is magical. I am left dumbfounded and speechless. Ian laughs at me for I am in a trance. He leads me along as I have stopped dead in my tracks. I try to take pictures but the guard stops me, this is not allowed. We continue on to the Basilica that is lined above with mosaics of the royal court of Justinian and Empress Theodora. They are lavishly decorated in robes with geometric patterns and draped in precious stones and jewels. Ian explains that this is the height of the Byzantine style. I am amazed and don't want to leave. Sensing my excitement after so many Christian churches and religious art, he buys me a book from the vendor with pictures of all the buildings we have just seen.

"Here, for you." He writes inside it, "To My Bella, so you never forget. Ian" He takes a turn driving, as I clutch my book in the back seat and watch the unimpressive town with it's incredible hidden treasure fade away.

Fortunes of Venice

We park the car and carry our bags as a ferryboat takes us into the city. We hang over the edge to see the sites and catch the breeze. Along the Grand Canal, ancient buildings in faded shades of ochre look as if they are melting into the water. There are boats carrying fruits, bushels of fish, and cases of Coca-Cola. The wet air feels wonderful as we are transported across the Grand Canal. We find our hotel through a maze of tiny streets and drag our suitcases up three flights of stairs. Joan curses the entire climb. Our rooms are tiny but who cares, we're in Venice. It is like Disneyland for adults. In the Piazza San Marco we sip cappuccinos and watch the tourist take pictures among the pigeons. We visit the Basilica and the Bridge of Sighs where prisoners take one last look at the Mediterranean before being locked away in jail.

Ian and the Michelin Guide lead us to a little store front restaurant where we eat a meal of bruschetta with tomatoes and olives, fried calamari, stuffed artichokes, and grilled zucchini blossoms with two bottles of Prosecco, and for dessert a plate of cheese, fruit, little cookies and fig jam. For a two star restaurant it is wonderful.

After, we take a boat to a remote island to see the casinos. In the casino, the women are dressed in the most elegant fashions sparkling in jewels. Men in fine Italian suits toss thousand dollar chips onto the table with little enthusiasm. It is remarkably quiet. The Blackjack tables are serious business as eyes stare from face to face. There is an infectious boredom to the casino. No one is having any fun. Smoke swirls around lifeless humans as they slowly drink pink Champagne and blue cocktails. It is a bizarre carnival in hell, where the creatures have been twisted to abnormal proportions. Their grotesque faces stretched and exaggerated from decades of plastic surgery stare out from eyes that cannot blink and lips that cannot smile.

I'm beginning to feel like the cheese and squid I ate for dinner are trying to swim upstream through a sea of Prosecco. I head outside for air and breathe deeply in the salty sea mist that has now cooled the heat of the day.

An old woman, a fortuneteller, calls out "Doralina sees all, Doralina knows all and Doralina can tell your fortune. You are not well, are you love sick? Perhaps love sick?" she asks slyly as she points to her hand for payment. I give her the last token I have from the casino. It is worth twenty dollars but I don't care.

She reaches for my hand and studies the lines through squinted grey eyes.

"Past, Present, Future," she traces the lines of my palm in the dim light. "What Doralina sees is very interesting." She presses a thumb into my palm. "You are guarded; a man in the past has left too soon. So you choose men not too seriously, you fear they too shall leave. You seek adventure you do. Hmmm interesting, you travel with a man; he is not your lover but can show you much. Learn what you can from him, but he is not the one for you..."

She follows another line, "I see you shall one day have a lover with great passion." She spits on the ground and mutters something in Italian and looks at my other hand. "He too shall teach you about life, but, it will have a price as all things do." And then she laughs all knowing, "You will find love and live a long life and see the world. I see two children in your future. Yes, Doralina sees all..."

CHAPTER 5 - MANHATTAN WORKING 9-5

At 6th Avenue and 48th Street I enter one of the skyscrapers and take an elevator up to the 45th floor. It is like flying up - invigorating.

I enter a glass door etched with the title:

HAMILTON WRIGHTWOOD TEXTILES,
HUMAN RESOURCE DEPARTMENT

"Please sit down," (Mrs. Baker comes into focus. She looks like a woman from the Venice carnival with a long thin nose and high lace collar under a navy blue suit.) She gestures to a chair and hands me a heavy corporate binder.

"On behalf of the Hamilton Wrightwood Textiles, we are glad to have you on board." She recites her routine almost unconsciously. "I am here to help transition you into your new position with our corporation."

"Hamilton Wrightwood Textiles is an old name in manufacturing with factories and cotton mills in South Carolina. Our New York office handles design, sales, showroom and financial. Not in that order of course." She fidgets with her fake pearls.

Just a week before Mr. Jameson interviewed and hired me within 20 minutes. He flipped through my portfolio mumbling something, not really seeming interested. I try to explain the giant mushroom, as a concentration in line drawing, but he moves on quickly. Then he stops and looks at me carefully, "Hey I know you; you're one of the bakery girls from Roberti's Pastry Shoppe.

My wife and I shop there every Sunday after Church. Best jelly donuts around!" He closed my portfolio abruptly not even finishing to look.

Suddenly I remembered he came in every Sunday afternoon and ordered eight jelly donuts in a box and a seeded rye bread sliced. I usually worked the 5 a.m. shift but I did recognize him as well. Seems the bakery recognition for once would pay off. There was a position available in the art department, it paid $225- a week to paint samples of woven textiles. I had been hoping for a position with the print department but it was a good company and there was a chance for mobility. Mr. Jameson showed me the art studio where he announced upon entering...

"This is where the children play." There were about a dozen artists, all women that looked up from their desks. You could tell they found Mr. Jameson rather annoying. "They have the best view in the house." He pointed out the windows and he was right. The studio had a panoramic view of the Hudson River across to New Jersey.

"On a clear day, you can see the George Washington Bridge to the north and World Trade Center and Statue of Liberty to the south," said a woman sitting by the window. I thought that this wasn't so bad for a corporate job.

"We run a tight ship here, but I hope you don't suffer from sea-sickness." Jameson a former marine talked in seaman terms.

"When it gets very windy the building does sway back and forth. We do have Dramamine if it gets too bad." Said the women in an apron who ran the studio.

In the next three days I took a physical, which included a chest x-ray, blood test and urine sample and exam, all to be a painter in a studio? Upon passing the tests, I was called to come in to sign the welcome aboard papers.

"I see here you have passed your physical and drug test, very good. On behalf of the company, welcome aboard." She shook my hand ceremoniously. "Now please turn to the third page of your welcome package. You will be on probation for the first quarter, a trial period where we will review your performance and conclude if you will be offered a permanent position. After the second quarter you will receive your complete benefit package."

We turn through many pages and I hear, phases like "3 days off after this, 2 days off after that for a total of 5 earned holiday days off the first year, advanced notice always in writing, permission and rules of conduct." Mrs. Baker adjusts her fake pearls again as she proceeds to tell me about the rules. My favorite is the retirement package. If I stay with the company for 5, 10, 20 years I can rest assured that there would be matching funds and a tidy package upon retirement. If I invest in their plan it can grow to a tidy sum. To me it sounds like a death sentence being with the same company for that amount of time. The room gets smaller and I feel the sickness of the Venice casino come upon me. Mrs. Baker keeps talking about retirement and pensions and her nose keeps growing longer. I wonder if anything she is saying is the truth? Words go by in a blur passing over me. I already feel seasick. What have I gotten myself into, I wonder?

"Sign here and sign there. Initial this, and this and this." She turns pages and pages of text and staples the pages together three times. "Now let me take you on a tour of your new home away from home. Think of us as one big happy family." She walks me around a maze of grey corridors, with executive name plaques on every door. We pass the accounting department, logistic department and corporate offices; room after room of little cubicles each with workers who kind of smile and say hello. Each worker has a cup of coffee, matching office supplies and family photos. We pass the sales department and I am introduced to six men in matching blue suits and diagonal striped ties. They seem to be part of their own tribe.

The lunchroom is small and painted bright orange. There are vending machines, a pot of stale coffee and posters on how to be a more efficient worker and what to do when someone is choking. There is fire extinguisher and dusty pictures of the mills down south. I wonder which would be worse to choke to death right now or wait 30 plus years for the retirement package to kick in. I think choking would be the way to go, I feel sick.

In the far north of the building was a caged room where they kept all the office supplies and sales material. In the shadows, an attractive man was flirting with a girl over the copy machine. Upon seeing Mrs. Baker, the girl quickly gathers her papers and rushes off blushing bright red.

"Nina Page is joining our art department." She says to the man who comes out of the shadows. "Alfonso can handle all your copy needs." Alfonso glides towards us. He is tall and thin, with a long ponytail, clearly not one of the suits. He has deep brown eyes and mischief written all over his face. He smiles devilishly as his eyes look me over.

"Very nice to meet you Ms. Nina Page, call me Alfie," He goes to shake my hand and an electric spark flies between us. "The copy machines build up a lot of static electricity." He says with a smile, "always nice to see you Mrs. Baker, that's a very flattering scarf you have on, works well with the pearls." He winks at her and she is clearly flustered but likes it.

We continue down a long corridor and out of earshot she whispers, "I warn you, our Alfonso is quite the ladies man. He is a writer, comes from Italy." I turn around to take one last look. I can still feel the spark on my fingertips. Alfonso is leaning against a wall watching, smiling, devilishly handsome. I quickly turn around. He is unnerving.

Mrs. Baker finishes her tour and we are back to the elevator banks where the salesmen sit. As if on cue they all look up to check out the new girl at the same time. Their expression reminds me of a pack of hungry wolves at feeding time. I feel undressed and cover my breasts with my binder feeling somewhat violated by their stares.

"I will see you then on Monday, come to my office at 8:20 a.m. sharp." As we say our goodbyes the salesmen also all say goodbye.

"See you Monday."

"Yes looking forward to Monday."

Mrs. Baker reprimands them "Get back to work." Like a carnival ringleader she pretends to whip them back into their seats, "You naughty beasts!"

The elevator doors close to their laughter. I push the one button and plummet 45 floors to street level where I throw up behind a bush in Rockefeller Center.

Village Life

At dinner with Ian on Bleeker Street in the Village, we toast with beers as we wait for pizza at John's Pizzeria. We have a seat by the front window overlooking the line of people trying to get a table on a Friday night. They gawk at us through the window.

"Well congratulations on your first job, we should go some place special for dinner next week. There is a steak house I would like to try out that has just gotten a great write-up in the Times." Ian always knew where to eat.

"Ian, this IS someplace special for dinner! Really, I hardly fit into my clothes as it is. I had to borrow this suit from my mother," I say as I reach for a slice. "I am not so sure I am ready to celebrate, I think I just signed on to a death sentence. What was I thinking taking a corporate job? I thought school was a jungle but these people are scary. Some of them are in cages and the others belong in cages!"

"Nonsense, we have to celebrate. Tradition is that the person with the new job gets to pay!" Ian says through bites of pizza.

"Great, then it will be a small dinner. I need new clothes." I reach for another slice.

"You could save money on commuting if you moved in with me," Ian said in a matter-of-fact way. "I have plenty of space you could use the second bedroom for all your stuff."

"Ian, wow thanks but I …I'm not sure I'm ready for that. See I made myself a promise that I wouldn't live with someone until I lived alone for a few years."

"Oh well living alone is not what it is cracked up to be, believe me. Just think it over, you could roll out of bed and be on the 7th Ave. subway to work in less then half an hour vs. an hour plus each way on the Long Island Railroad to that little town you call home. We can share expenses, be roommates! What do you have to lose? You'll love living in the Village! We can throw a Halloween party and announce our co-habitation!" By the end of dinner I agreed and Ian started to plan the party menu.

Creature Comforts

Months passed quickly living downtown. I love the atmosphere of the village, a parade of artists, intellectuals, gay pride, freaks and me. At night every corner is a happening with something going on.

Every morning I would leave the apartment for work, kiss Ian goodbye as he read the morning paper under the mobile of utensils. I'd grab half a bagel from the kitchen and smear it with cream cheese. The kitchen window overlooks the movie theater on Greenwich Street. Traffic was already making noise as people filled the streets heading off for their day. It was my favorite place in the apartment to sit and people watch. I liked to shake the fork and spoon mobile above the table and make it chime.

"I was thinking fish and chips for dinner, what do you think? I could make fresh coleslaw with it, yes that does sound delicious. I should call my mother's housekeeper and get her recipe. She makes the best, adds a touch of cayenne pepper and caraway seeds. Or maybe some finely chopped carrots and beets with fresh ginger, like we had in the restaurant you liked so much? No coleslaw it is." Ian always had dinner arranged in advance. "On my way to drop off the laundry I'll go to the market. How does that sound?" He had already made up his mind, what could I say?

"Perfect." I said not really caring about dinner before I had breakfast.

Ian loved housework and brought the laundry to the cleaners once a week. I paid for a few utilities but he covered the rent and our eating out which we did twice a week. When we weren't going out he cooked and took the time to teach me. His job was easy and he had lots of spare time on his hands. On Tuesday afternoons and all day Saturday he worked in his studio. On Sundays he'd roast something or simmer something or assemble something for hours and fill the apartment with incredible smells. We would spend the mornings reading the Times over Bloody Marys or Mimosas. In the evenings, if the weather permitted we would walk around Washington Park and take in the street performers.

"Mother has offered us her tickets to the opera next week. It is Wagner, not one of my favorites but it would be a good experience for you to go to the Lincoln Center." He was always the teacher with me, sharing his world as a good experience. I would always be the student in his eyes in need of instruction.

"And we have been invited to the Taylor's for Sunday brunch. They have just come back from Greece and have invited a few couples over for Greek food and a slide show. I know that Jack is an ass but I like Susan's photography. She's very good. I said yes without asking. I hope you don't mind." He turned the pages of the paper not even looking up.

"Sure, whatever you want." I grabbed the other half of the bagel. We were like an old married couple confirming schedules. We socialized a lot, dinners, weekends in the Catskills, art openings, theatre, there was always an event scheduled. Ian was social director and the calendar was always full. He bought me a stylish suit and a new dress so that I could be dressed properly. He never asked what I wanted to do, just made plans and let me know what to wear accordingly.

Let's do the Time Warp

His colleagues were 20 to 30 years my senior, all painters, teachers and therapists, I enjoyed their company and the conversation. There was always a debate. They showed me their world each teaching me something along the way. In return I dragged them all one Saturday at midnight to see the Rocky Horror Picture Show on West 4th Street. They were curious but needed someone to take them. I had seen the show a dozen times in college. It was cheap theater, a movie and a sideshow all in one. So one night, whilst six teachers and I sat in the front and watched the movie and floor show, we were bombarded with toilet paper and sprayed with water guns hiding under our newspapers. They loved it and were glad I made them go. I recognized some of the cast from years ago; it was surreal. The following week we gathered to discuss the Freudian good and bad, dark and light, sex and religious taboos that the film portrayed. I missed my old friends who just laughed at the pageantry without all the analytical crap.

It was difficult to keep my old friendships. Everyone scattered, got married, went back home, or was traveling through Europe. Only two remained. On Halloween, Ian and I dressed as Sonny and Cher and threw a costume party. We tried to mix our friends. One of my friends hated the history teacher who had failed her. She confronted him at the party, calling him 'an ass' after too much vodka-voodoo-punch, and stormed out declaring this to be the end of our friendship, and it was.

The Fashion Institute of Technology hosted the Fashion Awards gala evening and Ian's mother got us tickets. I was awestruck at the sight of Mary McFadden, Calvin Klein and Betsy Johnson. As we exited the show with hundreds of people looking for their limos, we gave up on finding a cab and started to walk downtown. From the crowd my name was yelled out and there were a few of my high school friends behind the barricades. They rollerbladed around us as we all headed downtown. They wanted to know all about the event and why we didn't have a limo. I told them we were in the cheap seats, which annoyed Ian. It was good to see them being goofy and having fun. They seemed so young and I seemed so old in my gown. In time Ian's friends became my friends; it was just easier.

A Cog in Something Turning

Although Ian kept my calendar full, I was growing bored and complacent. In some ways it became very comfortable, our playing house. We functioned as a couple; Ian & Nina, Nina & Ian, and once a month we even slept together. I guess just to make it official. But it was awkward to say the least. Days passed unconsciously, routinely, I was dying a slow death and I didn't know why.

Out on the street I headed to the subway underground. I'd catch the uptown express train at 14th Street and take a window seat to watch the stations go by 23rd, 28th, 34th, 42nd, 47th, 50th Rockefeller Plaza. I admired the mosaic signs along the way. In the afternoon I would walk 40 blocks home through the city streets to experience each of the neighborhoods. I loved being a part of Manhattan, the streets hummed with energy and every block offered a new surprise, a demonstration, a movie shoot or a parade.

I related to the Joni Mitchell song *Woodstock* and felt that I was a cog in something turning and maybe it was the time of year or maybe the time of man? Somehow, I had lost track of who I am.

Working in the heart of Rockefeller Plaza was a wonderful place to be at lunchtime. On a beautiful day, everyone would come out of their buildings and fill the little parks and plazas and eat lunch on their laps. I explored the neighborhood each day taking off in another direction. To the west there was Times Square and the excitement of 7th Avenue. Heading east past Radio City Music Hall was Rockefeller Plaza. The sunken plaza was a restaurant by summer, a skating rink in winter; it was my favorite place to people watch. Beyond the plaza were the shops of 5th Avenue and St. Patrick's Cathedral where on rainy days, I would go in to light a candle or watch a mass. To the north was Central Park. If I hustled I could get to the zoo in time for penguin feeding and back to the office in my hour lunch.

I settled into my new job with the help of my supervisor Miriam leaning over my shoulder, correcting my every move. Miriam had been doing this job for 20 years so she knew all the shortcuts. I quickly learned to mix paint to match color charts. The paint was then strained into glass jars and labeled with the customers name and the season. Miriam worked with me to get the right consistency of paint to flow evenly through a ruling pen. She taught me to use T-squares and gauges to count off ends and picks that would represent yarns of a fabric.

First you painted the stripe and when it was dry an adhesive backed clear film was applied. The cross stripe was then cut with an X-Acto knife and the area was sprayed with paint in an air gun. The colors from the two cross stripes would blend and create the plaid or woven effect. For dress shirt fabrics we used a fine spray for an oxford fabric a coarse spray. It was kind of magical as first. But I couldn't see spending 20 years doing the same thing.

Day after day I kissed Ian goodbye. As he planned my social calendar, I rode the subway, sat at my desk and painted stripes and plaids. I feared that this was all there would ever be to my life and I felt I was losing my mind. Everywhere I looked the world was in a grid pattern and my eyes turned these into plaids. The skyscrapers reached to the sky in plaid patterns, the grid of the streets below created plaids, the store windows featured everything in plaids for the season, just to mock my pain.

I looked up from my desk, dizzy and nauseous. When my eyes needed a break, I focused in the distance at the amazing view. Boats went up and down the Hudson River all day long. In the evenings the sunset lit up the sky in orange and pinks over New Jersey. When the wind blew and the plaid buildings started to sway it did make me seasick. I told the supervisor that I occasionally smoked, she looked at me with great disapproval but allowed me 10 minutes break two times a day. If you smoked you needed to go outside. The elevators would drop 45 floors to the lobby and out to the courtyard. In between the smokers one could get some air. I went for the air and to meet Alfonzo.

When my work was finished and dried, it needed to be logged in a master book and include a color copy. That meant a visit to the cage of Alfonzo. I found I rushed through assignments just to get time at the copy room. Miriam, my supervisor, always frowned upon my return for I took too long, but I was her fastest painter and my work was always done ahead of deadlines.

Within a few months, Alfonso became one of my lunchtime friends. A few of us would head outside the building when the weather was nice and eat in the park. There was something about this Alfonso that was like nothing I had ever encountered before. He was foreign that was for sure. He was charming and devilish.

Everything about him was elongated, almost delicate. He could look rugged and scruffy one day and elegant and handsome the next. He always looked a little stoned. I learned he was copy guy by day, playwright by night. He was part of an experimental theatre workshop that performed his plays Off Broadway.

We were very different but seemed to have a lot in common. We were both living with other people but it was temporary. The people we were with were not people we were in love with. As we walked around midtown on our lunch breaks we talked about being artists. We struggled with an unfulfilled feeling of being a cog in a big corporation that would go on and continue if we were not part of it. I found it was easy to talk to him and I told him things I didn't even know I was thinking. He challenged me to see a bigger picture for my life.

One day we were alone for lunch.

"So what would you do if you could do anything?" he asked as we ordered falafels from a street vendor.

"I always wanted to go to Parsons School of Design and have my own studio apartment, be an artist and see the world." I said as we sat down under the trees in a small park that had a waterfall feature. One could walk through a plastic tunnel surrounded by water on both sides. We stood under the tunnel as the cool mist sprayed into the air. We were so close; I thought he would kiss me.

"I'd write a horror play" he said with his best count Dracula accent "and have it performed right here at Radio City Music Hall." He smoked Kool cigarettes inhaling every drag as if it was exotic nectar. He intoxicated me and I found myself daydreaming I were one of his cigarettes. He caught me staring, "Would you like one?"

"Yes." I don't know why I said that? I guess I wanted to seem cool but coughed on the first drag. "I haven't smoked in a while." I lied.

"Kools are an acquired taste, you may want to work up to them?" He took the cigarette away from me and smoked it himself.

"Tastes like you and cherry lip gloss. I like it." He made me nervous and I could tell I did the same to him. We were just friends, just friends I kept telling myself. But we watched each other very carefully.

Heading back to the office we both reached for the elevator button at the same time and again an electric spark connected between us. We jumped.

"We do that a lot," he said as he leaned into me and looked deeply into my eyes. I thought he was going to kiss me when someone stopped the doors from closing and a crowd of people entered separating us to opposite corners.

The Owl and the Pussycat

Valentine's Day lunch, Alfie and I ran uptown to see the animals at the Central Park Zoo. Alfie bought me a cupcake, which we shared watching the seals play in the water. On the elevator going back up to work, we kissed for the first time. Our bodies melted into each other as one. We held that kiss for 45 flights up. The passion and the nonstop elevator ride left us dizzy as the doors opened to our floor. The pack of salesmen immediately read our expressions and started to howl like barking dogs.

"Way to go Alfie, don't know how you do it?"

"Ms. Nina, not you too?"

"Must be that Latin charm, women just fall for that." They whistled and banged on their desks.

After work I saw Alfie with his girlfriend leaving the building. He looked back at me as she snuggled up to him. She had wild curly red hair and a furry coat in the same color. It was hard to tell where the coat ended and she began. I walked the 40 blocks home alone depressed thinking of our kiss and how she would have him tonight, not me.

That evening, back home with Ian, we dressed to go out to dinner. He was taking me to a local Spanish restaurant. Ian was deciding on which sweater vest to wear that would match what I was wearing. He always wore wool sweater vests over a dress shirt and with his silver hair he looked older than his 40 years. He also liked to match my colors, which drove me crazy. At the last minute I change to something red, which throws off his balance as he is in black and white. With reservations set, there is no time to change. I like to throw him curve balls when I can.

"Well," he said as we sat down at Gulliver's Restaurant. "I was inspired by the Taylor's trip and was thinking we should go to Greece this summer? We can see Athens and then join a sailing flotilla. I've always wanted to learn to sail."

"Wow that sounds like a major trip. You have the summer off but remember, I have a job with 3.5 vacation days left until I die." I say sadly.

"Well you can take a leave of absence or better yet quit your job. You said you don't like it much anyway. Come with me to the islands of Greece."

He gets down on a knee to recite a poem:

"The Owl and the Pussy-cat went to sea
In a beautiful pea-green boat,
They took some honey, and plenty of money,
Wrapped up in a five-pound note.
The Owl looked up to the stars above,
And sang to a small guitar,
"O lovely Pussy! O Pussy, my love,
What a beautiful Pussy you are,
You are, you are!
What a beautiful Pussy you are!"

"Ian, oh my god! Are you kidding me? Get up, please, you are embarrassing me." I say as he is attracting glances.

Ian gets up and ever the teacher gives me the facts. "Do you know that poem? Edward Lear in the Book of Nonsense wrote it in the 1800s. He was an artist hired by the London Zoological Society to illustrate birds…"

"I've heard of the poem." I snap, hating when he goes into teacher mode. We are silent.

Ian orders a large pitcher of Sangria. "Well if you want to travel you have to make time for it," he calculated, "we have three months to save."

"I don't know Ian, I'll have to think about it," I twisted the napkin under the table. I couldn't stop thinking of that kiss today and how electric I felt next to Alfie. Ian searched in this jacket pocket for something as the Sangria was brought to the table and our glasses filled.

"We'll have the paella for two." Ian orders without even asking what I want. "It's a traditional dish with rice and chicken, chorizo, clams, shrimp and lobster all in a saffron garlic broth. You'll love it."

"I did want to try the veal cutlets in mushroom sauce…" It was too late the waiter was off.

"I'd like to make a toast to us. We have been together for almost a year now. We made it through Europe and have been comfortable living together. We make a good team, and I have so much to teach you. I think it is time we made it official." He took out a beautifully sculpted ring with my birthstone. "It is not a traditional diamond, but you are not a traditional woman."

"It is beautiful." I said with great resistance.

"Designed by one of the faculty especially for you," he reached for my hand, it fit perfectly he made sure of that.

"But Ian, this is a big step, maybe we should talk about this…" I twisted the ring off my finger. "I do admire you and care for you but I am just not sure of what I want right now. I have been thinking about going back to school, and what about the promise I made myself to have my own apartment some day?"

"Living alone is highly overrated. Come on we're great together, all my friends say so; even Tomlin thinks you have calmed me down. I am definitely less anally retentive around you. You make me more spontaneous and I bring you stability."

Flustered I almost spill my glass of Sangria but he catches it before it falls. "See we make a good match." He could be very persuasive in any argument. I down the glass of Sangria.

"Ian I think the world of you but I am not ready for this." I was panicking. The smiling waiter refills the Sangria glasses.

"Well then take the ring out of my love and deep affection for you. We'll just call it a friendship commitment ring, ok? When you are ready, you will be ready." He placed the ring back on; it sparkled in the candlelight. I agree to take it.

No sooner had I put the ring back on, than he tells the waiter we were committed to be engaged. They send over the mariachi band to serenade our table. Ian takes my hand and starts to cry with his other hand on his heart he sings along with the band. A giant bowl of seafood is set between us. I really wanted the veal.

I think of Alfie and drown my guilt with more Sangria.

CHAPTER 6
– POSTCARDS FROM THE EDGE

Spring fills the city with tulips and azaleas that fragrance the air. It is a picture-perfect New York day.

Sunday's French toast and sparkling wine is eaten silently over the N.Y. Times. Sunday and the N.Y. Times is my favorite ritual.

"I see the Joffrey is doing something experimental at the Joyce, we should make an evening of it." Ian says over his glasses, over his paper, over the remains of breakfast.

"Did we meet them at the art opening two weeks ago?" I am not really listening.

"Meet who?" Ian asks.

"Joffrey and Joyce, were they that hippy couple? You know the one that painted the close ups of his wife's body parts. A bit obsessive if you ask me. Some things are not meant to be so in your face! I don't think I could spend a night with them after seeing her you know what blown up and plastered all over the gallery walls. Hard to find topics of conversation after that." I say, but in truth I envied lovers with that kind of obsession. I longed for that kind of intimacy.

"No, no, no, that was Jeff and Jane Ann" Ian laughs, "I was talking about the Joffrey Ballet performing at the Joyce Theater."

"Oh sure, whatever." I felt pretty stupid and went off to make more coffee as Ian switched from the Times to his maps and guidebooks.

He has been planning our summer trip for months. He had made four possible itineraries already, which were tacked to the library bulletin board. Although I agreed to the trip I had grown tired of the plans and was thinking of Alfie's face when I told him I quit my job.

After Valentine's Day I told Alfie that Ian and I were pre-engaged. At first he seemed to be upset.

"Just as well," he said after calming down. "We want different things. I have no interest in traveling and you have gotten spoiled on fancy dinners and art openings. Besides I have a girlfriend that I am quite fond of. Why mess up two good things?"

We still met for cigarettes and lunch but invited other people to join us so we would not be tempted or alone. Still my heart skipped a beat every time I saw him. Every time his fingers touched my hand in any way, the sparks continued to fly.

In May, I gave my job two weeks notice. They said they will consider it a leave of absence until the fall. I know I will not return but agree anyway. There was an hour of closing papers and procedures to endure. This is my price for freedom.

I met Alfie for a cigarette at 3 p.m. and told him that I had given notice. His calm demeanor turned violent, a side of him I had not seen.

"Now what am I supposed to do?" He threw the lit cigarette on the ground and left me standing there. The next day Alfie didn't show for work, or the day after, or the day after that, and by Friday he quit.

So I finish my last two weeks without him. I walked all of our old routes missing him, our talks, how he made me laugh. Around him, I didn't feel like I was a student with so much to learn. Alfie made me feel like a mysterious women that held a hidden secret. He noticed what I wore and loved my scent of perfume. There was passion in how he looked at me that unnerved my confidence and I liked it.

It is just as well I guess. It is easier this way, I told myself as I feed the birds part of my lunch in Central Park. But there was emptiness without him. I missed the way he flirted with me and made me feel feminine. The way he held a cigarette, the way he leaned against me in a crowded elevator gave me goose bumps… and then there was his kiss.

In A Beautiful Pea-Green Boat

Ian had his farewell lunch with his mother where she handed him the summer check. He sublet the apartment to another teacher and we were off to the airport for an adventure in Greece.

Decked out in sailor attire with a blue striped Italian shirt (Ian bought in Venice last year) white pants and sailor's cap, Ian boards the boat with more luggage than I have. Of course almost one entire suitcase is dedicated to guidebooks. For the past two months I have watched him pack and repack, plan and revise the itinerary. It is the first trip he has planned without a crowd of people, just the two of us, a breakthrough Tomlin called it.

Throughout the spring, Ian checked the maps, cross-referenced the guidebooks and practiced Greek words with *Anyone Can Learn Greek*, a record he bought in the Village flea market. On Friday he'd cook Greek or Mediterranean foods. He bought books on sailing and practiced his sailor knots. I was completely 'Greeked' out before the plane even landed. I tried to immerse myself in all of it but I felt I had left something behind.

We travelled to Athens where it was 105 degrees in the shade. We walked up to Mt Olympus where the wind blew dry sand into the tourists' eyes as they all positioned around the Parthenon for pictures. Pictures they would all take with eyes closed. Everything was roped off and in scaffolding, no workers on site, anywhere, and a common sight I learned for Greece. A hundred work sites and no one was ever working?

"The guide books say that most of the decorative carved stone frieze is on exhibit in London." Ian guides the way, as other tourists that speak a little English follow along. Soon Ian has accumulated a group as he leads us around the Parthenon.

I wondered why we didn't just go to London and view the art in an air-conditioned museum? Sweat drips down my face and back, I spit out some of the dirt that blew in my mouth.

After three days of the hot sun and city heat, we take a small plane across Greece to Corfu where we make our way to the dock. We are assigned a pea green boat and meet our captain. Captain Grayson Jones had a cockney accent, really bad skin and a red nose from way too much drinking. He smelled green and a bit pickled.

"Welcome aboard! I will be sailing aboard your boat by day and returning to the mother ship at night. We will have two or four hours each day to sail and reach our destination. In the afternoon, the flotilla will anchor near a small village, where the locals will prepare dinner. In the afternoons you will be free to swim, nap, windsurf, or go to shore and explore.

"The locals set up their crafts and wait for our arrival. The older women knit shawls from the wool of their lambs with beautiful skill. Local pottery and ceramics are abundant if you like that sort of thing. Everywhere are tributes to the naked male athlete, most statues have extremely large penises. These over-sized phallic symbols are said to bring fertility and good luck! For over 2000 years the Greeks have not moved forward but have held onto their ancient heritage with complete pride. Their phallic symbols are a favorite. For this, they were most proud and it is reflected in slogans on their t-shirts." The Captain has us all laughing.

"Ahaaw... Love to Love You Baby..."

We sail the first day in the hot sun silently as the wind pushes us effortlessly over the aqua blue waters. It is a magical day.

We anchor in a cove and row a dingy to shore where we dine. Town is a single road lined with a few shops facing the sea. The road would be cleared of goats, and set up with tables for dinner. By midday, lamb roasted on a spit, being slowly turned by an old man for hours. Moussaka baked for hours with layers of cheese, eggplant and potatoes. And giant bowls of Greek salad tossed with feta cheese, sweet onions, tomatoes, tart olives and slivers of salty fish. There are the same confections at every port, cakes and cookies covered in nuts and fruit dripping in honey. I order baklava every chance I get. Just as with Italy, I find it hard to fit into my clothes as I eat and drink the nights away.

After several days, every island stop is the same. The same food, oversized phallic tourist items, and elderly women knitting shawls. The men would tend the herd and the fire as they turned the roasting lamb. It was clearly a society where the women did most of the work behind the scenes and the men drank a lot.

Ian buys me a t-shirt that says 'Greece is for Lovers'!

During dinner, a small band would sing a selection of Greek favorites. After dinner the tables would be cleared away, and the street became a dance floor. Entertainment consisted of loud pumping disco music played over and over again '*Turn the Beat Around*' amplified over a scratchy PA system and with not much else to do, we all danced the *Hustle*.

At night the stars come out making a perfect dome for our disco. The breeze off the sea cools us from the hot day as we recover from the abundance of food we just ate. Dinner is followed by larger bottles of Ouzo, which we would empty. Captain Grayson at 52 had lived many lives and would tell stories of his life in the Peace Corps, or his time as a radio pirate. He could captivate an audience and make us all laugh with his adventures. We got silly shit-face drunk most nights and danced the night away.

In our flotilla there were 10 American fighter pilots and their lady friends. They were a wild bunch on a mission. One of them had cancer and this trip was his big wish before starting chemo. By night, they matched shot for shot with Captain Grayson further inspiring his storytelling. By day the men were up early and ready for action. You could never tell they were shit-faced the night before as by midday they were sailing their sailboats in a V like formation, as they flew their military jet planes.

On the last night, over the loud speakers, Donna Summers' sultry voice starts moaning "Ahaaw, *Love to Love You Baby*" seeps seductively into the night air. After hearing the same sound track every night on every island, disco was getting old, but Donna's *Ahaaw, Love to Love you Baby*, was the call to dance. Chris the man with cancer, asked me to dance. We danced close and slow. He was such a hunk of a man it was hard to believe he was sick as he had an erection worthy of a Greek God. I could feel that through my summer skirt. I didn't mind.

"So really, what is it with the old man?" Chris howled in my ear over the sultry sounds of "Ahaaw, *Love to Love You Baby*,
Ahaaw, *Love to Love You Baby*."

I looked over at Ian who was dazzling an old knitting lady, teaching her his amazing knot tricks and learning hers.

"What do you mean?" I asked knowing very well where this conversation was going. He is dancing very close but I don't mind, I've enjoyed dancing with each of the fighter pilots. It feels good to have a man in my arms that packs heat between his legs.

"Life is an adventure," he says as he twirls me around, pulls me close and grinds into me. "You're young and beautiful, why settle? Go find yourself a man closer to your age that can fuck the hell out of you." Under the dark of night I am sure I am beet red. "Don't get me wrong, Ian is a great guy... really great guy, and everyone likes him. But, you are young and full of light and energy; so don't settle for an older man. Find someone who can be your equal, your best friend. Sex is for the young, you shouldn't miss out." I thanked him for the dance, the grind and his advice.

Around midnight the bar closed, the music stopped and by tomorrow morning, the dance floor would be a street again filled with goats.

Blinded by drink, Ian and I stagger back to our dingy and paddle back to our boat. Ian snores all night making it hard for me to sleep. I wrap a sheet around my naked body and head out on deck to watch the stars. The air is chilly but it feels good on my sunburned body. I let the sheet fall off; I am naked under the stars, alone with the moon.

I think about dancing close to Chris, how vital he seemed, his erection pressing into me, and how warm his body felt. I think about all the things he said. Ian was a great guy and I had seen so much of the world with him. However I would always be the student and he would always be more interested in his guidebooks than my body.

"Sex is for the young," he had said. I longed for a man who wanted me as a woman should be wanted. I ask the stars to show me a sign. Should I stay with Ian or look for a new adventure? Just then a school of dolphins swim by the boat and laugh at me. I curl into the sheet and sleep on deck where I dream of naked Greek gods competing at the Olympics with giant penises and I get to choose the winner. I wake with the sunrise and head off to bed.

Lightning Strikes

On the last day of sailing, we reluctantly head back to home base. Our boat trails the pack. Up ahead, the fighter pilots are motoring in their V shaped formation with their flags flying one last time. Ian still has a hundred and one questions for Captain Grayson and requests that instead of motoring, we sail back to port. Out of nowhere a dark storm cloud appears in the distance racing towards us.

"Oh, that doesn't look good," said Captain Grayson. "Quick, take down the sails!" he hollers. The sea turns angry and grey and the swells are rough. We lose sight of the boats up ahead. The wind whips the sails in every direction as we fight to tie them down.

Captain Grayson yells, "Batten down the hatch!" We scramble to pack the sails away as the waves toss us around. The sky and water turn ominously black. We put on life jackets and Captain Grayson orders us to tie ourselves to the rails while we ride out the storm. We hold on for dear life.

Lightening cracks the sky and thunder shakes the boat. Ian forgets how to tie the knot and the last sail flaps wickedly in the wind. Captain Grayson orders us to tie ourselves to the boat.

Tied to the sailboat we are tossed around in the storm like a weightless cork. I fear this is the end. I am going to die here, now, today! My life flashes before me. What have I accomplished? What mark would have I left behind? I never went to Parsons or had my own place. I was going to die before I reached twenty-five.

I imagine my obituary, being read by Lannie the Crossing Guard to all at the bakery who will listen: "Young Bakery Girl, Lost in the Ionian Sea. What a shame," she would read, "what a shame," and they all would agree.

"Please God, if I make it out of here I'm going to follow my dreams, go back to school, and live on my own." I say to my God, whomever he may be, as I hope somewhere someone may be listening. Suddenly a sense of calm takes over my body. If I die, I decide, this would be a poetic way to end my life. So I face the wind and heavy rain that stings my face and with a strange calm, I ride the storm like a windsurfer and prepare for my demise.

CHAPTER 7 – A PROMISE KEPT

A Vintage Walk-Up

'Take the F Train to Queen's read the ad in the paper.
'… Loft living can be found in a vintage walk up, studios and one bedroom apartments still available'.

The subway rushes through the stations of Queens; Jackson Heights, Forest Hills and Kew Gardens. I get off at Union Turnpike to meet a realtor that has agreed to show me loft spaces within my budget. We drive to a building next to the Long Island Railroad tracks.

"How far are we from the subway?" I ask as we climb the stairs to the third floor. "About 10 blocks, but you are right near town. There is a bus on the corner, everything you need is here, greengrocers, laundromat, and the LIRR is only a few blocks away," says John as he checks his stats.

"Heat is included, you pay electric, new security locks (there were three), and it is rough, but has lots of potential. Based on your criteria I immediately thought of this place." he looks up from his clipboard puzzled.

"Will you be moving in by yourself?" he asks incredulously.

After undoing a bunch of locks we enter a long hallway, which opens up to a large room with two windows, another hall leads to a large bathroom with a claw foot tub, and a second room he describes as the bedroom. The space isn't huge but I can imagine a bed in the main room and still have enough room for a cozy couch and a kitchen table. The room for my studio has large windows that once cleaned would give me southern light.

"What about a kitchen?" I ask.

"It does have a small refrigerator and you could set up a counter for a hot plate or now everyone just uses a microwave. My wife would be lost without her microwave," he reassures me.

"This will need a good cleaning," I look around a bit discouraged, but truthfully my heart is racing, as this is just what I had imagined.

"As a girl alone, wouldn't you rather I show you a nice one bedroom apartment?" he asks looking through another folder.

I respond, "If they will take $500 a month, I'll take it." Back at his office, after a phone call, I sign the papers, hand over two checks, one for the realtor who takes a month's rent and one for the landlord for 1st month rent and security. This doesn't leave me a lot of money in the bank but it buys me freedom and a set of keys.

Back in Ian's apartment I explain to him that I have rented a place.

"Just like that you got on the subway and rented the first place you saw, are you crazy? You just started making some money why blow it all on rent when you can stay here?" This was true, after Greece I never went back to my old job. Instead I started freelancing and one of my first accounts was Levi's. "You're only 23, what if you don't make a success out of it…? Businesses take five years to get off the ground. What will you do then? I think you should cancel and think this through."

"This is something I need to try. I told you from the start this was a promise I made to myself. It is time I live on my own. We can still see each other I don't want to be out of your life, just out of your apartment." I take off the ring and hand it to him. "I cannot promise long term with you, Ian. I am sorry; you are great. It is just that I am still searching for what I want in my life and you have already found what you want.

"I want you!" He refuses the ring, "I bought this for you, what am I going to do with this find some other girl with the same birth stone?"

"Ian, I am sorry, I do love you. It's just I'm not in love with you. I am not ready to settle down and well, you are. I need to grow up, be on my own a bit. I know deep down you do understand."

"Tomlin was right. He knew you would leave me some day," he says looking out the kitchen window as he smashes the mobile of forks and knives. "Ian this one is going to need her freedom someday. She is a bird that will need to fly. He says I just date younger women who are in awe of me for a spell then end up needing to spread their wings. He said you needed a father figure and when you got tired of a father, you would leave for a lover. Are you leaving me for a lover? Have you found a lover?"

"No Ian, there is no 'lover' in my life. I have thought about this since Valentine's Day, and this is what is right for me." I reach for tissues and take his hand. We are both crying.

"Tomlin says it is the sex thing? I told him you did not seem to be satisfied. I know that is important to you. But in time that won't be so important. Look at what you have here, a place to stay, shared expenses, we are great traveling buddies, and I'm making cheesy cornbread and black bean chili for dinner. It is one of your favorites. You're willing to give up my black bean chili? You must be crazy," he laughs and tries to smile. "Why don't we both go to Tomlin and talk about this? I'll make us an appointment."

"Ian I want to thank you for everything. You have given me such memories I will cherish all my life. But we are just at different places in our lives. You want to get married and start a family and I am just not ready to take on all of that. I wish I were because I do think you are wonderful and will make some woman, the right woman, very happy." He smiles and doles out hot chili with a dollop of sour cream and sprinkles slivers of scallions on top – I will miss his cooking!

We promise to still see each other but after two dinners and a movie, we stop calling, as getting together becomes awkward. I hear from friends that within a year Ian is engaged again to another student and has plans to get married. I wish the best for him.

Above the Tracks

I move into the apartment in Queens and start by cleaning the place up. Rusty water comes out of the pipes at first and big water bugs are in the bathroom and hallway. It is not paradise. I buy cleaning supplies, roach traps and bug spray. I scrub.

I have very little, a sleeping bag, a few mismatched cups and plates, an electric wok and chop sticks that Ian gave me as 'a parting gift'. I set up my drawing table and arrange art supplies on a makeshift shelf. I buy a vintage table from the Salvation Army and chairs from the 50s, colored sheets to make curtains, and a toaster oven, which actually works on 3 settings.

My mother brings an air mattress and a blanket my grandmother's knitted. She thinks I am crazy to pay so much for this dive of a place... but knows stubborn women run in our family. We buy paint. On the street, I find end tables, a big easy chair and a gaudy brass lamp I decorate with beads. I pay two guys to bring up an Empire couch that is in the trash. I find everything I need or it finds me. One day along the alley I find some old leather suitcases and curled up in one, is a kitten! He has one green and one blue eye; I name him Hobo. Together with Hobo rubbing my ankle, I clean and paint and soon the place comes to life. Kitty and I are happy as fall sets in.

The neighborhood is mostly filled with Hassidic Jews with big families. Like Mother ducks, the women take the lead as all their ducklings spread out in a line behind them. The women are covered from head to toe, long skirts, and heavy stockings, with no elbows or hair showing. Their daughters are dressed the same. By marriage, the women have shaved off their hair and wear wigs. *Sadie's Hat and Hair Emporium* has a constant stream of ladies who go in and out of the shop all day. The young men and boys are all dressed alike in long black coats, old-fashioned brimmed hats with long curls that hang down in front of their ears. The old men have long beards that hang down to their chest. On Friday evenings before sunset the men all head to temple where they pray.

The men and women are often separated except on Saturdays and Holy days when they put on their finest hats and wigs and as a family walk to the Temple. Outside the baby strollers line the courtyard until after services are over.

I find some of the men to be lecherous and when their wives are not looking they smile and flirt with me. The women rarely smile they have to keep track of too many kids.

For such a conservative neighborhood, the movie theater features XXX adult films only and there are not one but two adult video shops in town. Along with a large Jewish population are Indian families. In contrast to the turtlenecks, long skirts and drab colors of the Hasidic women, the Indian women float down the streets in layers of magenta, tangerine and lime silks covered in geometric patterns. They decorate their ears and noses with gold. They have a red dot on the center of their forehead and arms covered in colorful bracelets that jingle as they walk. Some are beautiful creatures with long dark hair braided down their backs and dark eyes that are accented with heavy charcoal eyeliner. They are exotic and I love watching them float down the street past the Hasidic families that waddle along like ducklings.

The neighborhood has great swells of ethnic cuisines. Chinese takeout food, Mama's Jewish Delicatessen features potato pancakes and stuffed cabbage, Joe's Pizza by the Slice and coming soon an Indian Palace. It is an interesting place to live.

In my building, the neighbors are strange. Above me is a flamenco dancer, alcoholic who entertains men on Saturday nights. Till 1 a.m. you can hear her shoes tapping away on the wood floors above. After the floor shows you can hear her men grunt and groan as the floor squeaks. She has a son who stands over 6 feet tall with big teased up wild black hair. He scared the hell out of me one night when I returned late. On Friday nights, he rehearses with his David Bowie cover band; they may look the part but they have little talent. I think they would be better to be a Kiss cover band and hide behind heavy makeup. I take it he and his mother take turns over the weekend as to who has the run of the place.

Next to my flat is a woman named Myrna, who I try to make friends with but when she sees me on the stairs she hides back in her apartment and I figure I should just leave her there. My bed is next to her wall and at 8 a.m. before work she practices piano and does her scales for one hour. Religiously from 8 to 9 a.m., every morning she practices, except Sundays. Her piano is so badly out of tune and well, so is she.

At 8 a.m. on the dot 'bong' in a minor key radiates through the walls. That first horrid note that starts the hour long rendition of her scales 'ah ah ah ah ah ah ah, bong ah ah ah ah ah ah ah' bong goes the second out of tune key and one more round of scales. The woman has lungs. By the time she reaches the high notes my cat runs into the closet and I put on headphones trying to drown out the screeching but there is no use. The sound penetrates through the walls like acid.

Once I was out on the street shopping early at the greengrocer as she was rehearsing, and you could hear her down the block. People in the store remarked that it was the worst sound they had ever heard. They covered their ears and shook their heads as if in pain. Yeah, right next to my bed behind a wall was this women and her piano.

On the first floor are two Indian families living in a small space. To support their families, the women start cooking Indian samosas filled with potatoes, peas and cumin that floats through the building and tickles your nose. I buy four for a dollar and they include a spicy red tamarind sauce on the side. I am a steady customer, for a dollar I have two meals. Within a few months they are forced to leave, as the smells of cooking have bothered some of the tenants.

I believe the complaints must have come from Harold Walker, retired schoolteacher, who lives alone. Many things bother Harold, including the sounds I make at night walking above him. He likes to bang on his ceiling to remind me that he is there.

As my business grows, I work through the night and the sound of my air gun makes him pound on the ceiling. I try muffling the noise of the compressor by putting the machine on top of a few towels and in a box. I try to save my spraying to the daytime hours, as I understand he is an early riser. Sometimes that is hard to do if I have to meet a deadline. My cat is also a night runner and has taken to running across the room, up the walls, makes a flip and at full force nosedives into me. (I plan to get him declawed and fixed... I hear this should calm him down.) It is his 3 a.m. ritual which sets off Harold who bangs on the ceiling some more. I don't understand why he has no issue with the piano soprano and the tap dancer and her rocker wild-haired child!

The LIRR train is constant; it rattles the foundation of this old factory building with every train that rushes by. When I paint precision stripes, I need to lift up my ruling pen until the train passes. The windows rattle, the dishes rattle. Some nights, when it is hot, I like to sit on the fire escape and watch the trains go by. I think of all the lives, rushing from place to place. I imagine the train carries my lover and I wait for his return. I know that sounds a bit Freudian, but I am lonely.

Sitting on the fire escape I breathe in the night air, imagining I had a man coming home to me. It starts to rain a warm Indian summer rain and I stay put until I am soaking wet. Yesterday I met Mom at the station and showed her the town and my new place. She was not so pleased that I left Ian. All she kept saying was poor Ian, poor Ian. She did understand the sex thing when I explained it to her. Still, she was supportive that even in this place I was following my dream. She hated the place, but I think she was proud of my independence.

Strange Encounters

My Levi's account grew and soon I added a few more customers. I was able to cover the rent and buy art supplies. I am saving to go back to school and start the paper work to apply to Parsons. By word of mouth I gain more customers. The Ralph Lauren group becomes one of my new customers. I paint stripes for the men's dress shirt division who connected me to the home furnishings division. Today's assignment: paint tartan plaids on fine paper that can be applied to plates and mugs for their showroom. Seems their sample delivery out of China is all yellow and there isn't enough time to ship new ones. I have one week to create two-dozen samples of red and black buffalo plaids with a twill effect. It is difficult to create without cutting the fine paper with my X-Acto knife.

Why anyone would want to eat on red and black twill plaids, I don't know but at $50 for a red plaid, this is a great assignment. For one week I have plaids drying everywhere in my apartment trying to make this deadline. Because it is Ralph Lauren, they have to be perfect. In the past a studio of eight people would need the whole week. I am exhausted as I ride the subway, portfolio in hand, with two-dozen samples done.

Ralph Lauren corporate offices occupy an entire brownstone on 54th Street. The receptionist buzzes me in and I take a seat. My designer is in a meeting, so I'm told I can help myself to some coffee while I wait. In the kitchen walks Ralph lamenting to a small group of followers that there are never enough vanilla yogurts!

"Please make sure you order extra as I am tired of only finding strawberry." He says with a smile to his assistant who writes down his every word. He is much shorter than I expected, very tan, very handsome, very determined. I smile as they pass by, though awe struck, I say "Hello". He smiles back as he and his followers leave the room franticly writing notes in their day planners.

Everyone in the office is absorbed in the Ralph Lauren culture. It must be a pre-requisite that to work for the company you must buy your clothes from the Ralph Lauren sample sale. They appear as if they came out of a print ad featuring country casual. The women with their long hair held back, wore full paisley or plaid skirts below the knee with beautiful riding boots, white shirts and blazers with big shoulders. It is the featured look for fall. The men are in button down shirts that all have embroidered polo ponies on their cardigan sweaters, corduroy pants and penny loafers.

My designer is crazed with deadlines before the new showroom opening. I have 'saved the day' and she is thrilled that I have met such a tight deadline. I give in my assignment still dumbfounded from being so close to Ralph. She takes my receipt and rushes me out the door. This job will cover rent for next month and I am very happy, my business with Ralph Lauren has grown nicely.

On the street I spot a little French bakery and in the window are my favorite almond croissants. I buy one as a reward for a job well done. I sit at the little counter and eat it with a cappuccino. The croissants are filled with butter, oozing with almond paste, heavenly. I buy three more and head to the subway. As I am waiting for the light to cross the street, still licking my sugared lips, I see Alfonso in a car waiting for the light as well. He sees me too and pulls over half way down the block.

He looks me over as if undressing me and shakes his head. "Wow, back from the world and look at you. Turn around and let me get the whole picture." He gets out of the car. "You're like a walking cupcake. What did you do, eat your way through Europe?"

I catch my reflection in a storefront window and he is right with my pencil stripped skirt and billowing top I do look like a giant cupcake. "Very funny, looks like you've gotten skinnier." I hide the bag of croissants behind my back.

"Unemployment will do that to you. Turn around let me look at you," He reaches back in the car for his cigarettes.

"I will not! What are you up to?" He offers me a cigarette and I take it.

"Just dropped off a friend and thought I would cruise the porn shops on 42nd Street and see what I could find. So, here you are!" he leans against the car all confident and sure of himself.

"So why did you just up and quit your job?" I ask bluntly.

"There was no reason to go back if you were not there." He exhales slowly. His breath makes me nervous.

I ask rather quickly, "still seeing your girlfriend?" and feel like an idiot.

"Oh, Gigi, she took a job in the Caribbean as a dental assistant. She wanted me to join her but I wasn't interested. I hate traveling. The whole sand and sea doesn't interest me. I drove her to the airport; she dressed in killer heels, a mini skirt and a low cut top. She wanted me to know what I would be missing. When she got off the plane, the dentist's wife took one look at her and she was fired on the spot. She's living on some houseboat with some guy and wants to come back. What about you, still with your professor sugar daddy?"

"No we broke up. I'm living in Queens now." I am so relieved that Gigi is no longer in the picture though I didn't need the visual description.

"Oh really, he opens his eyes wide. Do tell more..." He sucks deeply on his cigarette. I hold my breath until he lets the smoke out of his mouth. He unnerves me.

"Well I broke off the engagement, I mean commitment, after we came back from Greece. Traveling was wonderful. It is amazing how he picks up languages and always finds the best places to see and well obviously eat. He wanted to get married, have children, but I guess I didn't feel the same. We got along great but in some ways we weren't compatible." I couldn't believe I was telling him all of this and so quickly. I take a deep breath.

Alfie offers me a cigarette and I take one. As he leans in to light it, I can feel the heat of his body. I am sweating down my back and I try not to cough as I take a hit of the cigarette.

"It was the sex, right? Jewish men just don't know a thing about pleasing a woman. It is not in their DNA. That's why they buy jewelry and houses. If they could fuck, the women would need for nothing." I couldn't believe how blunt he was at times and well, how right. "So where are you now?" He touched my arm and my skin quivers with goose bumps.

"I just took a studio in Kew Gardens." I was blushing, his presence made me nervous as it always did. I deeply inhale the cigarette as a form of Dutch courage.

"Oh, I know that town, don't they have an X-rated movie house. I'd like to see your place. Maybe see your work…" he inhales the smoke deeply and continues to scan my body. I am uneasy and excited. I tug on my clothes feeling like nothing fits. "You know, I have a thing for beautiful Raphaelite women."

"Oh really?" Nervously I drop my bag of croissants to the ground.

"Ah the evidence, I see now my Cupcake, your weakness is sweets." He grins and brushes against my breast as he retrieves my bag. I am not sure if it is an accident. As he hands it back to me he doesn't let go and we stand there staring into each other's eyes. In the heart of Manhattan, on this busy street, time stands still. City noises all slow to a hum. We are in a new dimension where there is only the two of us and the beating of my heart. I take the bag back.

A police officer hollers from his car "Hey bud, if this is your car, move it or get a ticket! This is a no standing zone!"

"No problem officer, just leaving" Alfie heads to the car. "Wanna get some coffee? Can I give you a ride somewhere?"

"No I'm catching the E train." We quickly exchange numbers and agree to meet next week. Entering the subway I give my baked goods to a homeless man who devours one whole and licks his fingers in approval. He smiles broadly with missing teeth. Better him then me.

I catch an E train and watch the stations go by as I head back to Queens. I keep shaking my head in disbelieve. My face is still flushed. I can't decide if it was meeting Ralph Lauren or being close to Alfie that made my day? I love New York. You never know what is around the corner. I decide it is time to start a diet!

CHAPTER 8 - FIRST DATE

I put on some soft music. The cat stretches on the newly painted blue rocking chair. This is my home and I like what I see. It reflects the new me, a colorful work in progress.

Onions and garlic sizzle in the electric wok, I cut up and add the diced tomatoes, and it all comes to a simmer before adding basil. I add salt to a pot of water on the hot plate and set it with a low temperature. I wrap buttered Italian bread with fresh garlic in tinfoil and throw it into the toaster oven. I have managed to cook a dinner without a stove. I take one last look around the apartment. I dance around adjusting little things. By the fire escape window are the sunflowers I bought from the Korean market down the street. They were a splurge but well worth the price. The table is set with my grandmother's tablecloth and linens. I have been collecting mismatched Fiestaware and Bakelite utensils from the thrift shop. The table is full of color. I wash the two wine glasses I bought at the thrift shop, and set them on the table. Chilling in the fridge is one of my favorite wines from Tuscany. The sun is setting and the evening light starts to glow.

Alfie is coming for dinner. He is an hour late. For the third time, I change my clothes and put on a dress that is way too tight. I reach for a kimono when the rose-colored lingerie falls off the hanger. I hang it on the bathroom door, just in case I may need this later. I smile. I change again into leggings and an oversized top. The buzzer rings, as I add the kimono on top. I dance in my kimono to the door and hit the buzzer.

"Yes. Who is it?" I sing into the intercom.

"Who the hell are you expecting?" his voice crackled over the speaker. This wasn't the tone I was expecting. I buzz him in.

I check my reflection one more time. "Whatever… Why the hell did I cut all my hair so short? I have lost a few pounds. Good but not great." I say to the cat, he never answers but I talk to him just the same.

Alfie comes in like a tornado. He is all nervous energy and immediately lights a cigarette. I grab a bowl for an ashtray before his ashes hit the floor. He doesn't even notice. He tells me that Gigi has come back and with no place to go has moved in with him. He lied to her and said he was with his mother. He couldn't reach his mother so now he is nervous that she will find out. What if she goes over looking for him? I thought things were over between them but obviously they are not. He assures me this is only temporary, till she finds a place or can move in with her sister. I have never seen him so upset.

"She is nothing but trouble," he says, "nothing but trouble!"

"Well then why did you let her come back?" I ask.

He throws me an awful mean look, "She had nowhere else to go. What could I do?" He eventually calms down as we start to eat. He has lost a lot of weight and is hungry.

"What kind of sauce is this? No meat?" he turns up his nose. "Where is the Parmigiano Reggiano?"

I place the garlic bread on the table and get the butter and Kraft imitation powdered cheese.

"You call this cheese? This is cheese colored cardboard." He takes it reluctantly. "Americans…"

"Well it will have to do. I'm on a budget and a little limited here with a wok and a hot plate." I am offended by his attitude. The night goes on quite the same.

His Nonna made the best sauce in the world. He calls it gravy. He went on and on about being a boy and the smell of good food cooking for hours. His Nonna was a genius in the kitchen. Nonna devoted her life to take care of the family. Seems she raised him. Nonna was the most selfless woman he ever met. All other women just can't compare. Saint Nonna was the salt of the earth.

"She was a saint, a pain in the ass, but a saint. Lived till she was 90, drove everyone crazy. But cooked till the day she died. "

We sit down to eat and he tastes the garlic bread. It meets his approval. He slathers on the butter. He tries the pasta and gives it great thought with every bite.

"Guess it's not so bad?"

"Well at least it is not from a jar, you get points for that. Not bad. Most American women I have met know nothing about how to cook. Gigi eats only cereal bars and yogurt." I'm getting tired of hearing about Nonna and Gigi. I open the wine and offer him a glass. "I don't drink, detest the smell of it."

"Wow a man who doesn't drink, we don't have a chance." I wondered if I spoke too soon. He gives me a strange look and smiles in that way that makes me nervous. I quickly changed the subject.

"I always liked to cook. My mom went to work after my father died. We lived above a diner so I spent time in the kitchen and learned how to cook. Gus would tell me adventures of growing up in Greece while I watched him cook. By the time I was twelve he paid me a dollar an hour to peel vegetables and make soup. When I was sixteen I got a part time job in the town bakery which I had till I got out of school" I was talking fast and I knew I had already told him most of my life story.

"That sounds very suburban." he says, "We shall have the salad after the pasta." He pushes away the wooden bowl. "Americans have no sense of timing. In Northern Italy where I am from, there is a pride to cooking and a rhythm to eating. Americans throw everything at the table at once and everyone just jumps on in.

Food is like a play it needs to build. An appetizer wets the palate, it sets the stage, introduces the characters. The main course is the heart of your story, followed by something savory to set up suspense before you are gratified with the sweet dessert. In Italy, we ate fresh fish every day from the Mediterranean Sea. Have you ever had fish caught that day and served for dinner? There is nothing like it. We grew vegetables on our property. Food **is** love in my country. You can taste it in every bite. You Americans with your fast food and microwaves know nothing of cuisine! Cooking is a passion, an art, everything else is just …substance."

"Yes Italians do have a love of food. When I was there I couldn't stop eating pasta. I had pasta for lunch and dinner. Ravioli, filled with mushrooms, or cheeses, pumpkin filling was my favorite." I was babbling about nothing.

I felt defeated. This was not turning out like I'd had hoped. He was so uptight and I felt so nervous, like I was on the defensive about everything. I poured a second glass of wine as he lit another cigarette and stared at me intensely.

"Do you want to know why I never touch the stuff?" he went on before I could even answer. "My father died an alcoholic when I was eighteen. Liver disease sounds much more noble then saying he drank himself to death. Of course not before having an affair with the downstairs neighbor and knocking-up both my mother and his mistress. Some balls, two women in the same house. Good old dad! By the age of 13 I was left here in New York with my pregnant mother and grandparents. I think my mother did it on purpose hoping to keep him but he left anyway. That is how she caught him in the first place getting knocked up with me.

My grandfather hated me. He was a bricklayer and lived to do manual labor. My brother Giovanni is a lot like him, working in construction. He was my grandfather's favorite. He didn't 'get' me at all. I read books and liked to write stories. I don't think he could read at all. My mother and Nonna waited on me hand and foot." He takes a long drag off his cigarette, "I will never forgive my father for abandoning us that way."

When the timing was right, we ate our salad in silence. I realized we both were missing fathers in our lives. Something we had in common.

We move to the couch and Alfie rolls a joint that we smoke. After this we both calm down.

"Why would you get a cat? I hate cats!" he shakes the chair from which the cat is sleeping. The cat jumps off begrudgingly flashing Alfie the evil eyes.

"Hobo was in an old suitcase I found on the street, he needed a home. I'm more of a dog person but a cat fits better with a studio. He's been my companion these past few months." Hobo jumps on my lap as if on cue and starts to purr.

"I hate dogs even more then cats," Alfie sneezes. "I am allergic to cats," he takes a look around, "not a bad place. I like how you have a space to work. I've lived in a one-room studio underground for five years. The past two years with Gigi, her stuff was everywhere. I pay $300 electric included. My landlord is looking to sell the building and wants me out. I don't know where I'll find such a great deal. What does this run you?"

"Around $500 a month with electric," I admit no longer thinking I found a great deal.

"Why didn't you look in Brooklyn? You can find some deals in Brooklyn. When I came to this country, we lived in Hells Kitchen. I went from playing along the Mediterranean Sea to Hells Kitchen. My childhood was beautiful until I was 6. But my parents ripped it away from me and dragged me to this country where we didn't even speak the language. To live with a view of people's laundry and garbage cans. I'll never understand why they left Italy."

"I grew up on Long Island, my dad died of a heart attack when I was around 14. My mom went to work as a secretary and worked her way up to a legal assistant. It was a really small town with only one main street running through it. Everyone knows everyone. The neighbors all kept a watch on me. Mom always had to work but in the summers we would pack a picnic and take a bus to Jones Beach. I loved swimming in the Atlantic Ocean and dreaming of traveling across it to foreign places."

"That explains a lot, Cupcake," he kids.

"What do you mean by that?" I felt defensive.

"Just a nice conservative background, small town, uptight, Long Island girl." he says mockingly with a Long Island accent.

"You don't have much of an Italian accent, why is that?" I ask.

"Oh, I adapted once I hit high school as the kids made fun of me. I became Americanized. That's when the kids started calling me Alfie. I hate it but everyone butchers Alfonso so here I am Alfie with no accent and no real home. My brother on the other hand was born here and still is called by his Italian name Giovanni. Why people can say Giovanni and not Alfonso I don't know." He paces. "There was a point where the show Happy Days was popular and everyone started calling me Fonzie. I hate this country, I hated that name!"

"Fonzie?" I laugh but clearly this is not as funny to Alfie as it is to me.

"I started to refer to myself as Alfie and well it just stuck."

Alfie relights the joint from his cigarette. We are high enough. He inhales the heavy smoke just as he does his cigarettes. He looks around and then moves to the blow up mattress and signals me to join him. This man has been my fantasy for months and finally he is here in my apartment. Forgetting the awkwardness of dinner, we start to kiss passionately. He tastes like tobacco that reminds me of my very first kiss behind the train station. In seconds his hands are under my shirt flirting with my breasts and unhooking my bra. He kisses my eyes, my nose, my mouth. His tongue tickles down my neck. I surrender to him knowing this is what I have longed for and dreamed of.

I excuse myself to the bathroom to find my birth control and put on my beautiful rose-colored Italian gown. The gown is a bit tight but I squeeze into it. I fluff up my hair and my breasts and quickly brush my teeth. When I return, the lights are out except for the candles on the table. He is completely naked. He lights another cigarette. He takes my hand and leads me to the bed standing in front of me with one hand on his cigarette, the other stroking his cock. He turns profile. I try to stay calm but he is quite endowed and clearly very proud of it. He is like one of the Greek statues of Priapus, God of Fertility with his enormous phallus. I was sorry I didn't buy one but now I may have my own.

"Take off your gown, slowly" he purrs, "I want to watch you undress." I do what he says, feeling awkward and shy with my overweight body I struggle. I can't stop staring at him as he can't stop staring at me. The music has stopped and there is only the sound of the wind outside and the rattling of the windows as the trains pass below. My heart pounds loudly as it rushes blood through my veins.

"You are beautiful, so young, turn around" he says in Italian and motions with his fingers. He takes one last drag of his cigarette before resting it on the ashtray by the nightstand. He lays me down on the bed and slowly crawls on top. He caresses my body with his hands, my nipples with his tongue, slowly. I feel his weight, his skin is hot and smooth and soft. He is sweating; we shiver at each other's touch. I have never been so excited. He takes his time touching me all over.

I am scared. It has been a while since I have had a real lover. I feel shy and frightened like a sacrificial virgin, a virgin who is ready to give it up completely. I feel he is about to enter me when Hobo out of nowhere runs full-force up the wall and lands with nails out on Alfie's back. Alfie screams and grabs him by the neck and flings him with all his might across the room. The ashtray falls to the floor and ashes scatter everywhere. The cat bounces off the wall and screams, landing on all fours stunned and bug-eyed. Shaking itself off it runs around the room a few times before dashing into the studio. Alfie hides behind me. He has scratches running down his back and is bleeding. I put on my robe and get him peroxide to clean his wounds.

Along with the Italian curses I understand, "...Fucking cats!" I do my best to calm him down. He is violently mad. "Oh this is great! What the hell else can go wrong today?" The lit cigarette burns through the air mattress puncturing it. A slow hiss starts to grow. I run to put out the cigarette but it is too late, the mattress starts to deflate.

Alfie gets dressed and our evening is clearly over. Still cursing his bad luck he sneezes twice. "Nina it is either me or that god damn cat!"

"I guess you need to go, I choose the cat." Alfie curses as he leaves slamming the door behind him. The commotion wakes up Harold downstairs who starts banging on the ceiling.

"Great! Just fucking great!" I see the rose-colored gown on the floor where it fell from my body. I will never get laid in this gown, it is cursed. I pick it up and throw it behind the couch. I blow out all the candles and proceed to finish the bottle of wine in the dark. Hobo lies fast asleep on my lap purring. He looks up at me content now that he has me alone. I swear he is smiling. Cats are so much smarter than humans.

CHAPTER 9 - BURGER HEAVEN

Under the Mushroom

After a few weeks Gigi was gone, and Alfie calls to say, "let's meet up". The E train lets me off at the Roosevelt Avenue station. I climb up the stairs and wait in front of a barbershop. It is spring but we are having an early heat wave. I am sweating from just climbing up the stairs and had hoped to lose weight, but clearly that has not happened.

There is no Alfie so I wait. After about 10 minutes I see him at the newsstand across the way. He was hiding behind a magazine watching me, kind of creepy. When we do finally connect, he kisses me hello on both cheeks, smelling like incense. It is too hot to walk so we take an air-conditioned bus a mile or so to his apartment. He lives in a house by the airport that has three apartments; his is in the basement. It is dark until he finds the light switch that illuminates a cozy cave. The air conditioner has been running making it 30 degrees cooler then outside. It feels good. There are movie posters on the walls; a sofa and hexagonal card table with chairs. The focal point of the room is a big brass bed facing a tiny TV. As he locks the deadbolt lock he tells me the landlord has been known to walk in. I am nervous.

The kitchen sink is filled with dishes covered by a blue towel. The bathroom is damp and disgusting there are roaches. He lights a candle, and some incense, he then lights a joint and hands it to me. I am not sure if getting high will help my tension. I look at the brass bed and start thinking of that song '*Lay lady lay, lay across my big brass bed...*' I can't remember any other lyrics as that one line plays over and over again in my head. '*Lay lady lay, lay across my big brass bed...*' Why can't I get to another verse?

'Why wait any longer for the one you love when he is standing in front of you.' Yes, why wait I say to myself, take on this lover.

Alfie puts a record on a turntable and plays some soft jazz. He turns to face me as if to dance, God why didn't I learn to dance? I am clumsy and can just shift my excess weight from side to side. God why didn't I lose some weight? Why did I wear this dress? Why did I bun up my hair? I look like a nun.

He lowers the lights. "Take down your hair." I do what he asks, somewhat lost in his spell. "Now take off your clothes very slowly." I tremble and start to unbutton my dress. It has been so long since a man has wanted me. Alfie leans back and watches me carefully. He smiles. It has been so long since a man has desired me. I know I am standing but feel light headed as if I am a giant balloon filled with air and my tiny feet do not touch the ground. I am naked. My giant balloon body is trembling. He holds me close and caresses my hair. Softly, gently we sway back and forth.

He whispers softly in Italian, I don't know what he says. It sounds good. It feels good. Everything is all right. The world is good.

Our shadows dance on the wall, me a balloon bopping from side to side, him a thin line swaying and circling all around me. The incense has a sweet smell and the pot has filled my head. Totally surrendered to the moment, I see a cockroach as big as my thumb. It crawls up the wall over a poster of Bela Lugosi as Dracula. Bela and the cockroach look down upon me, watching, smiling all knowing. I close my eyes and decide to just ignore all outside interference, including my thought pattern that is exploding in a hundred directions. Am I worthy? Will I disappoint? Do I remember how? I shake my head of all of this to concentrate only on this strange man about to make love to me.

My blood pressure races, I am flushed in the moment, light headed. I remember I used to like sex. So why am I so shy and uncertain? I am not even sure if I remember how to be with a man? My mind wanders back to the cockroach, I open my eyes but it has gone. I look around to see where it has gone. Alfie runs his hands over my body, exploring the many hills, yet not so many valleys. He is long and lean, skinny next to my round frame. He makes me feel comfortable, still nervous I give in to him. Pulsating, panting, perspiring, hours go by in foreplay in this underground lair. Tense, excited, ready, wet and wanting. We have sex. We start on the bed, head to the couch, over a chair, on the floor and under the table.

Exhausted, we stay under the table. Alfie changes the music to the sound of a rainforest. He brings the pillows and blankets and for another hour we hide under this toadstool table and pretend we are horny frogs. We hide from the world in our dark makeshift forest. I never want to leave.

Alfie lights a cigarette and we both smoke.

Something about smoking a cigarette after such an encounter seems right. I am inhaling and exhaling. The taste of tobacco on my tongue tastes like his mouth. The same mouth that was just all over my body bringing me such ecstasy, as I had imagined it would. I love watching his mouth as he brings the cigarette to it inhaling, exhaling. I think I will start smoking after this. The refrigerator sputters as the air conditioner hums pumping frozen oxygen into the room. We listen to the sounds of rain and cuddle under the blanket. A candle illuminates the smoke as it floats and swirls through the air. We fall asleep in each other's arms like frogs in a rainforest under a mushroom, watched over by Bela Lugosi and his pet cockroach.

"Ya want fries with that order?"

Four hours later, exhausted and starved, we head to the Jackson Hole Diner by LaGuardia Airport. It is a rundown 50s metal streamlined diner with blinking neon signs of cowboys and airplanes. We take a booth with a jukebox. The cook behind the counter knows Alfie, "Hey Alfonso! How's it going? How's your mother?" They switch to Italian and talk at length.

Finally the waiter asks, "What can I get ya Al, the usual?" He writes down the order without an answer, "cheese burger, fries and a Pepsi …and for the new pretty lady?"

I check out the blackboard specials "I'll have a Greek salad." I really want a cheeseburger and fries but after this afternoon, I am back on a diet. At the last minute I change to what he is having, I add mushrooms and a diet Pepsi. Like that will make a difference to the calorie count of the coming meal.

When we are alone I say to Alfie, "I figure I must have burnt off a thousand calories this afternoon. I earned a cheese burger and fries."

"You should regain your strength," he says all knowing. I blush at the memory.

"I'll just start a diet tomorrow." A phrase I have been using for the last few years.

The waiter brings us our drinks, "I don't know how you do it Al always a pretty lady buying you a meal." They laugh but I am not amused. It is true, I will be paying for lunch. Alfie hasn't had a job in months and has no money. By the look of him, he has not eaten much lately.

"So Al," I ask when the waiter is out of range. "Is this where you take all your pretty ladies after having your way with them?" I ask not really wanting to know the answer. He smiles like a Cheshire cat. "How many pretty ladies are we talking about?" He ignores my question and offers me a cigarette. I decline.

He leans in close and changes the subject, "I like you, just as you are. Nice curves, you are not fat you are voluptuous. Cherubic like the goddess Venus, I would say." He looks me up and down as if I don't have any clothes on. "I like my women nude as well." He puts his hand on my leg. Even his stare drives me crazy with desire and I feel myself blushing again. If he wanted I would have let him take me right there on the countertop. "I must confess," he whispers, "I like my women full bodied and curvy, hell I like them large, like the painter"

"You mean Botticelli?"

"Yes, Italian men like their women to be women, not little girls. Not like these American stick figures with big hair, lots of padding and no tits. We like something we can hold onto, something to sink our teeth into." He says as the burger specials are placed in front of us and he takes a big bite. I blush.

I can't believe all my life I have hated my body for being bigger than other girls in school. Now I find a man who rejoices in my being pudgy. I have never enjoyed a cheeseburger more.

"I have news," I search through my bag for my acceptance letter, "I have been accepted to Parsons. I've been on a waiting list and it seems someone has dropped out."

His mood changes quickly, "Waiting list, sure. They are more than happy to take your money. What's the big rush to go back to school?

"Hey, this is pretty prestigious. Parsons is a big deal, I had to show a portfolio and take an art test that was judged. They don't accept everyone you know," I protest pointing a French fry in his direction. "Parsons is a dream comes true for me."

"Oh great, I'm a little old to be dating a schoolgirl... really Nina? You're going through with this degree thing? Can I ask why? Where are you going to get the money?" He lights a cigarette and inhales I watch his mouth. I am stuck on the word dating.

"I have the first semester taken care of, some financial aid and student loans after that, I guess. I do have my freelance business and well, I'll manage somehow. If I have to, I'll move back with my mother. I don't know I haven't thought this all through, but now that I have been accepted I guess I have to figure this all out." I say rather quickly surprised at his disapproval and my need to defend myself. "Do you have plans for the fall? What are **YOU** going to do for money? Did you contact that temp agency?" Joe the waiter winks at me as he takes away the dishes.

"Thanks Joe." Alfie crushed his cigarette in the ashtray and throws me a nasty look. "Yeah I have to go down on Monday for an interview with some non-profit company. It is just what I always wanted to be a 35-year-old temp. I'm looking forward to it."

"You'll do fine. You need to find some work. I like a man I can sink my teeth into as well. You could use some meat on those bones. And why are you so anti schoolgirl all of a sudden? I thought you would be excited for me, you know what this means to me." I folded the letter back into my bag.

"My first girlfriend went back to school when we lived together. She wanted to be a therapist. It ended our relationship. You meet people who have different experiences. It changes a person. All she wanted to do was psychoanalyze me and socialize with other would be therapists." She finished school and left me. A year later she married her professor and in no time she was pregnant."

"Well I promise not to psychoanalyze you. I have already done the professor thing. I may want to paint you?" He likes that idea.

"She would visit me once or twice a year just to get laid. Especially when she was pregnant she got really horny. It was a turn on to fuck a pregnant chick. When the second kid came she stopped coming around. So, what was the point of an education, if she turned around and just became a baby machine? Last I heard she was on number three."

"I know I had a friend in college from a wealthy family and all she wanted to do was to get married and live in the same town she grew up in. She could have had anything, gone anywhere, been anything. If I had money I would travel and see the world." I say.

"Travel is overrated. Can't we talk about anything else, it turns my stomach, people who make their whole life about having kids," he snarls. "I hate traveling, I hate kids and animals. When are you going to get rid of that fucking cat of yours so we can go to your place next time?"

Joe casually pushes the check in my direction. I snarl and pass back a $20.

"Shall we go back to my place for dessert?" Alfie says with a smirk, I can't believe he wants more of me.

Autumn Leaves Must Fall

It is a hike back and forth to school. I take the E or F train from 14th Street to the Union Turnpike station. My apartment is eleven blocks away. When I have too much to carry or the weather is really bad, I take the bus. This week money is tight, and I cannot afford the double fare, so I walk taking the route along the cemetery. The oak trees are starting to change color and are dropping their leaves everywhere. The streets are dark and I feel a bit frightened, I drag my feet so as to hear the rustle of the leaves and because I am tired.

Back to school I struggle with freelance assignments and school projects. My life becomes nonstop deadlines. With what is left of my money I buy a loaf of bread and some peanut butter. I thought the Fashion Institute of Technology was a struggle but Parsons is demanding in a very different way.

At FIT, I learned to create textiles through mathematic formulas and design patterns in perfect repeat with precise measurements. We learned the business of being a commercial textile designer and it was these skills that allowed me to get my first job and now freelance. Except at Parsons I needed to forget all the rules and learn to express myself artistically. Forget the borders and boundaries, the rulers and charts, and create art in freehand. I struggled to get 'out of my box'.

Alfie lands a permanent job at the non-profit agency. He hates it. One weekend I have no freelance so I stay over. In his lair, we get high, have great sex, and hide away from the world under the mushroom table. No one can reach us. We watch old black and white movie on his VCR. He teaches me about Film

101

Noir over delivered pizza. I stay an extra night not wanting to leave this decadent getaway. I'll catch up with work tomorrow.

When I returned home I realized that I had left a window open and Hobo had jumped out. Three floors down, there is a patch of dirt ground where he might have landed. I walk around the streets calling his name and I spend the next week looking everywhere but he has gone.

Alfie is downright thrilled that now he could stay at my house. He offers no comfort as I moan about my lost little buddy. He stays over most weekends now as I have work to do and he can lie around and watch TV.

"We should move in together," he says one night out of nowhere, "now that the little beast is dead."

"Hey, have a little heart I really liked that guy." I keep searching outside the window for weeks to come. Hobo has moved on.

"Look I didn't want to tell you, but my landlord is selling the building and wants me out by end of month. I figure I can give some new landlord all my money or move in with you and help you pay expenses here. We're together all the time anyway Nina, why should we keep two places?" I am shocked and say nothing. "Cupcake, why don't you answer me? I'm serious, we should move in together." He tries a gentler tone.

"I don't know that I want to live with anyone right now. I have school and work and well… I'm just not ready to share my space. I love being with you but I like living alone."

He is far from pleased with my response and we start to fight. After a while he regroups. "Here's the deal, I need to vacate my place by the end of the month. I just need a place temporarily until I find my own place, ok Ms. Independence…? While I am here I'll help with rent and utilities."

I must admit we are spending all our free time together. The sex is great. And I do need some help with rent and utilities as school supplies and transportation are killing me. "I don't want to share my space." He leaves annoyed at my 'attitude'.

Two weeks later he is moving in. Upon arrival we have a fight when I show him a drawer that he could put his stuff in temporarily. Silently we assemble the brass bed.

I wonder, … what have I got myself into?

CHAPTER 10 - PARSONS

I fly up the subway stairs by twos to reach 14th Street and 6th Avenue. The energy and excitement of Manhattan is contagious. Vendors along the street hawk their wares. Neon signs blink from shop windows. Colorful bins are filled with flip-flops, sponges, plastic dinnerware, fabric, toys, beepers, jewelry, perfume and clothes.

'Dress for success' they say. I am on a mission and choose a persona fit for riding the subways. Military garb is in fashion as is street chic. At the Salvation Army I find a cargo coat with hundreds of pockets, some high top sneakers, black leggings and some oversized men's shirts. It makes me feel edgy and hides that I am a girl. Alfie hates my new look.

"God gave you breasts for a reason. If I had a rack I'd be showing it off," he said on the first morning as I dressed for school.

"I need a bit of an edge to ride the subways," I say proud of my butch persona. I feel old at 25, broke and struggling but determined. I run a freelance business and go to school full time; it is a constant struggle. A struggle I seem to always be losing. As the semesters move on I lose most of my freelance customers. One by one, Ralph Lauren, Liz Claiborne, my top accounts, all drop me. By the time I return from a day at school my answering machine is full, but when I return their calls the next day, they have found someone else. After a while no one calls.

My one steady client now was Martin, a stylist who creates collections for sportswear firms like Levi's. Martin merchandises a collection of patterns and pitches the color changes from which I paint new samples. Before school started I would sit with him to style the line. He liked teaching me why something would work and why it would not. Everything needed to coordinate back to khaki pants and jeans. For different seasons, different color palettes would be created. I would mix these colors in paint in little plastic containers I got for free from the photo labs. As the seasons went by, there were hundreds of plastic containers in bins around my studio.

I juggle school deadlines with work deadlines and am constantly on the run to deliver assignments. It was an insane amount of pressure.

Alfie, my temporary houseguest, has now permanently moved in. We see each other for dinner and then I go to work and he goes to sleep. By midnight I go to sleep and he stays up late in my studio working on a script till 3 a.m. We are like roommates on different shifts. Some nights I have late classes and some nights he's at theater workshops. He is terrible with money. He spends his paycheck first at his dealer, then hands some to his mother. He does buy take-out food, which I gladly eat as I complain about what he has spent. As the months go by, less and less goes into the house fund and he also needs token money to get to work.

Masculine vs. Feminine Side

Parsons is crazy expensive. Almost all of the students are from rich families, whose parents fill up bank accounts easily accessible through any ATM. It must be nice to get whatever you want when you want; art supplies, pizza, a drink at the bar, and drugs. They just walk across the street from school where a machine in a wall spits out 20s. I live on ones and fives; twenties are like hundreds to me.

"What should we do this weekend?" "Who is playing at the Limelight, Mudd Club, or CBGBs?" "No let's check out what's going on at the Palladium!" "Sure you don't want to join us, Nina?" They say to be nice as they argue down the hall off to the diner for lunch.

"Thanks but I have work to do" which of course I always do.

"Let's do Indian for lunch" they agree.

"You pay for lunch and I'll pay for cabs…but lets stop at Citibank first." They all agree.

In truth I like when the 'gang' goes off to lunch. It means that the silkscreen tables are all mine. I unpack my apple, crackers and cheese and get to work. I unpack the sheet sets that I bought at a discount store on 14th Street and pinned them with T-pins to the printing tables. There are two refrigerators that store pigment paint in jars. I use the recycled colors to save money and choose soft rose, a light teal, and a buttery yellow for the feminine side of my sheets. I put on my Walkman with some Pretenders and wildly start to paint. Starting from the upper left and the yellow, I use big brush strokes that pull the pigment half way into the center of the sheet. With smaller brush strokes I overlap the other feminine colors. From the right side I do the same with deep greys, burgundy and violet. I think of being with Alfie, the different roles we take on, the way he makes me weak. I work ferociously until the fabric is complete and the colors have covered the entire fabric. It is an explosion, represents the passion I feel. I am pleased with the results when I notice people have gathered around to see. I tag the table as wet paint. While it dries I run to my art history class.

In my surface design presentation I talk about the melding of masculine and feminine sides, sex, and sides of a bed. The students were excited about the concept but the teacher gave me a D. He said he didn't get it. My supplies were cheap and my colors looked secondhand. Later on, Alfie said, "what did I expect, he is gay and must have taken offense at the masculine and feminine sides of my presentation."

Lesson learned in design; you must know your audience and design accordingly. I take my sheets home and try them out on our bed they work just fine and Alfie gives them an A as we christen them!

A Fashion Shoot Deep in the Forest

Alfie collaborates on some of my projects and helps write my papers.

Photos are needed of my masculine and feminine sheet collection. Deep in Forest Park we tie the hand painted sheets to low branches. The wind brings them to life as I take pictures in between the wind gusts. A group of horseback riders come up the path. The moving sheets spook their horses and the riders turn and gallop away.

We finish taking pictures and fold up the fabrics into my bag before heading back through the park. At the point of the pine forest we pass by rangers on horses and they ask us if we know about the fashion shoot in the woods. We deny knowing anything and continue to walk on laughing hysterically when out of sight.

On the way home, we pass Raibman's Antique Shop noticing an old wooden drawing table out front. The owner wants $150, I get him down to $100 we turn over $25 as a down payment and return the next week when I get paid. It is in pieces and takes two trips to carry up the stairs. Assembled, I polish it with Old English oil till the wood glows. It is the most beautiful thing I have ever owned as I place it by the window, and in no time it is cluttered with half-finished work from Martin.

I take an art history class on Impressionist painters. We spend most of the class viewing slides in the dark of Picasso, Monet, Modigliani and Matisse. When pictures of Van Gogh's sunflowers are projected on the screen, I smile. I remember the train through the South of France and the fields of sunflowers all bowing to the sun. I use my drawings and photographs of sunflowers from my trip to Italy in a final project. I argue that Van Gogh was a realist more then an impressionist. My presentation gets an A; that helps balance the D.

Neon Lights in SoHo

Second year I take classes in Industrial Design, Computer Graphics and Neon Sculpture. My favorite class is in a glass factory in SoHo. On the street level, it is a gallery of beautiful glass sculptures, bowls and vases organic in design. They are displayed by individual color and reflect a rainbow in the afternoon light. Illuminated by the sun they glow with life. Upstairs is the glass workshop artists manipulate bubbles of molten ooze on the ends of metal rods. These are placed inside of furnaces blazing with fire. They twirl the rods back and forth expanding the ooze with gravity, colors are added, and with a blow of air into the rod they can be altered and create shapes. The ooze cools and is tapped like magic off the rods as beautiful pieces of glass. I love to watch the glassblowers work their magic.

In the back of the studio is my class in Neon Sculpture. It is my second semester with the same teacher, Diego Perez. He helps me create a piece that is a face. One side has hard bends and lines and the other side is softer with flowing hair.

"The melding of masculine and feminine, I get it." He shows me how we can make two pieces that hang together and use different colored gasses to create different colors. I follow my pencil drawing that maps out each shape. Over an extremely hot gas flame, tubes are heated and with just the right pressure will bend into angles. There are industrial fans humming away in the windows pulling the hot air out, still, the thermometer reads 105 degrees. Everyone is down to shorts and t-shirts intensely focused on the work as sweat drips down our backs. There is something very exotic about being in this furnace. The ratio of men to women is favorable. My teacher is hot literally and figuratively. He has beautiful skin that glistens with sweat and under his T-shirt you can see his nipple rings. He touches my arm and helps me to get the bend in the glass I am trying to achieve. As class is ending, Diego announces a party this weekend at his loft, and invites us all to come see his latest glass installation.

Saturday night Alfie and I take the F train into the city and head to SoHo. We fight the entire way. He hates parties, hates crowds and hates people who drink. He starts to go into a panic attack as soon as we leave the apartment and just wants to pick a fight. This is how he gets out of things, with drama and conflict but I am not buying into it. He climbs the subway stairs as if it is his last mile.

"We will need to get more cigarettes," he announces to let me know that I should buy him cigarettes to get through this.

"I can't believe you dragged me all the way into the city for some stupid teacher's party. Who is this guy and why the hell are we going? What is it with teachers and you?" he says as he packs his new pack of cigarettes against his leg and rips open the cellophane with his teeth. Feeling uneasy, I have one too.

"How often do we go out? We never go out, I thought it would be fun to be in SoHo, do something in the art community." I say as we make our way up Houston past a saxophone player wailing to the traffic. His music is haunting but no one stops. "The night is beautiful, look at all the lights in the skyline." I take his arm to lead him on, "…and please try to relax."

The party has overflowed onto the street so we know we have reached the right place. We climb through a sea of people on the stairway. The stairs go straight up as we head to the 3rd floor. A heavy metal warehouse door is open to a huge loft. The place is packed with people. They play Cheap Trick "*I want you to want me*" the DJ scratches into a new song "*Strange Brew*" by Cream. There is a video on the wall behind him showing the glassblowers at work. Alfie is not interested.

Along a brick wall are Neon light sculptures ablaze in reds and blues. They hum with electricity even with all the noise in the room as if they are energizing the party with an invisible vibration. Smoke fills the air, all kinds of smoke. We get a drink of some sticky punch, and see that all the food is gone. I see my teacher Diego. He is surrounded by a bunch of admirers but breaks away when he sees me.

"Nina, you made it. Great I wanted you to see my work, meet my friends." He takes my arm ignoring Alfie completely.

"This is my boyfriend Alfie. Alfie, this is Diego, my Neon Sculpture teacher. This is quite some place you have here!" I yell above the music. Diego looks him up and down. Alfie snarls his lip like Elvis as he says hello. I recall how those lips used to turn me on. Now I find it rude and annoying.

"Oh I see your masculine and feminine theme now, he's hot." Diego acknowledges Alfie's presence. My partner Steve and I live here." Diego may flirt with the ladies but finally I knew that he had a mate. It is impossible to talk, with so many people. Two girls in angel wing costumes roller skate by, they accidentally brush by Alfie, he spills his drink down the front of his pants. It looks like he peed! Alfie heads to the bathroom to clean up, cursing. There are people everywhere. The crowd is into punk, neon Mohawk haircuts, cut up clothes held together with safety pins. Diego shows me his work as he holds my arm to lead me around. Alfie, still snarling, finally catches up with us.

"Sorry about that man, nice to see you Nina." He gives me a kiss on the lips. "Stay for the light show. It's a gas!" He laughs at his own pun. I turn bright red and Alfie notices.

"Let's get some air." Alfie says which I know means he wants to leave. We head to the stairs though we had only just arrived.

"Nina we are leaving now! Don't ever take me to another one of these freaky punk parties, OK! I'm too old for this shit." Someone hands Alfie a joint and he stops complaining long enough to take a hit. When the joint is finished we leave and walk back to the subway in silence. He is full of rage, which scares me. I get quiet when he gets in these moods. If I talk he will explode on me or if enough time passes he will calm down. Back in Queens we just miss the last bus as it turns the corner leaving us to walk home.

"Great night out, Nina! A fuck'n three hour commute, just to climb three flights of stairs and have a drink spilled on me. I hate drunken idiots. There wasn't even any food left? I am hungry! … And then some fag teacher kisses my woman. …And she liked it!" OK, here it comes.

"Alfie you have nothing to worry about, Diego is gay, he just flirts with everyone. He thought you were cute too!" This makes Alfie smile; maybe we are over this. "I am sorry we didn't stay for the light show."

"Fuck the light show. And fuck your stupid teacher. And fuck you. Don't include me in any more of your schoolhouse rock activities. I told you Nina I have no patience for this bullshit. You owe me!" He says in a dark voice.

When we reach the cemetery on the top of the hill, Alfie pushes me in. I protest but he insists. He backs me up against a headstone and kisses me hard.

"You shouldn't forget that you are mine." He bites my lip and turns me around violently holding my arms behind my back tightly as he has his way. I tell him he is hurting me but he holds on tighter. "So that you don't forget."

Cohabitation

Living with Alfie is intense. His mood swings are extreme and sometimes I don't know who will open the door or come to bed. He says he loves me passionately yet when we fight he calls me such names. Names even a whore who had just robbed you would not deserve. He is spoiled, brash and cocky, yet shy and terribly insecure. He is a strange creature, like nothing I ever encountered before. He can fly off at the slightest thing just to make a scene. I avoid scenes and am always trying to appease him like one would a bad tempered child.

I call him 'Beast' as a pet name, for I never know when the violent animal in him will come out. He has fits of rage that at times can frighten me. He could sleep in the day and be up all night. He is a slob except for his most prized possessions: his pipe, pot, cigarettes and lighter. These things he arranges in a row all perfectly symmetrical to one another and always in the same order and evenly spaced-out. The rest of his life is chaos.

We are total opposites. I like to do things ahead of time, get up early, make lists of to dos and cross things off. He is easily distracted, leaves everything to the last minute. When he does get to something, there is always an excuse as to why it couldn't be completed. Something always seems to come up, as in what happened to his share of the rent.

This temporary situation changed when the brass bed arrived and was assembled in the corner of the main room. Not wanting his grandfather's bed to be junked it had to come too. I knew when the bed arrived that he wasn't going soon.

I insist that I still need my studio for work. He patches up the old air mattress and makes a bed in the corner of my studio so he has a place to go at night. He says he is writing but now under the Dracula poster is his little TV and VCR. He smokes through out the night. Martin has mentioned that the paper of my freelance work smells of smoke.

Once the rent is paid I save for the supplies I need at school. He mocks me but never plans for tomorrow, always runs short and borrows a few bucks till payday. It is a trick he learned from his mother. Money is what it brings you that day. Here today, gone today. One should be spontaneous with life, live care freely, and indulge in one's passions whatever the price may be.

He was the man of the family before he was a teenager. He watched his father destroy his life and thus leave him to care for his mother and brother. He holds such anger for being made to be the responsible one. These issues have stayed with him, preventing him from taking on any extra responsibilities as an adult. He can't hold a job, can't finish a script, he never wants kids or a wife. He commits to nothing, afraid to make a promise he can't keep. As his 'girlfriend' I am not sure where this leaves me. For the time being I don't care for a commitment but now my once airy apartment is cluttered with dirty dishes, laundry on the floor, wet towels in a heap, a clogged sink and garbage overflowing in the kitchen, -that only I seem to throw out.

"Italian boys are raised as princes. Nobility by right of birth." He says in argument of why he never cleans up after himself. "They are prized and taken care of. It is women who should do the tasks of a household. That is why they were built from a rib, to be a part of man, to assist as he journeys through the world. Not as a man but as a part of man." He says coming up behind me to hug as I am once again doing the dishes. I laugh at the stupidity of it.

We fight a lot, but are great at making up later.

"You live here too! Why is it my task to save for the bills, go to school, make money and have to come home and clean? Why do I get cleaning on my list of things to do as well? You use dishes; you need to wash the dishes! You wear clothes; you need to wash your clothes at the Laundromat not just the sink. You are stuck in the 50s when a women's place was in the home. I have a full life of my own. I didn't sign on to be your personal wash girl!"

"Your personal wash girl" he mimics me as he puts his hands up my shirt. He pushes all my boundaries, emotionally, sexually and financially. I know he is wrong for me but I have fallen for his charms like a moth to a flame. I am willing to burn. His touch silences my argument, as it always does.

Zsa Zsa

I asked Alfie once to describe his mother. "She is like Zsa Zsa Gabor, over the top, always embarrassing. A flamboyant drama queen! A character. 'Darling this' and 'Darling that', you will see when you meet her next week." Alfie said as he announced it was time to meet his mother.

We meet Sophia at Macy's on 34th Street, during her noon break. She has worked in the intimate apparel department for a decade. We meet in a restaurant in the basement where she can use her employee discount. Sophia is a beautiful woman in her late 60s with a ton of makeup. Worn around the edges, you could tell she was a beauty. As a woman working for Macy's she needs to present herself as a woman of fashion. She dyes her hair red, teased up high and sprayed with an acrylic hairspray. She is locked in a style from the 40s that is now her trademark. Heavy eyeliner, blue eye shadow, penciled-in eyebrows arched high, Revlon red lips and matching nails. I can see that most of her paychecks are spent at the beauty parlor. The rest is owed to the company store that offers a discount, minimal payments and monthly interest rate. After ten years at Macy's, she owes her soul to the company store.

Everything about her is over the top, she is loud, boisterous, a true presence. She adores her son as he endures her. She boasts of his talents, his looks and his inherent style. He orders his usual, cheeseburger and fries.

"Darling, you could use a new bra. You should come see me and we can fit you correctly. Yous know, that most women do not wear the right size." She reaches over and cups my breast; right in the middle of lunch, right at the table. I jump about 6 feet in the air. Alfie laughs. Like mother like son.

Over coffee, they smoke, he lights her cigarette in such a way… in an almost seductive ritual between them. She holds his hand and looks into his eyes, in such a way? It is uncomfortable for me and I look away.

Although they invited me to lunch neither of them have enough money to pay the bill. I wonder why we went to such an expensive place for lunch. Sophie puts it on her account and leaves a big tip. It is all about the show.

Like mother like son I learn. Alfie like his mother, theatrical peacocks living beyond their means. Alfie has style and looks like a million bucks on most days but he never has more than train fare in his pockets and that he would spend on cigarettes. Paychecks are cashed, and spent at his dealer. Our bills begin to pile up.

Sophia believes God tells her to play Lotto every Sunday. She goes to church dressed up for her savior and prays that he will look down upon her from the cross, recognize her pain and suffering and grant her the winning lottery numbers. But God never seems to listen as every Sunday night at 10:05, after Channel 5 news announces the winning numbers, the phone will ring and "It is I Sophia," she says all breathless and dramatic, "It is I, Sophia and I need to talk to my son."

"Zsa…" I whisper, handing him the phone.

Sternly, Alfie will get on the phone, "Si Mamma."

I can hear her through the phone, and even in Italian I can pick out the words senza soldi – she has no money, patire la fame – she is starving, venti, trenta - $20 or $30- would do…

"Si, si, si Mamma, si, faro quello che posso." He slams the phone down.

It is like clockwork these Sunday calls, and every Monday evening, Alfie stops by on his way home and gives her what he has. Then he hits me up for cash. Like Ian, it is a strange mother-son dynamic centered on guilt and money. I find out months later that in exchange for cash, Sophie refills her Valium subscription and gives the pills to Alfie. Giving Alfie her Valium has been a mother-son tradition since his childhood. Only now she asks for money and he gladly pays her.

CHAPTER 11 – UNDERGROUND

By senior year, I had lost another ten pounds and needed to buy a few things at the Salvation Army. Things that had not fit me for years were now loose and needed a belt.

Over summer break I took on as much work as Martin could provide and worked two days a week at the antique shop. With the aid of another student loan, I pay off the balance of fall tuition with $16.72 left in the bank. Deeply in debt, I carry on like a tired soldier off to battle another year of war.

Alfie loses his job and lands a new one; he drops in and out of theater workshops. He loves the excitement of seeing his scripts come to life but he hates the socialization. Theater **is** all about being social. When his scripts are in rehearsals, he comes home late and calls in sick to work the next day. He pushes everything as far as he can, has used up all sick days, vacation days and bereavement days claiming his grandfather passed away. If I call during the day, no one can find him, for he is off on yet another cigarette break. It is a matter of time before he loses this job too.

Some nights a group from the workshop head to the Green Door Tavern, a dive bar in Hell's Kitchen where actors hang out. I understand that there is a dominatrix in the workshop that he finds fascinating. I meet Mistress Payne one night as she is taping her underground radio show *Girls Talk Loudly*. Mistress Payne buys us dinner after the show at a diner on 10th Street. It is the best meal we have had in weeks.

She and Alfie have hit it off. She lives quite comfortably on the money she earns as a dominatrix, but she aspires to be an actress…thus her involvement with the theater workshop. Alfie casts her in his play so they need to spend nights working together on a script. Alfie insists there is nothing between them, that it is strictly professional. However, he talks about her in a way in which I know he is intrigued. I remind him that he hates bars, hates loud people and doesn't drink. Still, he creeps in around 3-4 in the morning at least once a week. I see the clock but go back to sleep with a deadline to face in the morning.

On Friday, I have an early class so we leave together and head to the subway. He has had only 4 hours of sleep, and was prepared to once again call in sick. Reminding him that rent is due, I kicked him out of bed. Running late we bicker all the way into the city.

We miss the bus, so we walk the 11 blocks uphill past the tall oak trees that bombard us with falling acorns. He curses the trees for those acorns hitting his head. I try not to laugh. I do believe they aim for him! We pass the cemetery. I can still feel the pain of the night he took me by force among the dead. He killed something in me that night, and left me as cold as the tombstone.

At the station he has no money for a token and jumps the turnstiles. We run downstairs to the platform and just miss the train as the doors close in our faces. The train sits there with closed doors not moving. A little boy sticks his tongue out at Alfie from the window. Alfie goes into a rage and kicks the doors as if that will help. The madman on the platform frightens the boy and his mother; I sit on the bench and look the other way pretending he is not with me. The train rolls away as crackling speakers announce more delays.

Across the tracks I see the water stains over the mosaic station sign. The rusty colors gradate down the wall; it is a beautiful design. With nowhere to go, I start to sketch the station sign and stain on the wall. Alfie talks to himself and rants about bureaucracy and the conspiracy that is causing him to miss the train. He finds a copy of the N.Y. Post, turns to the Sports section and complains about the Mets instead.

Lost Arts

There is something beautiful about the tile work in the subways. I see there is a difference between them in each station. I make sketches in my notebook of the different border designs as I ride the subways back and forth to school each day. It helps fill up the time.

These murals and stations have been neglected. They go unnoticed in the rush of the day's commute. The volumes of commuters that pass by during rush hour pay little notice to their surroundings. They stand unconscious waiting for the train. For weeks I keep sketching and my journal fills up.

Underground we do our best to keep our space. Until a train reaches the platform we rush to the doors waiting our turn until the passengers have disembarked. In our rush, in our rush hour, we don't notice the details in the architecture or the decorative textiles that ornament the stations. The details like the antique turnstiles, the stationmaster's ticket office, the decorative plaques now hidden under dust, and years of paint drippings that indicate where the women and men's bathrooms used to be.

The underground commuters are busy with their heads in books or newspapers, (New Yorkers are media junkies) or they listen to music on portable Walkman. Some just close their eyes pretending to sleep, but are acutely aware of each other, like animals in the wild. We keep our distances as much as we can. Sometimes, in this rush hour time of day, when we all have a common goal to get someplace as quickly as possible, we invade each other's territory as we squish in tightly.

I rush into a seat by the window and watch the stations go by. Graffiti marks the billboard advertising with bold puffy letters drawn with black spray paint, tags from street tribes leaving their mark. Like dogs pissing on trees, they let the other dogs know they have been there. The subway smells like the piss of too many tribes.

In Manhattan, I get off at Lexington Ave and walk down the station admiring the columns and walls along the tracks. The stations are covered in tiny tiles that create geometric borders and large murals with station names. I am reminded of the mosaics I saw in Europe, not as ornate but still decorative. The borders are wonderful works of art but no one notices. I thought someone needed to document these hidden works of art before time gets the best of them.

That is what my senior thesis should be about: the art of New York City's underground subway! In my excitement I spend the weekend writing up my proposal, Alfie corrects it, and I hand it in. It is approved.

A week later, I return to the Lexington Ave. line with my 35mm camera concealed under my oversized jacket. My plan is to photograph the mosaics. I have 36 pictures on this roll of film and every one of them has to count.

I get off the train at the 33rd Street station and wait till all the people have left. I walk the platform looking for the best-preserved sign. The Lexington Ave. line, I learn, originally opened in 1904. This station has ceramic plaques of eagles holding the number 33. I step back as far as I can to get the best camera angle without falling on to the tracks.

I focus on the border design that runs the length of the platform. Both the uptown and downtown platforms are identical. I walk up and down the platforms looking for the best-preserved station sign. Carefully I compose each picture holding my breath to steady my body. A train pulls into the station; I hop on board and head to the next station. Each station is laid out pretty much the same with ticket booths and gates that separate the station from the platform. Astor Place has large plaques of beavers eating trees. I wonder what the reason would be to depict a beaver under the streets of New York.

Another train arrives and I am rushed downtown. I run out of film but continue to ride the train to see what details of interest the other stations hold.

The City Hall station is in terrible condition. People leave the platform quickly. It is dirty, badly stained by rusty water and smells like an outhouse. I have a bad feeling about being alone on this platform. I feel like I am being watched from the shadows. The station connects with the Brooklyn Bridge and must have been quite important at one time. The walls included marble and plaques of the Brooklyn Bridge with clouds, a sailboat and a distant view of the Statue of Liberty. It is unbelievable what is down here under the dust. Once upon a time this station was stunningly beautiful, I must return. I head upstairs to switch to the uptown tracks and head home.

Four days later I have my developed pictures and lay out my photos station by station. With the help of a subway map I mark the back of each one. I light a cigarette and study what is in front of me.

I will need more film, a lot more film. I will also need a flash to get the pictures that are hidden in the shadows under pipes. I see that those didn't come out as well. I am pleased with what I have so far. At school I comb through the library to find anything relating to the early development of the subways. I lug the books I can carry, home to research.

The librarian enjoys my enthusiasm and gives me an application for an Art Matters Grant. "Maybe they can help you with the cost of supplies?" I mail in the application and convert the photos into slides for their review.

Indonesian Techniques

Tuesdays from 9-12 a.m., I have a Printing Technique Workshop. Today, we have a guest speaker who shares with us textiles and photos from his trip to Indonesia. For show and tell, he has brought the most beautiful samples of batik wax resist on silk.

"Resists are common in Africa, India, Sri Lanka, but, the most beautiful examples come from Indonesia. These are from the island of Java that has a rich history of diverse cultures. You can see the influences in patterns, technique, and the quality of craftsmanship." He then proceeded to demonstrate how with hot bees wax poured into a cup attached to a strange pen you can draw on a piece of stretched silk.

"You can use anything, beeswax, melted candles, crayons or a resist paste to mask out the areas that you wish to retain the color beneath. Once dry, you wash over the fabric with dye and where the wax is, the dye is repelled"

He then takes a brush dipped in green dye and another dipped in blue and blends the colors over his wax design. Like magic the dye resists and the original image remains.

"See water and wax don't like each other and they resist. After the work is dry you can iron off the wax and your design will remain."

This gives me an idea!

Canal Street

I decide to create a life-sized embossing of one of the station signs. I want to show the scale of these signs as well as the intricate details. I decided the best way to do this is to emboss an impression, tile by tile onto paper. I can do this with crayons, lots of crayons and I will need a roll of drafting paper large enough to cover the whole sign.

I head to Pearl Paint art supply store on Canal Street and buy three large boxes of Crayola crayons and a large roll of vellum drafting paper. They accept my Parson's ID for a discount.

I pay my token and head into the Canal Street subway station. In advance, I have picked out the best sign on the uptown side of the tracks away from the booth. I measure the sign 8 feet by 2 feet and cut a long piece of paper off the roll. In between the rush of trains I try to tape the paper to the wall. I have 96 colors to choose from and take out a bright yellow green. I start with embossing the tiles that make up the letters C, then an A, then an N. I am on my toes stretching to reach the letters. People come and go. A woman stands behind me watching for quite some time. When I finish the lettering, she asks why I am I doing this. I tell her of my interest in documenting the mosaics and that I am motivated by the word C-A-N.

She slowly walks away; suddenly she turns and says, "You know, it also reads A-N-A-L."

Around the letters I choose a deep teal and feel for the outline of the little tiles under the paper. I choose a blue violet for the ground. I work for 3 hours and have only completed the center of the sign. I realize this cannot be finished in one day. I will have to come back and bring something to stand on to reach the top. I roll my paper back onto the roll and stuff it into my duffle bag. I catch the next train and head home; walk the 11 blocks and three flights of stairs to my apartment. I tape the sign up in the long hallway to admire the day's work. I sink to the floor and fall asleep in the corner. For two days, I am in bed exhausted.

The next week, when I have regained my strength, I return to finish the rest of the sign. Standing on a plastic crate I choose a bright turquoise and start on the border. Then to contrast I use a magenta red for another row of small tiles, finally a border of 1 ½" tiles in deep teal. After another three hours the sign is completely embossed. It is 5pm and the train back to Queens is packed with rush hour commuters, I sit on my crate exhausted. I spring for the bus ride home.

Back in my studio, I tape the finished sign securely to the hall wall. I pour some black dye into a plastic container and get a spongy brush. With a light touch I paint the entire surface black. Dye runs down the wall as I hold my breath. I have either just ruined the work I spent days on or created something great. The wax crayon starts to resist the dye and stains only the background paper; slowly the colored shapes of tiles emerge, creating a stained glass-like effect. I sit back and light a cigarette, pleased. After the cigarette, I crawl on all fours to reach the bed. All my muscles ache.

I am awakened at 3 am. It is workshop night and Alfie has just come home and wants to talk. I get up to see my finished embossing still taped up to the wall; some of the black dye has run down the wall, it has dried and the effect is still beautiful. I thought perhaps I had just dreamt of my adventure on Canal Street and that this never really happened; but here it was, real and on my wall, a life-size replica.

Alfie doesn't seem to notice this 8' addition to the studio as he continues to tell me about his night while searching for a snack. I fall back to sleep and spend the next day in bed unable to move.

CHAPTER 12 – HIGHER GROUND

The Brooklyn Queens Expressway is blocked with traffic due to a construction zone that narrow three lanes into one. I am late and stuck on the Manhattan Bridge.

The windows are all open and I am bopping away to the radio that blares out *"Walk Like an Egyptian"*.

I borrowed Alfie's car to drive into Manhattan. The car is a wreck, and as always he runs it on empty…much like his life. I buy $4- worth of gas, dump out the overstuffed cigarette tray and squeegee over the windows, which don't really make them clean, just streaked.

I put the car in park thinking I can save on gas, which causes it to die. This happens a lot lately. To say the least, this car could use some mechanical attention. It is the battery; I know just what to do to tighten the connections. I reach into the glove compartment and pull out the big pliers. I release the hood and step out of the car. A nickel in my pocket slips out and falls through a metal grate. It is all that separates me from the racing currents of the East River far, far below.

I back up against the car. I hate heights and freeze, just staring at my feet standing on the metal grate, looking down at the East River. My legs start to shake.

"You have to be fucking kidding me," the cab driver stuck behind me shouts, returning me to my harsh reality. A chorus of cars starts to honk their horns. I try to focus on the task at hand and walk to the front of the car. All I need to do is secure the hood, and tighten the connections to the battery, with my shaking hands.

"Please, please, please not here, not now, please work," I say to the battery God, as if he is listening.

I smile at the cab behind me; he is stuck and really can't get out till I move. Serves him right for riding on my ass. He is yelling, waving his hands at me and making obscene gestures. I try to ignore him and once again stop to see the water rushing below the grate, below my feet. I return to the driver's side and start the car.

"Thank you Jesus!" yells the red-faced cabbie behind me as I head back out to close the hood. "Don't give yourself a heart attack!" I yell as I step out of the car. "Thanks for your help asshole!" I slam down the hood. In the car I readjust my mirrors and apply lipstick with still shaking hands. I find a new radio station and take a deep breath to calm my nerves. I put the car in drive and once again am off. The guy behind goes ballistic on the horn and is still yelling as he passes me by. I turn up the radio and smile sweetly as I give him the finger.

As the cab passes, I see its bumper sticker has a smiley face and a caption that reads, '**Have A Nice Day**!' and another that has a red heart that reads '**I Love NY**!'

Still shaking, I get off the bridge and navigate downtown to the Lower West Side. I find parking till 4pm.

Plato's Last Retreat

I am late with my freelance assignment. I have pushed Martin this past year and he is pissed. It is Thursday afternoon and he needed to FedEx this package of painted madras plaids to Levi's in California for a Monday meeting. My being so late gives him no chance to make corrections. I assured him over the phone that the collection looked great but he hung up on me and said it better! I could tell I had pushed him too many times as I juggled my senior thesis and finals. I had to make it up to him and I was ready to do that now that school was finished. School exhausted me and wiped out all my savings. All my bills were behind. I needed work and fast. I was hoping he would give me an advance.

I parked the car at a meter and headed to his loft on Warren Street in the shadows of the Twin Towers.

Martin and his partner Paulo made good money and had bought this loft on the Lower West Side. After a year, they had finally finished renovating the place to look like as a Roman villa in Pompeii, complete with columns and fresco paintings of frolicking naked boys playing tag among the ancient ruins. It was recently photographed in a fashion shoot, decadent and over the top. Paulo meets me at the door and walks me past the fountain of a naked boy hugging his dolphin. I like Paulo a lot. He is the Director of Visual Displays at Barneys, very flamboyant with an angular haircut, long bangs and earrings. Martin was the more butch, and the more business side of the relationship.

"Martin is going through a difficult time, Nina," Paulo confided in me. "We are waiting on some news, on a friend." Paulo went on to tell me that a dear friend of theirs had taken very ill. They weren't sure what was wrong. "Times have changed," he said sadly.

Times had changed from the wild gay scene of the early 80s. The village was their playground and Christopher Street was a carnival of butch guys in leather biker gear and extravagant transvestites with big hair and killer heels. Everyone slept with everyone gay or straight. When AIDS arrived the party was over. People started to couple up, as everyone was sexually scared of what was out there. 1988 was a record breaker for marriage licenses.

I hugged Paulo before he went to the bedroom leaving Martin and me to talk. Martin grabbed the package of designs out of my hands and shot me a look that could have killed.

Martin laid the patterns out on the counter in groups. He did his best Scarlet O'Hara, "As God is my witness…Nina!" He steps back. "Ok they are good, … thank God!"

"Martin, I'm so sorry they are late. I haven't had much sleep with finals and senior thesis. My senior show took everything out of me. The exhibit and thesis are now finished. I am looking to take on more work. No late deadlines, I promise."

Martin left the paintings on the counter and walked me to the bright red couch, which stood out in the grey and white décor. "We have worked together for three years, and you know I am fond of you. It's just that I have had enough. The last year has been a nightmare for me dealing with all of this." He made a big hand gesture that circled his surroundings. "I have started to work with another artist and I will send you your final check in the mail once the job is complete."

"Martin I don't know what to say. I wish you would reconsider. Really you know it has been such a struggle getting through school, but it is over, I..." The phone rings, Martin turns white. He takes the call as Paulo joins him. The news is not good and Martin waves me away. We are finished and I am shown to the door. "Pneumonia, are you sure?" Martin whispers as he bites his nails.

Paulo shows me out knowing it is goodbye, he says with tears in his eyes, "Good luck Nina, you must be careful out there."

"You too, take good care of each other." I closed the door on the frolicking white statues, the Roman columns and hand painted murals, the plush red furniture and crystal chandelier. The doors behind me make a heavy thud. The elevator gate clangs shut, the sounds echo in the old factory building as the elevator takes me down. This is the end of a chapter, for all of us.

On the street, in shock, I look up and head like a zombie to the tallest thing around, the Twin Towers.

Windows on the World

I walk around the plaza and buy a ticket to the observation deck of the World Trade Center. On the top of the south tower, 107 floors above the world, I sit on the roof facing north to the uptown Manhattan skyline.

In the distance are the landmarks of the city skyline, the Empire State and Chrysler buildings. Uptown the Trump Tower slices the sky with its triangular rooftop. To the west the residential areas of the Village where I lived with Ian for what now feels like a lifetime ago. North is Midtown, Times Square and Central Park is just a patch of green. Harlem is beyond that. It is the end of a crystal clear day. I find a quarter and put it into the telescope for a better view.

To the east are the little bridges connecting the island of Manhattan to Queens and Brooklyn. Tiny cars and trucks run back and forth like someone is playing a toy game. Uptown is the 59th Street Bridge. Even from here I can see the traffic jam all around the entrance to the bridge. Maybe I will just stay up here till rush hour ends and traffic dies down.

Further downtown is the Williamsburg Bridge, designed with exposed steel that zigzags in a repeating grid. I love the shadows it cast as you drive over the bridge in the afternoon sunlight. It always makes me feel like I was part of the film frames of some motion picture.

I see the Manhattan Bridge, flashing back to earlier today when I looked through the grates of the road to see the East River rushing below. I guess it's the day for tackling my fears.

To the south is the Brooklyn Bridge, one of the oldest suspension bridges. Over a hundred years ago, it was the first bridge to connect the islands. A cruise ship leaving the harbor clears under the Verrazano Bridge. Freighters heavy with cargo line up to enter the harbor, while empty freighters riding high on the water return to foreign ports; all passing under the Verrazano Bridge.

I recall my job on the 54th floor looking out on Downtown Manhattan. I recall meeting Alfie and exploring the streets at lunchtime. I think of my time with Ian when I didn't have to worry about money and I was overweight from too much food. My stomach grumbles in hunger. I watch a sailboat circle around the Statue of Liberty and Ellis Island. I remember that day of the storm as we sailed in Greece. I had decided then to live my life to the fullest, without fear. What had I accomplished? My life was full of uncertainty and at the moment, many fears.

I watch as the Staten Island Ferry goes back and forth, tugboats haul barges up and down the Hudson River as the sun begins to set over the Statue of Liberty. My view turns black as the money runs out.

I walk around the edge.

I remembered being little when my Father took us to visit the new World Trade Center and ride on the Staten Island Ferry. He bought me a figure of the Statue of Liberty. He talked about being a kid and growing up in New Jersey where he explored woods and swam with the boy scouts in the Hudson River. He marveled at how the city was always in motion, always changing with the times. And through it all Lady Liberty watched over us he had told me. I wondered if she was watching now? I wondered if he was watching now.

I hadn't thought of that in years, how we looked out from this observation deck; much of the area below was still under construction. My Father pointed things out but I was more scared of being so high up above the world and held onto his leg. He said that in order to build this complex, neighborhoods needed to be leveled to accommodate the buildings and an underground transit system. Excavation for the site created so much excess material it was used as landfill what would later become Battery Park City. Father said that life was full of changes and nothing stayed the same in a city. He died the next year and nothing ever was the same.

When Mom and I would go to Jones Beach we would see the towers some 30 miles away. They always made me think of him. Maybe that is why I came up here today to be closer to him. I needed guidance and asked for his help.

With the setting sun, the wind kicked up blowing my long skirt in every which way. I didn't care. I was numb and the wind felt good on my legs. I tied the scarf around my head tighter.

This past year I had worked exclusively with Martin and finished my senior thesis. I didn't have time to take on any other customers. I pulled all-nighters to get Martin's work done. Now I had no other clients. I paid part of May's rent with money I received from graduation. I had exhausted all my savings. I had hoped to ask Martin for an advance but now I needed to wait 3-4 weeks to get his check in the mail. The last check and June's rent was just around the corner.

I walked around the perimeter of the observation deck wondering if the wind could lift me up and carry me over the edge. Carry me far away.

Graduation from Parsons was only just a week ago. I could see 5th Avenue where I watched my class parade in their caps and gowns. I was not one of them. The school charged for everything. There was a fee for taking yearbook pictures and a fee to buy a copy; there were graduation expenses, cost of caps and gowns and tickets for the ceremony. There was even a fee for the paper diploma to be mailed to you. Mom paid for the diploma. She offered to pay for graduation, but I told her it wasn't important to me, that the school had gotten enough of my money.

Alfie said it was an outrage how much the school charged, "What a racket! It's criminal how these institutions are buying up properties all over Manhattan and claiming their nonprofit status! God, in no time NYU will own Washington Square Park and charge people to sit on the benches! All the while ripping off stupid students, like you, who think a piece of paper will give them a brain. The great and powerful Oz dips into his bag and behold a piece of paper that says the scarecrow now has a brain."

Maybe he was right?

"As God is my Witness"

The lights come up on the bridges and the buildings start to twinkle with their windows aglow. I pick up a flyer about the Twin Towers. I am reminded of the medieval towers of San Gimignano in Italy, symbols of great power and great wealth erected by men needing to show their family's prosperity. Godlike, they grew from the earth and reached to the heavens with their sheer determination of will. What would Freud say about these large phallic symbols of capitalism on the island of Manhattan? He would say here is construction to honor the male with not just one phallic symbol but two. Twice as strong, twice as powerful twice as godly! That made me smile.

I wondered what I accomplished over the past two years. With every new semester I registered for, I heard Alfie's speech on how I was wasting my time and money. Every semester my student loans grew, sinking me thousands of dollars in debt. Now out of school I had already received the letter saying it was time to get back on the student loan payment schedule. These last two years were so difficult I couldn't even pay taxes on my freelance work. The IRS would also soon be after me. It was a depressing mess I had gotten myself into.

I felt small and fragile high above the city, like the piece of paper the wind was tossing and turning. I had lost my will and felt completely alone high above a city with millions of people. I had no job and a relationship that was going nowhere. I took a seat away from the tourists and started to cry. How peaceful it would be to leave all of this behind and just fly with my wings into the sky.

Maybe I should think positive when a door closes... "It slams tight," I say to myself. No, when a door closes, a window opens. Something like that, something closes, something opens. I thought about the last few months.

Senior Exhibition

I recall the week of my Senior Show, which had been very tense. I had work I couldn't get to and my senior thesis to assemble and mount. In early May, Alfie up and quit his job. In truth he was asked to leave and he was happy about it. He was fighting for unemployment. He hardly showed up, hid his work in a bottom drawer, took long smoking breaks and yet expected he was owed unemployment. With the government giving him a check once a week, his plan was to stay home for the next 6 months and finish his play. This of course meant less money a month and we were already behind. I had a bad feeling about this from the start.

Mom helped me hang my Senior Show in the Parsons Gallery. Together we secured the Canal Street sign. It just fit on the back wall. On the other wall we arranged my subway photos, some of which I had managed to enlarge. In February, I was notified that I would receive a grant for $1000 in April for my photography of the New York subway mosaics. With letter in hand I went to a photography shop and convinced them to hold a postdated check until I received the money. I told them about my interest and showed them some of what I had done to date. They granted me an account for $200. I bought a flash for my camera and rolls of film. When the grant check did come, I paid my bill first.

With my camera and a ten-pack of tokens, I ran all over the subway system. I'd pick a subway line and stop at every station along the way. At many of the older stations I would walk up and down the uptown and downtown sides of the track to find the best examples. I tried to find murals that were not damaged or repaired, stained by water damage or with dried paint that over the years had dripped down. Hanging now in my gallery space there is a collection of station signs, plaques, running borders, directional signs and even bathroom signs. I was exhausted and had killed my favorite sneakers.

With the last of my money I made enlargements of some of my favorite photos and bought a bottle of wine when I picked them up. I even splurged for a cheap pair of Chinese slippers I bought from a bin on 14th Street. I didn't let Alfie near the money though he fought hard to get an advance before his unemployment set in. He was pissed that I didn't rush to buy us some pot. We were hardly speaking lately and I tried not to be home.

On opening night, I wore my silly sandals with my Italian rose-colored nightgown. I tied my hair up with chopsticks. It was Parsons. I could be who I wanted to be. I had come a long way from the girl that first came to Parsons or the one that went to FIT. I had been allowed to stretch my imagination and pursue a personal artistic quest. As much as I was happy that school was over, I knew I wasn't finished with my subway endeavor. I couldn't wait to get more film and build my collection of photographs. I wanted to fill a book with every subway line. I wanted to continue to emboss the station murals. Now all of that would have to wait.

Alfie and my mother had to be cordial with each other hiding their distain for the sake of photos. Mom brought Fredrick, her long time accountant boyfriend. Guy and Diane were there, acting very proud; yet concerned at how much weight I had lost since they last seen me at Christmas. We all smiled for more pictures and went down to Chinatown for dinner. Fredrick was confused by what some students showed and how a large picture of a dictator could be considered art. He and Alfie got into an awkward debate. Fredrick wasn't too broad-minded in his view of the world. I often wondered what mom saw in him. But he picked up the check for dinner and that was enough.

Two weeks later, Mom helped me take down the show. Once again Alfie couldn't or wouldn't come. We packed the car and parked it in a lot. We went to a local diner for lunch, the diner all the students frequented that I could never afford!

"Nina, you look terrible." Mom hated when I didn't wear makeup. "You have a pretty face but you look old Darling. Some concealer would hide the circles under your eyes. It's that boyfriend of yours! How can he up and quit his job?"

"Mom, I know, school has just taken it all out of me and I'm totally spent. As for Alfie, what can I say? This is all so sudden; he'll find another job. Can we just change the subject?" I ordered a large lasagna knowing I could no longer eat that much. I would take half home to Alfie.

"This isn't sudden, you have been with him for a few years now. His type expects everyone else to do for him. He's lazy, can't you see that, he talks a charming story but he will never amount to anything!"

"He **is** respected in his theater group and he **does** have talent. Maybe he just needs to finish a script and have a lucky break!" I hated these conversations where I had to defend him. I was mad at him as well for quitting his job.

"Talent? What about your talent? You were raised to be a strong independent woman, Nina. You have now earned a degree. You don't need a man; I have taught you that much, I hope! Why would you want to take on a 'man-child'? Nothing will change, you will see. He will only bring you down to his level. Look at you, you're wasting away; you can't even finish your meal."

"Mom," I say rather abruptly, "it is hard to eat and defend my life at the same time. I have been busting ass to finish my thesis in time. I am just exhausted! Now that this is over I'll get a bit of rest and get back to work, and so will Alfie. For now, just please give me a break."

As we parted, she hands me a pink flowered makeup bag. "This is for you, you need some makeup dear, and get a haircut and eat something!" In the bag is $100 dollars. I pack up most of my meal and her salad, and all the bread and butter and a handful of sugar packs and napkins into the take-out bag, as Mom pays the check.

At home, Alfie attacks the bag of food before I am even through the door he starts complaining about what I ordered. "Couldn't you have gotten something with chicken?" Still he eats it with a vengeance.

"Being broke has kind of turned me into a vegetarian. I can't process meat any more. And by the way, you're welcome." I collapse on the couch.

"You should have ordered the Chicken Parmesan. You know how I like Chicken Parmesan." He tears off a hunk of bread and fights to open the butter packet. "Cut your hair? Why cut your hair, it's fine. I like long hair. Don't go mutilating yourself for your mother," he mumbled with a mouth full of bread. "It is bad enough you look so skinny, your Mother is right, you don't look very good. You used to be so cute and round. Now you just go up and down, no meat to hold onto, literally Nina, no meat!"

"I guess that is the topic then, no meat. Why don't you find a way to bring in some money and we will have steak for dinner! I will be more than happy to cook it for you on my wok. Or we could use the George Foreman grill your mother gave us. You know the grill that we never use because we are always giving her money every other week and never have any food! Just think we could sizzle the steak on both sides at the same time! That would be living Alfie! How about rustling up a job and buying some meat and I'll be happy to cook it right up."

We argue until he is finished eating. He needs pot and knowing I have money hassles me until I can't stand it anymore. I give him $50 to just leave. He takes another $20 as he runs out the door. I head down to the liquor store and buy a bottle of wine. Alone, I celebrate the hanging of my Senior Show. I toast myself in the mirror until the bottle is empty. I do look like shit, I finally decide. With the scissors from my studio I cut off all my hair.

High Again

My thoughts return to the roof, I take off my scarf and run my hands through what is left of my hair. An Asian man speaking in broken English approaches me on the rooftop of the World Trade Center.

"Take e picture, lady?" he says. I agree and a dozen Japanese tourist all repeat "cheeseburger!" and smile as they fight the wind. We go over this scenario six different times. They all smile, say

131

cheeseburger, giggle and bow, bow some more and hand me another camera.

After much bowing and many thanks, I am once again left alone. I turn to take one last look at the skyline. The lights are coming up, twinkling in patterns. I love this city. New York, my city, is so amazing. I am a part of its energy, which is somehow in my blood. This is the place to be, and I belong here. Manhattan is my home. I clutch my portfolio in the wind as a shield and head to the elevators.

Like Scarlet O'Hara in *Gone with the Wind*, I swear to the sky, 'As God is my witness, I will never go hungry again!' Someday I tell myself, I will crawl out of this mess, and be on top of the world.

A restaurant sign reads '**Windows on the World'** and I start to laugh. I am already on top of the world, only I can't afford to eat! Guess I got what I wished for. I must be more specific next time.

In the restaurant window I see my sad reflection; I drape the scarf around my head for a theatrical effect and head to the elevators. After a 107-floor drop I am back to my reality. On the street I return to the car with my newfound hope and stoic determination, only to find a ticket on the windshield. I shove it in the glove compartment. Again, the battery won't turn over.

CHAPTER 13
- THE SUMMER OF OUR DISCONTENT

If June was hot, July was unbearable. There simply was no air except for a breeze of dry dust when the trains rushed by. The air conditioner died a sudden death with a cough and a sputter. Alfie said the hardware store could recharge the system with Freon if we brought it in. We carry it down three flights of stairs the heavy relic he had insisted on bringing from his old apartment.

"Haven't seen one of these in years. Will cost ya about $75 plus tax to fill it. But, there is no guarantee that it will last. No I'd say chuck it and buy yourself a new one." The man in the store looked us over. "We do sell fans."

We left the store and headed to the alley to dump it in a dumpster. Alfie didn't want to carry it back upstairs and we started to fight about it. Inside the dumpster we find a *Drink Coca-Cola* advertising sign, some wooden cigar boxes, a standing magazine rack, and a Wrigley's gum display. We left the air conditioner and carried our new found treasure back to the apartment.

Upon returning to our building, seeing what was once a garden of herbs, marigolds and wild roses surrounded by a little iron fence, now held wooden frames filled with cement. Work permits were hung by the front doors. Word spread quickly that the old landlord sold out and there was a new sheriff in town. By the looks of things, this wasn't going to be good. We hurried on in with our arms full of stuff.

The old landlord shared his garden herbs with me and let some of the artists slide when we ran late on rent. I knew his wife and two kids and I always gave him baked goods for the holidays. I had a history of paying rent with him, except now I was free falling; behind, with not much hope of money coming in.

Otto and the Bloodhounds

Otto Bushwick, the new landlord didn't look like a guy who would give you slack. He had two ugly sons, Osgood and Olaf that stood on either side of him like lopsided Bloodhounds. Within days the herb garden became their personal parking lot. Every morning their three trucks would be lined up between the buildings. At 8 a.m. the hammer would bang, by 8 a.m. my neighbor would begin to play her scales on the out of tune piano. She now had to compete with the banging and became even louder – it was maddening!

Otto sent his Bloodhounds around on Tuesday and Saturday mornings to collect past due rent. At 8:30 you could hear them going through the halls. We were not the only ones owing rent. The knock on the door would make me freeze like a statue, as Alfie would head to the door.

"Better to head this off from the start." Down the hallway I could hear their conversation. Alfie would promise, "Yes we have a check coming in the mail. Should be here end of week. I am sure end of week. Yes we will see you then." The Bloodhounds would go away for another day of unbearable banging. There was no check coming at the end of the week.

We were too broke to go out and too poor to stay in. With time on our hands we grew closer like allies in a battle. We spent a lot of time at the library and in the park.

On Tuesday, Alfie and I climbed out the fire escape window and dropped to the back alley making a run for the park.

There was no money for gas. The car was running on fumes with just enough to move it across the street to avoid another ticket on alternate side of the street parking days. There were several unpaid tickets jammed in the glove compartment.

We escaped to the park. Some days we would climb the apple trees by the ball field where we could sit for hours without talking and watch the squirrels run around the bases. It was a place we could hide from the world. One day, hunger got the best of us and we ate the green apples that made us sick for days.

Some days we walked deep in the forest along the horseback riding trails looking for wild blackberries and raspberries. I wondered if squirrels could be stewed in my wok? The air was cool under a canopy of trees, we felt far from the city, deep in the forest, alone in nature. We stopped to take it all in and deeply breathe in the oxygen as we ate the berries.

Alfie turned me around and reached up my skirt. He had his way with me over a fallen tree. I worried about anyone passing by but we had seen no one for hours deep in the woods. The bark of the tree scratched my stomach as Alfie dug his long nails into my sides. Pain and pleasure all at once, I would wear the scars like war wounds of a battle I had lost and surrendered to. There were always scars. All that was left between us was possessive sex when he wanted it and the nail marks left on my skin.

As the sun started to lengthen, the shadows cooled the forest. It was time to go home. By 5 p.m. it was safe to head back to the apartment. From behind the trees we watched as the trucks of Otto, Osgood and Olaf barreled down the street heading home to Mrs. Otto who would have meat and potatoes for her men.

Out of the woods back to civilization on a Friday night, we walked hand in hand as if we were coming home from work on a pleasant summer night. Alfie picked leaves out of my hair, before we hit Metropolitan Avenue. There was something romantic about the struggle, us against the world. We found some containers of half eaten fried rice behind the Chinese restaurant.

Nightmares and Withdrawals

Alfie was used to smoking pot on a daily basis, and without money, he was going through withdrawals. I never would have thought that you could go through withdrawals from marijuana but this was serious. For days he had the shakes and a fever, he ached all over and was freezing. When he slept he had horrible nightmares. Dreadful nightmares. When he was awake, he became violently angry at everything and everyone. He ran down for the mail every morning hoping for a letter or check from unemployment. He believed his case would be won. When there was nothing in the mail but notices he would curse the Gods once again.

He had fits of rage, frightening trances, where he would curse the ghosts of ancestors past that only he could see. He would have long conversations with the dead blaming them for fucking up his life, as he paced the floor chain smoking cigarette butts he found in the alley.

"Damn you father, for dying and leaving me with this crazy woman to call mother." As if he had them all in the room he would turn to talk to each. "Damn you mother for seducing such an idiot. You got yourself pregnant and drove him to drink! Drank himself to death, just to get away from you!" He started to laugh. "And fuck both of you for dragging a child to a foreign land to try and get away from your mistakes. Do you know what a fucked up childhood that was! From a villa on the Mediterranean to the tenements of Hell's Kitchen what were you thinking?" He demanded. "And what did that make me …a constant reminder of life gone wrong? Of plans ruined and the years pretending to care for one another? All a lie, a charade with people's lives on the line; you took us all down with your lies." He would speak to them as if they were all sitting on the couch listening. "And then you couldn't keep your dick in your pants dear old Dad! No you go and get her pregnant again. Let's have another baby! 'Cos misery sure loves company! What was that for good luck, a fuck for old times' sake? Leaving yet another child marked with your legacy." He asks his father's ghost who seems to have moved to the rocking chair.

"Mom, you must have thought if I trapped him the first time by getting knocked-up let's do it again." He talks to a painting on the wall.

"But no Dad, you didn't even stay around for this one, no just up and left… and who was left to raise this child, and care for a hysterical woman fainting in the streets? In a country where I would always be an outsider? Me! That's right me! You just up and fucking left. How easy was that, and in less than five years, your guilt would be drowned in scotch and so would you, you selfish bastard? How easy was that?" His father had nothing to say in his own defense and just sat there like an overstuffed pillow.

When he ranted about his family, I was just the audience. He liked an audience. At times, he needed an audience. I sat very quietly so that he didn't notice I was there. If he saw me, sometimes the anger would turn to me. He resented loving me, blaming me for trapping him. He insisted he wanted no part of a conventional life. He knew in time I would have to make a choice to leave him. He wanted no obligations, no family, no 'little house on the suburban prairie' he would often say. I understood all of this and didn't see this as any place to bring in a child. I wanted out.

By the fourth day of no pot, no cigarettes and little food, we both slept curled up in a ball of sweat. At times he was delirious. I thought of taking him to the emergency room but he would not go. If he slept he had horrible nightmares. He was drowning, burning, falling, crashing. I did my best to keep him warm and nurse him, calm his fears and be there in the night when he screamed out. I was also dealing with my own demons and felt like I had the flu.

By the fifth day we were both hungry and there was nothing to eat. I pawned some jewelry at the antique shop. I walked a mile to the gas station in Jamaica that sold cheap cigarettes and I went to the next town to shop, as I owed everyone in our town some money. I bought a chicken and noodles to make soup, milk and coffee, bread and butter, bacon and eggs. I walked the mile up the hill with two bags of groceries, up the three flights of dust filled stairs trying to avoid detection by the landlord and not pass out. I ripped open a bag of bread and ate three pieces on the way home.

Alfie woke to the smell of coffee, bacon and eggs. He ate like a prisoner being released from jail. We ran our fingers over the plates to get every last drop of food. Once he had eaten, he apologized for all the things he remembered saying to me, and the things he didn't remember saying. He had lost track of days.

I would like to say that things got better when he sobered up but they really didn't. He was very short-tempered and mad. Without some kind of medication he was not the happy-go-lucky guy I once loved. He was full of rage. I grew to hate being around him more and more. In the morning, when he woke, he was most violent. Today I stayed in as it was raining hard outside. I was always amazed that he could sleep till noon. He slept with a headset that blocked out the building noise. By 1 p.m. he dragged himself out of my studio like a zombie, as it had been another late night. 'Writing', he would tell me, but I **knew** he was up watching porn. (Brandishing a cigarette in one hand and his cock in the other he could entertain himself for hours.) Last night he was up till 5 a.m., and in the light of day he smelled like an ashtray and looked like crap. To think this was an improvement from the week before…?

We kept very different hours. I was up early so I headed to the library to look through the help wanted ads. I hated being in the

137

apartment with all the construction noise in the day, and the fear of the landlord who at any moment could knock on the door.

We no longer slept together, taking turns in the bed. It was becoming a very strange relationship. When he woke, he picked a fight.

"What do you know, white bread from Long Island, with your nice suburban upbringing? What do you know from pain and suffering? What do you know from being ripped from the land you loved and dumped in Hell's Kitchen? In a country where you don't even speak the fucking language, a father who drank himself to death, leaving you a psychotic mother to care for and a newborn. What kind of a childhood was that? At 13 years old, other kids played on the street and I had to take care of Zsa Zsa and a crying baby."

I had heard all of this before and was getting tired of the broken record saga. "Alfie all of that was in the past. How many years can you carry this around? So they fucked up, lots of people fuck up, it is what we do as humans, we all fuck up! We are fucking up now. No one is perfect; you deal with what you have. You can't blame them for everything! At what point is it up to you to change things around? Why don't you grow up and start to take responsibility for your own life?"

The rain was pounding, the hammers were pounding, I may have gone too far but I was on a roll and there was no stopping. "You can do anything you want if you set your mind to it. We could go clean. You could find some work and help pay the rent, then we might be able to manage this place and not always be on the fence ready to fall at any moment." My heart was pounding.

If looks could kill, his bloodshot eyes sprang out of their dark sockets. Rage turned to silence and he backed down a bit, speaking just above a whisper. "I can't believe you said that to me."

"You may want to bask in your self-pity but I would like to do something about this. I don't like sneaking around where I live. I want to be able to eat and not salivate every time I pass the bakery window. I would like to have a job that could pay the bills, go out every now and then. Have enough money to buy supplies to be the artist I want to be. Someday I would like to own my own place and not pay a landlord. Don't you ever want a place to call your own, a house…?"

"Oh shit Nina," he paced back and forth, "next you will be telling me the names of our 2.5 kids and our dog. What do you know little Miss American pie? Don't make me part of your fucked-up fairytale. You are not going to trap me rotting on the vine in suburbia like some dead fruit. It is nothing but a huge cemetery made of ticky-tacky houses all in a row. Take a number, wait your turn, buy a plot in the ground, live where you die! Die where you live. Your father died, probably the only way he could get away from his mundane life, the burden of you, and your penny-pinching mother."

"Really Alfie, my father having a heart attack at 45 has nothing to do with me or my suburban upbringing. I think it had more to do with his family's DNA and a love for all things with gravy. Leave my family out of it!" I started to cry, but turned to hide the fact that he had hit a nerve, that would only make him dig deeper. I tried not to fight with him in this state, for he could cut like a knife and he would always win. However, my nerves were on edge today what with all the banging. The rain came down harder and my period was late.

"Cupcake, why can't you go to her and get some money? She works, she has it stacked away, enough to go on vacation with her boyfriend. Enough to drive a nice car! Why can't your mother help us? You are family, her only family! Isn't that what a family does? I don't understand you Americans! When my mother has it, she shares it with me. When I have it, I share it with her!" he declares.

"Alfie, your mother needs more than she gives. She is always calling looking for money. Our families, like us, are different. My mother taught me to work for what I want. I can't ask her for money, we don't do that. You have to earn it. My mother will ask why we can't find any work. Why are you not supporting me? What can I say?"

"We've hit some hard times that is all. Why wouldn't a mother understand that?" I ignore him.

"We need to find our own solution out of this. We need to find jobs so we can afford this apartment and afford to eat. You have been out of work for over two months." I knew this would set him off but I had to say it. Quickly I added, "You need to come to the library with me tomorrow and look through the help-wanted ads. On Thursday, I plan to get into the city and look at the job boards at school. Who knows, maybe I'll find something posted."

The day before, my diploma came in the mail and was sitting on the table under a stack of bills and final notices. I had just noticed that it was there and quickly opened it up.

"Oh look, a piece of paper! What did that fucking cost you Nina? $20,000? Really made a great deal of difference to the quality of your life now didn't it. You had a job but blew it on getting a piece of paper." I tried to ignore him but he just kept on. "Imagine that, a 'job board' where you can pick a job, how nice for you! Yes, do go into school and pick a job from a job board. Thousands of dollars for college tuition and they let you look at a fucking job board," he hissed. He looked at the stack of bills, which were nothing, but final disconnects and student loan notices. He threw them against the wall. "What were you thinking when you signed on to all those student loans. What a waste!"

"Well, what were you thinking when you up and quit your job like that? You didn't even talk to me about it! You move in here and expect me to pay the rent, pay the electricity, buy food, be your housekeeper and keep you in pot? What the fuck were you thinking?"

"It wasn't my fault they let me go and I didn't expect you would lose your job. Besides, I have a job, I am writing a play! I have ideas for my next project, so I am working on **two** projects!" He went to the fridge. There was nothing but two old eggs and three pieces of stale bread, a jar of jelly that had turned green. He throws it towards the garbage and missing sending jelly all over the wall. "Lot of good your college education is doing us now? I told you when you started it would be a waste of time and money, but did you listen to me?" He reached for my diploma.

"Don't you dare?" I grabbed it from him and hid it in the studio. It was all I had of graduation.

He combed through the cigarette tray looking for a butt to smoke. "I'd be feeling better if I could get my hands on some weed."

The torture of being locked away together was driving us crazy. So we did what we always did and headed to Long Island City. We postdated a check and told the dealer to hold onto it until his unemployment money came through.

He knew I would make good on it, ever if Alfie did not. Alfie would sell his soul for a bag of pot and I was too tired to fight any more. Sometimes it was better just to be high then to deal with the reality of our lives. The next day we hit the library to scour the papers for jobs and found a few leads. When we got home our phone was shut off.

CHAPTER 14
- THE GUCCI SISTERS
MOVE IN

A bit sober,
a bit stoned,
we carried on.

I freelance for the Gant Corporation, a job referral from a friend who was working with the men's knit division and remembered that I painted textiles. For two weeks I worked around the clock on a series of pastel colored tartan plaids for golf shorts and rugby stripes for knit shirts. This was a lot of work and a chance to make some nice money.

I put the art supplies on a credit card that I knew I couldn't pay. Exhausted from single handedly being a whole studio by myself, I finished the assignment in just two weeks, Alfie drove me into the city to drop off the assignment. The Corporate Office was located on 55th Street off of 5th Avenue above the Gucci store. After a week of being grungy in paint clothes, I quickly scrubbed in the shower and was still dressing in the car. My finger nails were embedded with cadmium red paint that I couldn't clean, I applied red polish as we crossed the 59th Street Bridge.

I borrowed $100 bucks from my mother, so we had a little money for gas, burgers and smokes. We were rich for a day.

Through security up to the third floor, Jeannette met me at reception and led me through a maze of connecting design offices. The showroom had cork walls where samples and color swatches

141

were pinned up for inspiration. The head of design came in and liked my work.

"You did a nice job with the plaids," she said after careful examination.

"Yes, I've been called the Plaid Queen by my friends." I joked and she laughed in spite of her very business demeanor.

"Good, we need a Plaid Queen, around here. I have another project for a Plaid Queen; do you have the time? I need these re-colored by Friday" she stated and went off to get the color samples.

"Wow, this is such a nice place. Thank you so much for the work." I said as I looked around at the different design areas in the open studio space. There was the swimwear wall, the men's shirt wall, and the denim wall with swatches showing a gradation of denim finishes from acid to stone wash, to suede, to chocolate indigo.

The head of design returns with a pile of papers and fabric swatches. Together we lie out the new collection and create a color palette that includes their chocolate indigo.

She hands me a dozen designs to recolor in three and a half days.

"My meeting is on Friday morning. These must be here by 9 a.m."

OK, three days. I was excited and skipped out onto the street. Alfie was leaning against the car smoking a cigarette like some criminal in a spy movie. He had a suspicious air about him, as always.

"What took you so long?" "I've already been chased from this spot once!" He was pissed off.

"Well I have good news and bad news. The good news is that I have more work. The bad news is I need more art supplies that we need to charge immediately before the credit card cuts us off." I take a drag off his cigarette. "The other bad news is that we won't see any money from this for a month."

"Are you fucking kidding me, a month! That's insane, how are we going to wait another month to see any money? That sucks!" He grabs back the cigarette and chucks it into the dumpster as he opens the hatchback of the car for me to put my portfolio in.

"Get in the car." He growls as if this is any of my doing. I'm tired and now have a lot of work in front of me. I'm not up for his mood. I breathe deeply.

"Are you nuts, you don't know what is in there!" Dumpsters intrigue me; one man's trash is my treasure. I climb up even with my nice dress on. Once inside the dumpster, there were body parts everywhere, which freak me out until I realize that they are mannequin parts from the Gucci's Boutique on 5th Avenue.

"Holy Shit!" I say.

"What's in there?" Alfie climbs up to see.

Franticly, before anyone could stop us, we pulled out arms, legs, torsos, and beautiful bald heads and stuffed them into the back of the car until we couldn't fit any more. With a turquoise Datsun packed with body parts, we drove over the 59th Street Bridge. Our spirits were high as we sang to a Pretenders song on the radio.

"There's one thing you gotta do
To make me still want you
Then there's one thing you gotta know
To make me want you so
Gotta stop sobbing now
Yeah, stop it, stop it..."

Passing cars stared at our strange cargo, as we head back to Queens. It was at these times I feel that I felt that we were in this together and that there may be a rainbow just hiding behind the clouds.

After charging more art supplies that cover my lap, as we drive home, we make multiple trips up the stairs carrying bags and body parts. There are enough parts for two standing mannequins and an extra pair of legs. Assembled on their stands they stood six feet tall and were stunningly beautiful with their baldheads. Alfie rubbed their faces with oil and their features came to life. He talked to them like they were his ladies and he named them the 'Gucci Sisters'.

I dressed them up in some clothes, not trusting him with them if they remained naked. With his strange sexuality I never know...

Flea & Food Market

Our eccentric collection of street memorabilia has filled the place we now call home.

143

By the end of July, freelance work stopped, as most people took vacation to get out of the summer heat. Alfie surveyed the mailbox each day for my checks. We were hungry. Alfie's Mom Sophia had cigarettes for him, which means he would owe her some money. That also meant that she had Valium for him. Since he was a child she gave him her prescription of Valium to calm down his fits of rage.

When I mentioned that his mother was his dealer, he blew up at me. He asserted that I don't know about family or taking care of family.

Alfie's habit was out of control. He stayed up every night high strung out on Valium, taking five at a time to 'take the edge off'. I was grateful something could calm him down. However his next 'morning mood swings' were getting tough again.

I sold two rings and a pin to the Antique Shop. The owner was a little Jewish man, who winked at me as he handed me twenty-five dollars.

"It is always nice to see you, Nina. How is that tall feller I always see you with? I don't see the two of you together any more. Are you single? I always like to see your smile. Come tomorrow to the Richmond Hill Flea & Food Market. I have a booth on the stage. You should come down. There is something for everyone, including dented cans and cheap food." He strokes his long grey beard and stares at my chest. I grab the cash and quickly leave the store.

The Richmond Hill Flea & Food Market is held every Sunday in an old theater. Two nights a week is regular Bingo, but on Friday's they double the stakes for Jackpot Bingo. The old theater was once a beautiful palace that featured vaudeville acts back in the day. Some of the old posters were still on display. The building had been seriously neglected throughout the years. In the main hall, all the seats had been taken out and the faded walls and ceiling still had the original plaster statues and ornate faded gold scroll designs, like an Egyptian temple in a low budget B-movie. The owner lived in the balcony that was up a grand stairway. Rumor had it, that on 'off nights' it was either a gay male brothel or a religious cult. The owner was an interesting character with twinkling blue eyes, a red faded beard, and cowboy boots, almost like Santa Claus, especially when he laughed. It was said that the twinkling in his eyes bewitched many a young lad to spend the night.

Early Sunday morning as others head to church to find religion, the flea market crowd unpacks the brick-a-brac and knick-knacks preparing for a day of haggling and bartering. Rows of tables line the main floor creating tight aisles. By 8:30 a.m. some 25 dealers have arranged their wares on tables. On stage is surrounded by red velvet curtains now faded and moth-eaten are the more 'serious' antique dealers.

Everything is a little moth-eaten.

The doors open at 9 a.m. and dozens of buyers rush in to find the day's treasures. Both Indian and Spanish families squeeze together down the narrow aisles and by 10 a.m., when we arrive, the place is packed with people.

"This is a fire hazard, Nina. I can't take the people, let's get out of here." Alfie protests. We made our way through the masses back to the front entrance. "Clearly someone has had to pay off the fire marshal."

Near the entrance in what must have once been a grand lounge and bar, are tables lined with food. Donated to a charitable organization these dented cans of expired food are for sale. We each take a basket and start grabbing them.

It's all uphill as we head home with bags filled with dented cans of peas, corn, chili, tomato soup, banged up boxes of pasta and cereal, bags of rice, dried beans, and Tang.

"Oh Heavenly Father," Alfie says as we hold hands about to eat. "We thank you and the spirits for our flea market windfall, Amen."

We stuff ourselves on rice, cream of tomato soup, saltine crackers and peaches in their own syrup. We toast our good fortune with Tang orange flavored drink in wine glasses and truly feel blessed.

Blood on the Tracks

I take the time to organize my studio. The room had been divided between my space and his. Along my space is my drawing table and the Canal Street sign hangs on the windowed wall. I have a system of racks for my paper, supplies and bins of old paint-filled film canisters. A wall of wooded crates acts as a bookcase for my art and textbooks. I definitely learned to organize from Ian! Alfie has his poster of Dracula and one of a large woman from outer space that is attacking Earth. Under that is the patched up, old blow-up mattress, which continues to lose air. There is a TV in the corner and his collection of videos and plays. A steamer trunk divides the areas of his and mine.

I opened the trunk where I kept a bag with the drafting paper and crayons that I had used to create the Canal Street sign. All my subway research and sketches were in this trunk. Why not create another sign?

I need to get away from this apartment and Alfie. He has the ability to suck up all my energy between his fits of rage, sexual demands and our constant poverty. He drains me. Everyday with him has become a balancing act, never being sure which personality within him will greet the day. He is raw insanity, pacing the floors at all hours, talking to himself. I am beginning to realize he feeds off drama and lives on chaos. He is his own worst enemy making everything more complicated than it had to be and making my life more complicated then I wanted it to be.

I knew in my heart that this relationship was going nowhere. I hated his bed in the corner and wished he had never moved in. Life with him was crazy. He operated only on crises, the rest of the time he lay dormant as if recharging for the next battle. It was exhausting day after day riding the waves of panic and swimming through the sea of despair. I dreamed at night that I was struggling under water, swimming with a heavy weight around my neck, unable to reach the surface. We had been through a lot this summer and I no longer wanted him near me. I could swim but with him I would surely drown.

One morning, while Alfie slept late, I rummaged through old bags and coats, and found enough change to buy a token. I tiptoed out of the house and made my escape. It was just after rush hour. I bought a token and hoped that I wouldn't need to get out of the station for I had no money to get back in. I took a seat and watched out the window as the lights and shadows created an effect like a stop action film. It was my film, my life; and at Grand Central station, I switched trains to the Lexington Ave. line. My destination is Spring Street.

At Spring Street, I walk up and down the platform looking to find the best-preserved station sign. I choose this station for it is part of one of the oldest subway lines. The mosaic murals have ornate borders with vines and flowers, geometric diamonds, squares and a checkerboard pattern all made of tiny quarter inch tiles. Built in the early1900s it is Victorian in style. I make a sketch in my drawing pad making a list of the colors I will need.

I tape paper to the wall as the Express trains rush by creating a vacuum of wind that almost takes my paper with it. I hold the paper to the wall until the train heads down a tunnel. I tape quickly before another train goes by. I have already pulled a few colors and begin to trace the letters of Spring Street.

The tiles are much smaller than those from the Canal Street sign. As an hour goes by, my progress is slow. I realize this sign will take a few trips to complete, maybe three in total. Another hour goes by and I have only traced the inner border. From the tunnel I hear high-pitched squeals from rats that scurry along, seeing big rats the size of groundhogs hobbling in the distance. I work on the bells next, trying to finish the top band but my body is stiffening up. I sit down feeling dizzy, my stomach aches in pain. Into the tracks I throw up the dented-canned tomato soup from last night's dinner as the rats scurry toward it sensing food. I roll up my work between the passing trains and pack my things. I take two trains back to Queens. I throw up again when I leave the station.

Walking eleven blocks and up three flights of stairs, I collapse into bed with pains in my stomach. I fall asleep and dream I am dressed like a Knight in Armor. I am fighting a rushing current of water as I make my way along the subway tracks. I search through a long dark tunnel, with a pole that I tap to find my way along the walls, and rats squeal behind me. I find rooms covered in moss hiding mosaic art. I have lost something dear to me and I franticly look for it. There are clues on the walls. Under heavy dust I find a fort, a bridge, a beaver and an eagle, yet I don't know what this all means. There are voices down the tunnel and I must hide.

Alfie wakes me up when he gets home. He says something about gas for pizza wheels? I hear him talk but cannot understand what he is saying. I cannot move my body, or lift my head.

"No thanks, I don't want pizza wheels." I hear myself say as I close my eyes. "I have no money to give."

I return to my dream wandering lost through the underground world of dripping stalactites and stalagmites echo each drop as they fall. They are florescent and glow in the darkness. I am on a quest. I understand this clearly. I fight a giant rat that takes a bite out of my side. I double over with sharp pains and there is blood on my hands, blood on the tracks. I have killed the rat.

I stagger on to an abandoned station. I see a magnificent fresco painted on the wall. I reach for it and my blood stains the wall. It is a portrait of the Virgin Mary illuminated with a golden halo, only it is not Mary; it is Doralina the Fortuneteller from Venice. She steps out of the painting and becomes three-dimensional. I apologize for the blood on her long velvet robe; she ignores it and leads me to a table set upon a stage. She pulls Tarot cards turning over three.

"This is your past: I see abandonment, and a great sorrow in your heart. This loss haunts you still it fills your heart with fear. You have built walls like a fort that you let no one enter. I see that the men in your past are not the right men. You must build a bridge like a beaver between who you want to be and who you are. You must choose the right path to follow and not let their negative current drown you. They are only here to distract you."

She turns over more cards, "Very interesting... I see a Questa, a Questa you have only just begun. This is the journey you are meant to take. You will find your eagle eyes from which you will see the beauty in the world. This is your gift and your calling. Be patient and the path will reveal itself in time. To what is around you now, pay that no mind."

"Yes, yes, I know I am trying to return to my quest but it is dark chocolate indigo deep within the tunnel, I have lost all my colors. I have forgotten where I put them. I can't proceed without colors to light the way" I hold my stomach in pain." I put down my shield and sword and kneel in front of her glowing body. "I have lost my way. Please make the pain stop."

She draws the card of death. "There are endings and beginnings to all things."

"Am I dying? Is this really the end?" I ask as I pick up my shield preparing once again to fight.

"You are with child, my Child, but it is not your time. This soul shall not go forth, no, not at this time. There will be others, when you are ready, there will be others." She reached to touch my stomach and the pain resided.

"There Child, it will be over soon. You are stronger then you think. You must rest now to regain your strength."

She draws another card from her deck. "This card represents the forces around you, it is the Hanged One. I see a tortured soul influences your life. You must choose between idealistic love and physical attraction." She turns two more cards. "Don't be fooled by this lover, he is charming yet deceitful." She flips over a few more cards; I see a devil. "Oh, this lover has demons. I see his addictions; the violent rage ignites his passion. He calls it love as he sucks you dry. Listen to me carefully, this lover will feed off your blood. Like a vampire; his charms will lure you as he drains everything you have. Don't be foolish girl, he is not the one."

"There is love…" I say weakly wanting to sound so much surer then the words came out.

She turns over the last card, "I see an adventurous spirit in your future. An eagle will come to guide your journey and be your lover. I see exotic lands to explore as one."

I wake covered in sweat. Alfie is standing over me, his long hair covering most of his face. The morning light shines on his earring fracturing the light in many different fragments. I smell the stale smell of cigarettes like death on his breath. I jump up frightened and the bed is covered in blood.

"Wow, didn't mean to scare you. You've been talking in your sleep for hours. Must have been some nightmare? You have a fever, drink this." He hands me some water with artificial lemon flavor and high fructose corn syrup. It tastes awful, artificial and bad. I don't trust him.

I go to the medicine box searching for something for cramps. All the bottles of painkillers are empty. Alfie has taken them all recreationally. I make a hot-water bottle and return to bed. For days, I have cramps and bleed extremely heavily.

Every time Alfie wakes me up, I remember the dream and jump up in fright. He watches over me but his presence scares me. This is starting to annoy him.

Pizza Delivery

Days turn into nights and I keep searching for what I have lost in my dreams. By Friday I am feeling better. Alfie brings me stale fig cookies and tea.

"Good to see you sitting up. Had me worried there for a while Cupcake." Alfie fills me in on what I have missed. He has a job delivering pizza at Wheelies Pizzeria.

"I'll bring you back a pie." He promises as he kisses me goodbye. I back away afraid to have him touch me.

I get up and look in the mirror. I am a mess so I take a shower and turn on the TV. We have only three stations that work. One is showing 'Life Styles of the Rich and Famous' and the other has Martha Stewart demonstrating her double chocolate cake recipe. I settle on the news.

In my studio, I unravel the Spring Street sign to see what I have accomplished. I haven't been able to get up and see this for days. So far, so good, I look to my crayon boxes to see what to add and prepare for the next trip. I have colors. I wonder if it was the dented cans or if I had a miscarriage. Either way, that dream still lurked in my mind.

Around 7 p.m. I get a phone call, and it is Alfie completely frantic. He has locked his keys in the car. I need to bring my keys to his job.

Feeling weak, I get dressed, and walk to the train. The stairs are endless between the street and the tracks below. By the time I get to Wheelies, the owner has already jimmied the car lock open with a coat hanger. Alfie and the owner are screaming at each other in Italian. I understand that Alfie calls Wheelie a dick and he calls Alfie an imbecile and that Alfie is fired. We head home and discover the six pizzas are still in the back seat. For a week we eat our fill of cold pizza!

When the pizza is gone, we go hungry again, until I finally get paid. We cash my check at the supermarket where they take out what I owe them first. We divided up what is left: a month to the landlord, $50 for his mother, gas for the car, and a small bag of pot. Not much left for dented cans...

CHAPTER 15 –

THE MASK OF KARMA

Wednesday is alternate side of the street parking, so reluctantly we walk five blocks up hill to move the car across the street. We fight all the way to the car, debating if we should sell it and who even would want to buy it. We are broke and hungry and take it out on each other, as we roll the car down the hill into another spot, trying not to use any gas, as the car has nothing but fumes. On the street near our new parking space we spot a black patent leather pocketbook shining under the evening streetlight.

Alfie grabs the bag and jumps into the car yelling, "Drive! Just drive the car!" We look around and see no one. The streets are empty as we quickly pull a right. The car chokes and sputters in a cloud of smoke. Eight blocks away we stop along the park in a desolate area where the streetlight has been broken. As we search through the bag a parade of men meet up and head into he woods.

There is a pack of Virginia Slims Ultra Lights. Alfie grabs the pack out of my hand, takes a cigarette and sniffs it like a dog. He tears off the filter and lights it with a pink Bic lighter, he inhales the smoke deeply into his lungs.

"It will do." He says as he sucks in the excess smoke like a dying man would reach for oxygen. I remembered I used to think that the way he smoked was sexy. Now I am repulsed by the amount of smoke he inhales in a day, and how now, I too, have a smoking habit. I light up my own cigarette with the filter and continue looking through the bag. Alfie grabs the wallet. Rummaging through it, he counts out twenty-two dollars.

"Sonya Silverman is a cheap bitch, she has two kids and a fat Hassidic husband. She is a card-carrying therapist, and belongs to the Jewish Society of Career Women." Alfie shows me pictures and cards. An overweight woman in horizontal stripes, brown lips and a blunt Barbara Streisand wig is in every picture. Below are captions that read Marshall's Bar Mitzvah and Sadie's Bat Mitzvah. "Poor Mr. Sonya Silverman, I feel your pain man. No wonder no one is smiling." Alfie throws the bag back to me. I continue to look through it.

There was an ugly mauve lipstick and matching nail polish still in its package from the drug store. There are prescription meds that Alfie grabs and shoves into his pocket. I try on the lipstick in the rear view mirror. It looks blue on my lips in the evening light. I toss it back in the bag. There is a pack of gum. Hungry, we each chew a stick, and moan, as it tastes like bad perfume, like Sonya Silverman's bad perfume! I roll down my window to spit it out and from the passenger seat Alfie spits his across my face and out my window.

I was guilty of invading this woman's life. It didn't feel right. On the street, guys continue to meet up with guys, and off they head together into the woods.

"I see we have found the gay connecting spot here at the park." Alfie counts the coins.

In the zippered compartment was a small purse closed with a safety pin. It was fat and jingled with the sound of money. We looked at each other as if we had found treasure. Inside the purse we unroll $600 dollars and several silver dollars. We were rich!

"See this bitch was loaded, carrying around that kind of money, probably meant nothing to her. Probably loses bags of money all the time. What should we do first?" Alfie flicked the cigarette out my window as well.

"Dinner!" We say at the same time.

"I feel like a king, let's go to White Castle," he said.

"No way. 'Belly-bombers' on an empty stomach, are you trying to completely kill me?" I head the car to Arby's and stop for gas along the way. We buy cigarettes.

Our Arby's routine is to go in separately, order burgers, fries and a coke and meet up at the fixings bar. With our backs to the registers we fill our bags with a ton of free stuff from the fixing bar. In little plastic containers we pack up mayo, horseradish, mustard, catsup, and pickles. We each grab a fistful of paper napkins, straws and sugar packets. I head to the car as Alfie calls his dealer at a pay phone to see if we can come over.

In the parking lot I am stopped by a woman in a brown UPS uniform, "Nina Page, is that you?" At first I think I am under arrest for stealing the purse until I recognize whom it is.

"RJ, how are you?" Rachael Jordan and I graduated high school together. She was a jock and I hung with the art snobs, but our lockers were next to each other.

"God! Wow, Nina Page it has been a while, look at you! You lost a ton of weight! I almost didn't think it was you. What are you up to? Last I heard you went away to art school or Europe or something?"

"Yes well I took a few years to work and then went back to school. I just finished at Parsons." I said wondering when Alfie would come out.

"Well you were always good at art. Imagine that. Do you have any kids? Just about everyone from school is married with kids," she said and started to name people I had not thought of in years.

"No, I'm not married yet. I hate this subject. "Are you?" She nodded no and laughed in agreement.

"I would have thought you'd have gotten married. This past year everyone paired up. Guess casual sex isn't as much fun when the risk of AIDS is on the line." We both nodded in agreement. "Cori passed away." She said suddenly.

"Yes, I heard that, he was so young." I said sadly.

"Took us all by surprise, rumors were he was gay. These things are such closeted secrets." I could tell she was keeping hers well hidden.

"Yes, until there is more research and a cure there will continue to be secrets." I agreed.

Just as quickly, she changed the subject. "You have really lost a lot of weight. Well I guess you're a career girl making the big bucks." I looked down at my bag of pilfered condiments and dinner bought from money stolen due to the absent-minded therapist with mauve lips!

"Yeah that's me, a career girl..." The phrase really annoyed me; career girl would stick in my head for weeks. It was something I had in common with Sonya Silverman and it wasn't making either of us smile. I thought of Mary Tyler Moore, the role model for career girls my age. She made it all seem so much fun. She had a great job, great apartment, perfect hair and a wardrobe of fabulous fashions. Reality sucked when you were undefined, wedged somewhere between housewife and career woman.

"Me too." She pulled on the collar of her uniform proudly. RJ ran track in high school and now she was running packages. I was sure she was a lesbian and I hoped she finally figured that out as well. "Did you hear about the reunion? We just celebrated 7 years. Can you believe it, 7 years already? A group of us get together every year. You should come next year. There is a committee looking to rent the Knights of Columbus and hiring the band Barry and the Leftovers. Hey didn't you and Barry go out one summer?"

"Um yeah, we hung out one summer." I was looking out for Alfie, he got very strange when I talked to people he didn't know. Barry was a few years older, the lead singer in a band. I spent one summer watching him perform in the drummer's garage - If you count that 'going out'. He would sing to me, which I thought was very cool. I was a freshman he was a senior. I was young and not ready to give out. He got bored and had lots of girls that would, so we drifted apart.

"Barry's got quite a following on Long Island. A bunch of us go to hear him play when he comes to Valley Stream. You should come by one night, I'm sure he would love to see you after all these years. You look really great!" she said as Alfie came up.

"Yeah maybe one night," I knew it would never happen. "Alfie this is RJ, we went to school together. RJ this is my boyfriend Alfie." They just looked at each other.

"Wait till I tell the gang I saw you! I need to grab some dinner before getting the truck back. Take care, see ya' at the reunion!" and off she ran.

"Sure! Take care, see ya at the reunion." I said just because I should.

"Leave you alone for five minutes and you're making plans for a reunion with some dyke. Was she picking you up? Clearly she was into you, I could tell." He seemed a bit annoyed that someone was messing with his woman.

"Calm down, we went to high school together." I said. "I am not her type."

"Well Jonathan is home and willing to see us if we get there within the next hour. He is off to CBGBs to see some band, Losers and Leftovers or something." We head to the car.

"You mean Barry and the Leftovers." I say with a smile.

"Yeah, how do you know? Losers, leftovers, whatever… It sounds like a really stupid name for a band, like some old diner, or the crap left over that they turn into meatloaf. Who likes leftovers anyway?"

I say nothing as we drive on the expressway eating our dinner out of bags and listening to Hendricks on the radio, as the windshield wipers slapped in time.

Found Money

The next day with gas in the car, we drive over the Manhattan Bridge to Canal Street. I need art supplies again. I budget one hundred dollars to buy paper and paint, so that come September I have supplies for work. Alfie tries to talk me out of being practical, but I insist. He agrees only if he too can buy some goodies. We park on a side street and feed a meter with our bounty of loose change. Along Canal Street we wander arm and arm through Chinatown, window-shopping. We enter an Antique Emporium, which is dark and dusty and filled with all sorts of odd things: carved skulls, gas masks, military gear, and a collection of Indonesian art. There were beautiful Batik robes and textiles and wooden carvings. A particular mask catches our attention.

"I see you like my mask, it is from Africa. They say every mask brings a spirit that protects its owner. This one was worn for prosperity to ward off evil spirits."

"We could certainly use that." I say as I try to lead Alfie away.

"What is your best price?" Alfie asks. The owner says $85.

"We need to think about it," I respond and pull Alfie out of the store.

Instead I take us to Pearl Paint. The multi-layered warehouse with red windows is a holy Mecca of art supplies. I breathe in the smell of oil paints and see the walls filled with colored pencils, markers, and tubes of acrylics, oils and gouache, pastels and cans of spray paint creating rainbows of color. On another floor are the papers, from tracing paper to heavy watercolor, shiny Mylar, Vellum and canvases in large rolls. I buy art paper, tubes of gouache, three large boxes of 64 color crayons and two fine sable paintbrushes. We put our purchases in the car, feed the meter and head to Little Italy.

Art supplies were to me like Italian specialties were to Alfie! We walk through Little Italy and buy fresh pasta, boxes of chocolate biscotti, cannoli and little cookies with pignoli nuts for his Mother. In a Deli he buys a solid hunk of Parmesan cheese and a hunk of salami, where he gladly orders in Italian.

We stop at an Italian café where little pastries fill the window display. We order espresso and the house special Tiramisu. I melt as Alfie orders in Italian, such a beautiful language. Tir-a-mi-su sounds seductive, and I find I am drooling as we wait for our treats. Today is a good day. The Tiramisu tastes as delicious as it sounds with layers of cake soaked in coffee and layered with cream.

Alfie mocks the waiter as he leaves, as he speaks with a southern dialect and not a classical northern dialect. Insisting we buy the mask, I think Alfie is out of his mind.

"We should save this money. We **do** need some real food," I say, as I savor every tasty bite and hot bitter coffee, like sex on my tongue.

"Can you stop being so practical for once? This is found money; we should have some fun with it. If you love the mask, Cupcake, just get it!" Alfie dumped a ton of sugar in this tiny cup making the coffee spill over onto a little saucer. He sucked this up with a loud slurp. We sit and people watch until we remember our car and the meter.

We walk back to the car with our arms full of Italian goodies and put them in the back of the hatchback next to all the art supplies. We feed the meter with more coins and return to the antique shop. After haggling with the antique dealer to get the price down another ten dollars, we walk out with the mask wrapped in Chinese newsprint. Alfie needs cigarettes so we go a little further to the newsstand where he considers buying a girlie magazine. He can't make up his mind which one and takes forever thumbing through the different issues. I remind him about the meter so he chooses one featuring big behinds.

We head back to the car, excited about all our goodies, but as we turn the corner we see two men rummaging through the back of our car.

Alfie yells and the guys take off in opposite directions. There is a sea of people and the guys are nowhere in sight. Alfie still tries to find them. I stay with the car. The hatchback lock is popped off and completely broken, which I secure with a bungee cord. In the garbage can next to the car I find all my art supplies and a large Purina Dog Chow bag filled with electronic equipment. Alfie returns and we stuff the bag in the back seat. We take the bridge home in silence.

I hang the mask in the living room. It looks back at me with a strange stare, like it was mocking me, as if it knew my guilt about the whole experience. Bad karma had followed us. Since we didn't return the money, now we too were robbed. I placed all the contents of the pocketbook into an envelope and addressed it to the name on the driver's license. I put the same address on the return label. Without postage I placed it into the mailbox and hoped it would be returned to its rightful owner. At least she would have all her pictures of her family and credit cards returned. Maybe that would help alleviate the bad karma.

I kept the lipstick, nail polish and a nail file but never used them.

The third notice for the electric bill came in the mail. We needed cash fast. I head to the local Antique dealer and sell the mask, hoping that the bad 'juju' would soon be gone. Alfie heads to Jamaica to sell off the 'bag-o-electronics'. He gets $80 and buys two cartons of Kool cigarettes and another hunk of Parmesan cheese from a Deli in Richmond Hill. Before coming home, he splits the cigarettes and some cash with his mother, forgetting all about the electric bill. We fight, as is now 'our thing'.

CHAPTER 16 – THE ADVENTURES OF INDIANA JONES

Alfie had a 'smoking friend' in Accounting that lied for him to the unemployment agency. He said that Alfie had been with the company for over a year and due to budget cuts was now let go. After much back and forth he would be entitled to receive unemployment checks for the next six months. Now Alfie was definitely not getting a job. Every Wednesday afternoon, after greeting the mailman at the door, he would cash his check in Jamaica and rush to his dealer to spend more than half on a bag of weed.

His routine once a week included meeting his mother so he could hand her $50. All the money ran through their hands within 24 hours no matter what amount.

On Sunday nights his mother would call heartbroken, crying that she had no money for the week and could only afford to eat pasta and beans. She was paid every other Friday but by Friday she owed money in so many direction there was nothing left. On Sunday, after praying at Church to her god, she would give the remainder of her paycheck to buy chances on lotto. By Sunday night, once again, she found herself destitute.

Alfie would curse at her but once he had money in his pocket he would head over and in return she would renew her Valium prescription and give him the bottle. They had a strange love-hate relationship. Like mother like son, it was feast or famine, never an in-between.

On Thursday nights Alfie was in Manhattan with a new theater workshop rehearsing scenes from his new play. It was a psychological drama about a man on the brink of suicide as a psychotic therapist berates him. I thought of the relationship between Tomlin and Ian but said nothing. Together, the man and the therapist plot to kill his wife, who coincidently seemed to be a lot like me!

I said nothing, a bit creepy, I thought, but it was a place to put all his demons. Life was a bit calm for the moment as the pages absorbed his wrath.

Thursday nights are all mine. On Friday mornings I head to the library or sit for hours in a local coffee shop, just to get out of the apartment. Even with the unemployment checks, we are behind on rent. Seems that was **his** money and since this was **my** apartment, rent was **my** problem…!

Survival of the Fittest

Otto and the Bloodhounds were evicting tenants one by one. First it was the piano player who left. The Bloodhounds smashed her piano into pieces that were stacked in the alley by the garbage pails. For this the tenants were both thankful and grateful. Other tenants left too, and we gathered their remains from the trash if they had any value.

"One man's trash is another man's treasure," Alfie liked to say.

Now construction was in full blast next to us, and beneath us. It was maddening.

In the fall I get a few freelance jobs and find a rep to take some of my prints. I find a freelance job with Izod creating presentation boards with little striped rugby and golf shirts. I need to learn the stitching detail and must show this with tiny little stitch marks. The little bodies line my windowsill to dry. The good news was, that I was earning some money again. The bad news was, that I desperately wanted to get back into the subways. Still, I couldn't turn down this work. With some money from Alfie and my freelance checks coming in, we started to repay the landlord a little at a time, and turned the phone back on.

By September, I had not yet finished the Spring Street sign. Weeks had gone by before I had a little time on my hands and started to regain my strength. In between freelancing, I worked on

159

my physical strength. At home I started lifting weights and doing sit-ups. I got a book on yoga and tried to hold the silly poses. I needed to be stronger if I was going to work in the subway again. I changed my diet as well, eating fresh veggies and less junk food, including nothing out of a dented can department. With Alfie out of the house, I started to meditate calming my mind, controlling my breathing and finding an inner peace.

Alfie still wanted to live off pizza and White Castle burgers but I had had my fill of both and no longer joined him. Since my awful dream, I didn't want to have sex with him, so our sex-life became me doing yoga in the nude. At night, he watched porn and jerked-off. I pulled away from him both physically and mentally, refusing to let him engulf me in his drama. I needed to get back to just being me.

Transforming my studio, I turned the walls into personal inspiration boards, all about the subways. I had a subway map on one wall marked with the stations I wanted to record, and color swatches on another. I tested crayon combinations and applied black dye. Little color swatches hung everywhere with the colors I wanted to use at each station. I reworked these swatches till I found the best colors, which maintained their brightness after the dye was applied. From the library I took out every book and made copies of what I could find on the history of transportation and the development of New York City. Everything I could find on the subways was hanging on my design inspiration walls.

I read The Post and kept track of patterns of crime in the city. I studied the psychology of criminals. I figured the best times of day to work were midday between rush hours. At these times, there would be less people on the platforms and I decided mid-week, mid-month and mid-morning were the safest. I found a calendar with cycles of the full moon discovering that when the moon was full, all the lunatics were about and the crime rate heightened. I thought about the times of the month when I was most desperate or when I felt physically weak. Never work the first of the month when rent was due. Never work the last week of the month, just knowing the beginning of the month was around the corner. Stay away from holidays; they made everyone a little crazy!

A Lifetime Membership

Using his unemployment money, Alfie joined a video store, paying extra for a VIP lifetime membership. He claimed it was to have access to the foreign film collection, of which he 'turned me on' to some Fellini films. This VIP membership also gave one VIP access to the hidden red room. A black velvet curtain hid the VIP erotica and porno collection. In this nice Hassidic neighborhood, where it was said men would not fuck their women unless a sheet was between them, the town hosted an XXX movie theater and two adult video shops. We had gone to the movie theater one afternoon. A few men were watching the film as we had sex in the back row. I remember how my shoes stuck to the floor, finding the whole thing disgusting. Now I won't let him near me.

"Cupcake, what do you expect me to do if you are not there for me. I am a man with needs," he said, defending his spending money, once again, that was promised for the house.

Just six months after opening, the VIP Video Store was closed for renovations and newspaper covered the windows. Alfie went through porn withdrawal, if there is such a thing.

A week later in the middle of the night, the store had packed up and moved on. Gone too was half the town's lifetime membership. Alfie stared into the window where the paper had fallen down. He was like a five year old, sad that the candy store had shut it's doors taking all the candy with them! We decided to head to the alley and see what they threw in the trash, where we found tubs of movie posters and promotional materials in boxes.

"These could be valuable. Grab everything Cupcake, and we'll sort it out upstairs." We gathered everything we could carry, making two trips. Alfie had hoped there would be videos but these were gone. He was so pissed that his source for porno closed. I was amused at 'the plot' that the storeowners slipped out of town stealing the VIP membership fees of these pathetic men. I imagined the storeowners going town to town, opening up VIP Video Stores for six months and disappearing over night, leaving hundreds of sad men empty handed. It was brilliant! What could these anguished souls do? Who could they complain to? All that was left was to longingly look through the newspaper-covered windows with their memories and despair.

I tried not to laugh at Alfie's despair, but it was funny how every time he thought he had 'one over' on the world, the world would always bite him in the ass. Naturally, I kept this to myself.

In the trash were movie posters for films: Ghostbusters, Beetlejuice, The Terminator, Aliens, Die Hard and Blue Velvet. Alfie hung these on his side of the studio. We found a can of red paint and the black velvet VIP curtain. I painted the bathroom walls red. I washed the VIP curtain in the bathtub and used it as a bed spread. In a canvas bag was promotional material for an Indiana Jones film. Inside there was a cargo vest, safari hat with flaps and a cardboard cutout with assembly instructions of Harrison Ford. These I could use in my subway expedition. I assembled the Indiana Jones cardboard cutout of Harrison Ford to watch over me and give me courage. I put this on my side of the studio.

TO WALL STREET

I dressed before Alfie woke. I had left my clothes in the studio, carpenter pants, cargo vest, and safari hat with flaps. The night before I had packed the canvas bag with my art supplies. From the kitchen closet I carefully lifted a garbage bag filled with bottles. They rattled a little, Alfie grumbled and rolled over, he had been out late last night, again. Quietly I unlocked the door and was free!

I gave the landlord money the week before, so he was not 'on my case'. I passed his Bloodhounds that each snarled a hello as they parted and let me walk by.

I headed to the supermarket to cash in my bottles. 5 cents apiece I had enough for one token to get into the subway. It was pathetic that Alfie had money coming in but by day two we were dead broke again. I had freelance earnings owed, but again it was a good week to ten days until I'd receive a check in the mail. I was a warrior heading into battle with my crate and bag of art supplies.

"What kind of work do you do?" the man behind me on line asked as I waited for the bottles to be counted by the guys in the back.

"What do you mean?"

"You have this determined look in your eyes and I can tell by the roll of paper sticking out of your bag that you are an artist. So, what do you do?" he motioned to my back.

"Well... I am interested in the mosaic murals that are in the subways. Today I am heading to Wall Street to emboss the station sign." It sounded crazy when I said it out loud, but he was interested.

"Where can I see your work?" he asked as the cashier handed me my dollar. I squished it into my pocket a bit embarrassed. "Nowhere yet, I'm just starting on my third piece. I would like to capture a few of the different decades in design and show it as a collection."

"Hey wait!" he hands me twenty bucks. "Let's call it an endowment for the arts."

"Thanks!" I don't refuse as we walk out of the store together.

"Good luck, I expect to read about you some day in the papers." We part ways.

With twenty bucks in my pocket my step comes alive as I head along the park to the Queens Boulevard station.

I take the E train to Wall Street. It is October on a Tuesday, a nice neutral day according to all my research. I find a New York Post on the seat next to me, and check the weather page. Good, it is not a full moon. I am too excited to read and save the paper for later. I count down every station, until my stop.

Wall Street Station is one of the first subway lines from the 1900s. It still has its wooden turnstiles and the original token-booth. The main mosaic mural included Victorian images of vines with flowers, and checkerboard geometrics just like Spring Street. However, I was going after the image of a smaller, less-detailed sign. Along the station walls, in between the mosaic murals were bands of marble and plaques with W's. Above these, a terracotta relief of a picket fence in front of an Old Dutch settlement. I had read that in the 17th century the Dutch settlers built a 12-foot stockade wall to protect the settlement of New Amsterdam against attacks from Indians. Near the station was a small directional sign **'To Wall Street'** with an arrow. It was only 3' x 1', easier to execute than the ornate Victorian mural. Today, this is what I was after, and I plan on finishing it in one day.

I stuffed my hair under the Safari hat and put down the flaps. Quickly I measured the sign and tore off some drafting paper, which I taped up to the wall. Using browns, greens and gold I started to trace out the letters, then the ground and then the double border. It took over two hours.

Someone left their empty coffee cup by me as they stood and watched. Then people started to put money in the cup. Within two hours I was heading home with a completed sign and a total of twenty-six bucks for the day. I felt it was a sign that the universe was providing for my quest and me. I hid twenty dollars in my box of crayons and spent the rest on an eggplant hero! I had started the day with returnable bottles and now I was taking the bus home with dinner. The universe for today was on my side.

I ate the entire hero and saved nothing for Alfie. I went to bed exhausted, content and full.

6TH AVENUE – 5TH AVENUE

I hand in my freelance work on a Monday and have a few days to myself. I set out to capture the directional sign on 42nd Street that connects 6th Avenue to 5th Avenue. This connection between streets was built in the 1920s and the sign reflects the Arts and Crafts style of its time. It was an easy sign to set up being away from the station platform and the rush of 'people traffic'. Without interruptions I set to work.

The sign measured 6' long by 1' wide. I tape my paper to the wall and I chose dusty colors beginning to trace the words and numbers. The sign has a colorful border that uses 2" tiles. I chose grey-blues, red-browns and ochre from my box of crayons; a palette similar to what is on the wall. The large tiles are easier to trace. In two hours I have achieved a great deal.

In a far corner is a pile of wooden debris roped off by yellow plastic 'Do Not Enter' tape. After two hours, the rubble in the corner starts to move. A homeless man rises and shakes himself off, comes over to see what I am doing. Now I wish this spot was not so remote.

"Very nice, I like what you are doing. I have been watching you," he says as he walks away. I note he has only one arm. "I'm going out for a cup of coffee. Can I get you anything?"

"Thanks, but I have no money." I say stepping off of my crate and stretching out my right arm that has grown stiff.

"No problem, I'll see what I can come up with." He whistled a little tune as if he didn't have a care in the world. I didn't see him again.

Once back in my studio, I dye both the 5th Ave - 6th Ave. and Wall Street signs with black dye. The wax crayons resist the dye and like magic, the colors shine through like jewels. I check with Harrison Ford, and his cardboard likeness smiles back! My goal now is to reproduce a new sign every month. I want to create a collection that shows the different designs throughout each decade of subway expansion.

34TH STREET – PENNSYLVANIA STATION

I am grateful when I do get freelance work but it does take me away from what I really want to do, which is to get back into the subways. Alfie is busy on a new script and has re-joined yet another theater workshop which now meets two nights a week. We are living separate lives.

In November, I set out to create an embossing from Penn Station at 34th Street. Constructed in the 1940s it has a modern bold streamlined design. Penn station is a busy platform with a constant flow of people making connections. I decide to work

165

between 10 a.m. and 2 p.m., thinking traffic may be slowest at this time. It is a struggle to get my drafting paper taped to the wall as so many trains pass through the station. I start to emboss the letters in a dusty orange color that I planned to contrast with a steel blue background.

From around the corner a violinist has set up to play. His sound echoes and moans in the ceramic cavern of the underground station. We are undisturbed, engrossed in our art as the trains rush by transporting hundreds of passengers through the station. He plays sweetly and soulfully, melancholy arrangements, as I trace the letters of 34th Street Penn Station.

Half way through the sign, a transit agent walked by concerned that I was defacing property. I said that I was only taking an embossing of the wall onto paper and the wall was not being harmed in any way. She left but was quite upset with me. I worked quickly to finish up. The sign was 9 feet long, much larger then I had expected. Around 1:30 with just the border to finish, I was exhausted when two transit cops came up 'barking' behind me.

When I turned around and they saw that I was a girl they calmed down. I explained, "I've been working on embossing a collection of murals that show the difference in style and design between the stations." I did also say I was a student at Parsons and that this was part of my senior thesis (a little lie). I talked fast.

"Hey that's a cool idea you should check out the NY Transit Museum. They would be interested in what you are doing," said an officer.

"The Transit Museum, where is that?" I ask.

"Boerum Place in Brooklyn, the museum is an abandoned subway station turned into a museum. You should check it out, ask for Ms. Leonie, she is the director." said the nicer officer.

His partner said, "Just hurry up and get out of here before rush hour. We will be back in an hour, so you'd better be gone." He said the last part louder so those that were looking on could hear.

"Be careful, this is really no place for a girl to be hanging around," said the first officer quietly, as they walked away.

"I will," I promised and continued to rush through the border. They made the violinist pack up and leave. We smiled to each other as he waited for the train.

Two days later I head to the Transit Museum in Brooklyn to meet with Mrs. Leonie. I had called her the next day from a pay phone (we never put our phone service back on) and she told me to come on in. I tried to tell Alfie about my appointment but he was in one of his moods so I didn't see the point.

I rolled my four signs into the cardboard movie poster tubes. They fit perfectly and had a seal on both ends that I taped for extra security. They fit in my Raiders of the Lost Arc bag; courtesy of the VIP Video Store.

At first, Mrs. Leonie is busy dealing with people and answering the phone, and then she asks to see my work. I carefully take out the mural and give her an end to hold as I walk away revealing Canal Street. She lights up with excitement and calls for some people to see it.

In no time, the small office is crowded. She asks me to repeat my story. One by one I unroll my murals and they gasp in excitement. They show me the gallery space where I can hang my work. A show in the spring, they have dates in April, how many signs can I have by then?

I am given a tour of the museum on the main floor that tells the history of New York transit. Down on the station platform the antique trains from years past are housed. Here anyone can feel what it was like to be a 'straphanger'. I try to take it all in, as there is much to see and learn. For the most part, all I can think about is, that they have offered me a show!

My mind races, as I head to the subway station home. The weather has turned cold and I only have a light jacket on. I take the subway home, watching the stations go by like old friends. I think about the gallery space and how I can lay out my work. I make some sketches on a scrap of paper.

Back in Queens, I climb up the three flights of stairs to the street and I call my Mom from a pay phone outside of the subway station. Her office machine picks up, "so sorry to have missed your call" I know she is spending the weekend in Pennsylvania with Fredrick and maybe they left early. I hear the message click and before the message "Please leave your name" I hang up. The phone booth returns my money plus 50 cents extra. The bus pulls up and I get two seats to myself. On the floor I pick up a five-dollar bill and quickly put it in my pocket. Maybe my luck **was** changing?

CHAPTER 17 – COURTHOUSE BLUES

I began working on the Christopher Street at Sheridan Square sign. I know with the Christmas holiday it will be January before I can return. It is the most ambitious sign yet, over 13' long and over 3' wide. I am exhausted and cold down to my bones.

I run out of colors and need to get another few boxes of crayons to finish. Worn out, I become depressed and think that maybe this is more then I can deliver. As the winter approaches fast, I know I need to give this up for a month or two.

Returning home, I drag myself up the stairs to find a notice for eviction plastered on the door. Alfie is home pacing the floor, pissed that I was out for so long. "Where the hell have you been?" He hands me a letter from our landlord's attorney. I put down my bags and with my coat still on; I collapse in a chair to read the letter. We are now three months behind with rent and have a court date. I had been focused on my art the past few months. In between the phone was again disconnected, as this was something Alfie had promised to pay.

"Evicted for Christmas!" Alfie paces the floor "What kind of an animal would do that to people?"

"We owe rent, why should he care what time of year it is?" I feel exasperated as I head off to the bathroom to wash my face and warm my stiff cold hands under the rusty hot water.

"Only a low-life evicts people for Christmas?" Alfie never thought he was in the wrong; it was always everyone else's fault.

I walk past him and head to the couch to reread the lawyer's letter and I spot the rest of the mail. Amongst the junk mail, is a postcard from Claire in France and a final notice from Con Ed. Our electricity is past due and about to be shut off as well. "I gave you money to pay this off last month! You told me you went to their office! Why on Earth do they say we still owe them all this money?"

"Well something came up." Alfie said sheepishly as he fumbled with his cigarette case offering me a cigarette.

"Alfie something always comes up. Why didn't you tell me? Did you think I just wouldn't find out? Alfie this is insane, we have no money, no phone service and it is a matter of time till they shut off electric! We owe money to just about everyone! What came up, another bag of pot? I can't live like this anymore!"

"My Mother needed some cash last month. She got herself in a little trouble." He claims, "She will pay us back at Christmas when she gets a bonus from work."

"We have a court date if we don't come up with the money we owe we will be out on the street." I grab the cigarette case, he throws me the lighter, we sit in silence smoking when the lights go out.

"Fucking great, what next?" he says as he exhales the smoke.

The next week is a scramble as we sell my drawing table, the Coca Cola sign, a brass lamp and my vintage hatboxes to the antique store. Alfie refuses to part with the Gucci sisters. I hated to see the table go. We walk a mile to the Con Ed office and settle our account by agreeing to a payment plan I knew we could never keep up. On the way back, I call my mom from a pay phone by the railroad station. Alfie sits on the stairs and smokes.

"Hi Mom, it's me," I say when she picks up. "I have good news and bad news. Which would y…"

"What's wrong now **Nina**?" She knows me all too well.

"The good news is about those subway signs I have been working on. The Transit Museum is letting me have an exhibit in the spring!" I say quickly, though for me all the joy of the event has been washed away.

"And the bad news **Nina**!" She says with **that** voice.

"Well we fell a bit behind this month. I need to borrow some money as we are facing eviction," I whisper into the phone.

A young mother rolls a baby stroller around the station. She looks exhausted as the baby sleeps soundly. A toy bear falls out of the stroller and Alfie comes to her assistance. He picks up the bear and flirts with the women in his usual charming way. She smiles back grateful for attention. He holds the bear before handing it over. I have seen this act before with him, the Italian charm, the routine, and the illusion.

"Choices made..." my mother yells in the phone. "These are the choices you have made Nina." There is silence between us, as I do not know what to say.

"How much do you need, this time?" she asks.

I whisper into the phone, "A thousand...?"

"A thousand...! Are you out of your mind!" There is a long silence on the phone before she continues to speak. "I have two hundred I can give you for the holidays, but that is all Nina. And what about Alfie, does this man have no responsibility?" I know she is at work but willing to yell at me just the same. "First you are supporting him, now **I am** supporting him! This is the last time Nina! This starving artist stuff is getting a bit old. You still have to eat! These plays he is writing, are they paying the rent? No! This Transit Museum, are they paying you anything? Nina...? No! So what good is this Nina? The two of you need to give up your art and get a job like everyone else! You both can't be artists while no one takes on the responsibilities! Grow up!"

I guessed this wasn't a good time to tell her about the offer for an exhibit at the Transit Museum. I hold the phone away from my ear as I have just given her an opportunity to get things off her chest. She goes on and on. Finally, I thank her and we arrange to meet in two days.

Alfie is annoyed, "This is all the help she is offering? Great!"

The next day, he heads to his mother's and she does give him some money. He pays just enough to get the electric turned back on then heads to his dealer on the way home. I never understand how a detour to Long Island City is on his way home from Jackson Heights. Upon his return, once again, we fight over money all through the night.

The Queens County Courthouse

It is a bitterly cold day with icy rain blowing sideways, as we make our way to the courthouse. We take a seat on a long, hard pew with the other deadbeat tenants. The tenants are to the left and lawyers in suits to the right. I think of church and the pain of sitting on wooden pews while the priest reminds the congregation that we are all sinners in the eyes of the Lord. I am feeling so like a sinner in the eyes of the Lord as we are all asked to stand as the Judge walks in.

"The Honorable Judge Morrison" the Bailiff sings out, "all rise."

As in church, I am wearing my Sunday best. Everyone else is in ill-fitting polyester tracksuits and sneakers. It looks as if Addidas is sponsoring this event.

A pregnant mother with two little kids sit in front of us. The kids squirm impatiently as they are told to "shut the fuck up and sit down!" An adorable little boy with dreadlocks keeps turning around to make faces. He is a mixed-race child with beautiful brown eyes. I make faces back to help pass the time. He giggles and screams in delight and his mother whacks him hard on the butt to stop. He sits down and whimpers as she threatens to do it again and flashes me a dirty look. I am heartbroken at the cruelty of his mother. I feel guilty for having encouraged him and head outside for some air.

"Who are you representing?" A man in a pinstriped suit asks me as he offers me a cigarette. We start to talk. He is cute for a lawyer.

"What? I'm not representing anyone but myself." He looks me up and down. I smoke half the cigarette saving the rest for Alfie.

"No way, you don't look like the usual riff-raff that lands up on the left...?" I am embarrassed as he walks away. I have earned a place at the riff-raff bench how much lower can I fall?

After two hours of waiting our case comes up.

"Walter Schultz vs. Nina Page!" shouts the officer so all can hear. We all stand and confront the judge.

"Who are you?" the Judge asks Alfie.

"I am her fiancé, Alfonso." I look to him strangely.

"Are you on the lease?" the Judge asks as he reviews the papers in front of him.

"No your Honor..."

"Then go sit down. I am dealing with Ms. Page." He smiles at me. "If we need you I know where you are sitting." Alfie does as he is asked, leaving me to stand-alone.

The attorney explains the case and how we are three months in arrears. The judge reviews the paperwork and turns to me.

"You look like a reasonably bright young woman. What is going on here?" He smiles again behind dark rimmed glasses. He must be someone's grandpa.

"Well, I just finished my degree at Parsons School of Design and have fallen behind with rent. I have yet to find a full-time job, but I am freelancing, your Honor. With freelancing, it takes over a month to get paid."

"So Ms. Page, how would you like to proceed?" All heads turn to look at me: the Judge, the Bailiff, the Landlord, his Bloodhound sons and their Lawyer. I want to die.

"I have half of what I owe in cash today." I say, "I can pay extra for the next few months till I catch up. After the holidays, work will pick up."

"We would prefer that Ms. Page vacate the property your Honor. This is not the first time she has been behind on rent." The Lawyer for the Landlord relays his client's wishes.

"Considering she has half of what is owed, and it is the holidays, I grant her three months to catch up on the balance. That will be rent due plus $300- every month. And Ms. Page, if I find you back in here I will have no choice but to grant Mr. Schultz an eviction. Do you understand?" I agree. "Well then good luck to you in this new year." He hands his clerk some documents which she stamps and we were ushered into a closed room where I hand over all the cash I have. The Landlord's eldest son winks at me. We sign papers and are free to go our separate ways.

I find Alfie on the steps of the courthouse pacing. He has a pocket full of half smoked cigarettes and offers me one. I decline. He is elated that we bought ourselves time. We walk home by the train station, and I imagine just hopping on any train going anywhere. I want to get away from him, from the apartment, and from the agreement I just made for money I don't know how to come up with. It starts to snow.

In the living room, Alfie rolls a joint and starts to get playful.

"Where did you get that?" I ask.

"Gift horse." He says joyfully.

"I'm not in the mood! How can you be in a good mood?" I push him away.

"Hey Baby, we dodged a bullet out there today, be happy!" he passes me the joint.

"We...? You get your hands on any money and buy this shit before paying off your expenses. If a bill isn't being disconnected you don't think you need to pay it! You constantly expect me to pay the rest, as I always do! Where do you get the **'we'** in all of this? It was **my name** called out in the courtroom. It is **my name** on the lease, **my name** in the records! It was me that stood up there facing a Judge, the Landlord, the Bloodhounds, and their Attorney. Where were you Mr. Fiancé, picking up used butts on the street!" I am beyond angry with him.

"The Judge told me to sit down. Oh who cares? Do you think all the other deadbeats cared about your name? They were too busy listening for their own names. Do you think there is some big bookkeeping score if you were late with your rent? Really Nina, in the big scheme of things you are just not that important. It's Christmas, the Judge wasn't going to throw us out for the holidays. He liked you, and that bought us some time Cupcake. So why are you still angry? Why do you even care?"

"I care! I didn't hear your name being called. I didn't see you come up with any solutions. Next month's rent is around the corner. How are 'we' now going to catch up?"

"You need to smoke some of this it will calm you down."

"Alfie, next month is 15 days away! See that's the difference between us. I am already anxious about next month. In the scheme of things this is my life and well, since you moved in it hasn't been much of a life. It's been a survival." I am mad and start to cry.

"Cupcake, Cupcake, calm down, you will melt all your pretty white frosting," he thinks he is so cute. "We got through this, and you never know what tomorrow will bring. There is no use worrying about the past and no need to be anxious about a future that has yet to happen. So relax. I could sell a script and be interviewed by David Letterman, or be hit by a bus."

"These are the options, fame or hit by a bus?" I scowl.

"That's life sugar! We will look back on this and laugh!" The smoke around his head swirls in the air like his twisted logic and goes up my nose. I try to sneeze it out.

"Look, every month there is rent and bills to pay. Like it or not they just keep coming. We have to have a plan of how to deal with this or we will be back in court again. Next time it won't be Christmas and that nice Judge will have no choice but to kick us out." I try to say this as slowly and calmly as possible hoping that maybe for once he will hear me.

"Alfie, you are my first love and maybe I have put up with more than my share because of that. I love you but we are very different. You like to live on the edge balancing on a fence. Every day with you is a possibility of falling. You don't even notice as long as you are high. I am tired of the balancing act. I want some stability. I want food in the fridge that doesn't come from the flea market or out of a dented can!" I slam the refrigerator door.

"I have eaten so much spaghetti that I can't stand the sight of it! I hate rice and beans! I want a hamburger! A fresh veggie salad or better yet I want seafood!" I open and close the cabinet doors hoping to find anything but pasta and dented cans of soup. "I want to pay my bills before they send warnings and threats of cancellation." I open a drawer stuffed with late payment notices, collection agencies and utility disconnection warnings and dump the contents on the floor. "I don't need a lot but I can't go on living with you like this anymore!"

"You are creative, you could weave these into a nice collage or something, get some museum to celebrate your shrine to poverty! They will think you are genius and write you up in the Village Voice. 'Brilliant artists make millions off of their poverty.' You will thank me then for the lessons I have taught you." I do not laugh.

"It is not funny anymore. I can't do this, really I have had enough." I sit down and put my head in my hands.

"So what are you saying? We are breaking up for the New Year? Oh, that would be really nice Nina. Even the Judge wasn't that cruel!" He continues to mock me.

"Alfie, do you even care about us? I mean really if you loved me, as you say you do, how could you be ok with letting us live like this? You know, I just can't go on anymore," I say vehemently.

"What are you talking about? We are just having hard times. Everyone has hard times when they start out on a career. Show some character, we will get over this. When I sell the rights to my play, you will see..." Again he goes to pet my hair and I push him away.

"I hate the play you have created for our life, my character is hungry and tired. I want more than to scrounge around in other people's trash and buy their dented food. Don't you ever want more out of life? This struggle sucks up so much energy. Wouldn't some stability be a good thing? Don't you ever want a home of your own, a job that could pay the bills? We need to rethink this. Why can't we be artists and get a job and pay some bills? Why do things have to be so hard? Why is it all or nothing?"

"Oh Cupcake there you go with those white girl dreams. Try not to be such a suburbanite. Dream higher than the hunger in your stomach! You'll see, some day we will laugh at this. When I am a successful playwright you will feel foolish for all the time you wasted hassling me with all your worrying about money. How will you make up for all the time lost bickering endlessly like this? When I am famous I will have to decide if I forgive you!" I head to the kitchen to put on some water for tea. The kitchen is overflowing with dirty dishes and his laundry lies in a heap behind the bathroom door wet from his morning bath.

"This place looks like hell. Can't you clean up after yourself? Why do you always leave everything for me?" I throw a towel over the sink full of dishes to hide the roaches. I recall how seeing that first roach in his basement apartment was upsetting but now they were everywhere in the kitchen and bathroom. Sadly, I was now so used to this. Without any soap we couldn't even do the dishes or laundry.

"When I become a successful playwright I will hire you a maid. Of course she will be plump and French and I can fuck her whenever you're not home. Then you will have your clean house, and live happily ever after." He is being playful, trying to kiss my neck. He smells of dead cigarettes and coffee. I want nothing of it and push him away.

"Beast, how are you going to be a successful playwright if you never finish anything? For all the years we have lived together I have yet to see a finished script. When is fame going to knock on our door and ask if Alfie can come out and bring his half-finished plays? By the time you see success we will no longer be talking to each other. In two weeks rent is due. If you plan on living here you'd better find a way to give me half, or find another cupcake to suck dry!" I head to my studio and lock the door.

CHAPTER 18
- IT'S COMING ON CHRISTMAS

On the night before Christmas, we wait till midnight and drive to Saint Nick's Church on Union Turnpike next to the White Castle. It smells so good that we buy a bag of burgers and onion rings. We eat them in the parking lot as we stake out Saint Nick's Church and plan our heist.

The parking lot is fenced in with the remainder of fir trees that didn't sell for Christmas. Everyone has gone for the night and only the biggest of trees remain. Alfie climbs the fence and picks out the largest tree on the lot and hoists it over the fence. He climbs back over acting like he does this all the time.

"Why one of the biggest? We have to get this up three flights of stairs." I ask as we tie the tree to the top of the car, looking out for the police.

"Well at this price, why not?" We tie the last knot and jump breathless into the car. Quickly we drive home.

By 2 a.m. the tree is decorated with little bows I made from fabric scraps. The Gucci sisters are in tartan plaid skirts and Santa hats. The table expands and I set it with my mismatched Fiestaware. We have been cleaning up for two days and finally the apartment is ready for company.

In a Christmas card from Guy & Diane is best wishes for a prosperous New Year and $50. Exhausted from fighting for days I hand Alfie $25 and he heads to his dealer on Christmas morning. I know I am enabling him but I also know I can't deal with things and have him in a rage as well. It is a vicious cycle.

As Alfie heads to Long Island City, I go food shopping. I buy a pot roast that is now simmering in the electric wok with celery, onions, and carrots for hours. Being broke has forced us to be mostly vegetarians. The meat smells wonderful and we are salivating like a couple of rabid dogs. I prepare potatoes on a hot plate, and in a large wooden bowl, I toss a salad. I arrange slices of clementine and figs that a neighbor gave me as a present on a pretty red plaid plate a sample from the Ralph Lauren collection.

Diner is set for seven but everyone is late. Alfie's mother enters. The first to arrive, she bringing a dish of ziti and gravy and her favorite Panettone fruitcake that no one but she seems to like. She is flamboyant as always, her hair is bleached platinum blond almost white, teased up with a ton of hairspray and long red nails fresh out of the beauty parlor. Alfie helps her take off her coat. She is wearing a wrap-around jersey animal print dress with lots of ruffles. It is a size too small for her ample body. She covers up her smell of cigarettes with a ton of Jean Nate perfume that lingers in the air like a rotting smoky lemon bomb. I open a window for air.

Alfie's brother, Giovanni follows. He is the complete opposite of Alfie. While Alfie's body is long and willowy, Giovanni's is muscular, rough and stocky. Alfie glides through the air with a delicate touch; his brother thumps into the room with heavy feet. He has none of Alfie's charisma or brooding good looks. He is blond with big features and bad skin. I wonder if they are even from the same father. Giovanni places two bottles of Chianti on the counter and I like him instantly!

"Wine is just what I need to get through this night!" he says loudly. "Someone get me a corkscrew." He looks me over, up and down, talking to my boobs.

His wife Camille is last up the stairs carrying a Poinsettia. She is a rather plain woman, a little older then Giovanni and is completely out of breath. When she puts down the plant it is clear she is pregnant.

Giovanni announces the surprise, "Yes, yes, Camille is pregnant. She is having a girl." He slumps into a seat and clearly he is not happy about their news. He pops the cork open and pours a large glass of wine for himself. I push a glass towards him as a hint to fill mine too. He looks confused. I pour myself a big glass of wine. It's going to be a long night.

Sophia gets overly excited to cover the awkwardness of her son's announcement, "Oh Camille, I can't believe it, a little baby. This will bring good luck, wait and see. I thought you were just getting fat, dear. I will be a grandmother! Oh dear, that will make me old," she laughs. "Never mind that, baby's bring joy! When will this be?" In a thick Italian accent she gestures wildly with her hands, spilling her red wine all over the table cloth.

I rush to get the fabric in hot water. All I have to cover the table with is a flowered bed sheet.

 "Beginning of April," says Camille. "I haven't been able to eat a thing." She helps herself to some bread and then reaches for the plate of clementine and figs that I was saving for dessert and proceeds to eat all the figs before cutting a big slice of Panettone cake. So much for not eating a thing!

"Oh, a baby in the family, how wonderful for both of you! When I was pregnant with Alfonso it was the happiest time of my life. You Giovanni, well that was another story…" she says as if spitting a pit on the ground. "So now it is your turn Alfonso, when am I going to see babies from you and your Bella?' he was clearly her favorite and she took every opportunity to say so.

"I am busy finishing up a script, and besides I got to raise Giovanni, remember Mother? That was enough for me!" He could be very curt with her and she never seemed to mind. Sophia just went on talking about when she was pregnant with Alfonso in Italy and how beautiful a baby he was.

Meanwhile, I busied myself in the kitchen mashing potatoes.

There was a strange connection between Sophia and Alfie. This became more and more obvious as the night went on. She thought the world of him. He was a star in her eyes and could do no wrong. His brother was a contractor and was building an extension onto their house. To her that was ordinary, however I was impressed that he had a house and a contracting company. Alfie reminded her of her husband, who in retrospect she idolized as some god who could do no wrong. Giovanni looked just like her and acted just like her father. When not in his presence she referred to him as 'that piece of shit' for he never gave her money and his wife 'that old woman'.

Everyone enjoyed the meal eating absolutely everything. His brother took the last piece of meat, before Alfie could get to it. After dinner, Alfie lit a cigarette for him and his mother. There was a weird ritual of lighting her cigarette that was oddly disturbing. The way she held onto his hand longer then she needed to light her cigarette. It was more like a ritual between lovers not 'mother-son'. I brushed it off as just my imagination, but I see I was not the only one to have noticed. The room filled with smoke.

"That was delicious Nina. I see Alfie found himself a good cook, like Nonna used to be. I wish Camille could cook. She has a modern kitchen that I built but not a clue what to do with it," Giovanni said disapprovingly as he opened the second bottle of wine with a loud pop. Camille pretended not to hear him and helped me clear the table.

"Oh her cooking is alright, it's getting better," said Alfie. It seemed compliments were not easy to get from the men in this family.

"That was a feast, dear." Sophia hands me her plate as she puts her cigarette out in the second helping of mashed potatoes that she left. I hated wasting food. "Please make the coffee, Bella." She waves me along as she holds court with her sons. Camille and I cleanup like good little servants.

I plugged in a pot of coffee while Camille sliced the Panettone.

"I see you landed up with the brass bed after all," said Giovanni motioning to the corner of the apartment where Alfie had set up his bed.

"She left it to me, I am the first born." Alfie protests.

This launches the family into a heated conversation in Italian over inheritances wasted, a property that went into foreclosure over back taxes and what went missing to pay off mom's loan sharks. I catch some of the conversation having now learned a few Italian words.

"You should come to Connecticut and visit before the baby is born. We're so close to the Long Island sound." Camille eyed the Gucci sisters with uncertainty. "Do you always dress them up?" She smiled politely.

I said, "It is better then leaving them naked." We laughed. "I'd love to come to Connecticut, I haven't been out of New York in years." Alfie flashes me a disapproving look from across the room. It was a look that said clearly 'no how, no way!'

"We should all go to Connecticut!" Said Sophia "We would have such fun!"

When it was time to go, his mother thanked me for everything. "Bella, next year I want baby news from you and my Alfonso. With Alfonso's good looks and your pretty smile, Bella, now that would be a beautiful baby!" She gushed as Camille looked on sadly. "Oh you two will also have a most beautiful baby." She said in consolation but her heart was not into it. "All babies are beautiful and bring such love."

Alfie laughs a wicked evil laugh from the other end of the room.

We exchange presents. I wrapped a scarf I had bought in Greece for his mother and a pair of mittens for Camille. These were things I already had. Sophia wrapped a snow globe of Venice for me that I had once admired at her apartment. They gave Alfie a carton of cigarettes, and for me, a bottle of wine. To the side I saw she gave Alfie cash, and a small bottle of prescription pills which he quickly put it in his pocket.

"Merry Christmas! Merry Christmas!" Sophia lets Alfie help her on with her fake fur coat. He walks them downstairs as I wash the glasses and bring out the recycling.

When Alfie returns, he falls onto the sofa and exhales, "Babies bring such love. Ha! How she can go on, that foolish woman! Babies didn't bring my father love! Babies only made him drink more! Having my brother only made him leave us. Being trapped by a woman just to have a baby. That was love, sure!" He paces back and forth as he inhales a joint.

"By the way, we are **not** going to Connecticut! I refuse to drive for hours in a car with my mother, to spend a weekend with my brother and **that** woman! He cares nothing for her. He loves her sister who is married to one of his friends. He screws her too, nice arrangement! I may look like my father but he acts like my father. We are not going to Connecticut that is final!"

"No" I said, "we are not going to Connecticut that would require gas in the car and money for tolls. That will never happen!" I finished washing the wine glasses and handed him a towel to dry. He shot me a look, as if his rage excused him from helping.

"Don't you ever want to go anywhere? You just want to stay locked in here until they physically throw us out on the streets? This 'no money thing' takes such energy away from the things I really want to do." I shake the snow globe and watch the flakes of white fall down upon St. Marks Square within the glass dome. After a long silence I ask, "Do you ever think of visiting Italy again some day?"

"Italy? Why, I wouldn't fit in there as I don't fit in here. I am a man without a country lost somewhere in the middle of here and nowhere. What do you know of immigrant struggles in a new land? No, you come from a nice little American town on the cross roads of boredom, suicide and hell." I had heard all of this before.

"Alfie, there is so much of the world to see, I would love to travel again and see the world! Don't you ever want to go anywhere? Lately you won't even leave the apartment unless you go to see your mother or the dealer. When my friends from school call, you never want to go out. You make me turn down all invitations. Now no one calls and how could they with the phone disconnected? I want to go someplace, any place! I feel trapped here with you. How can you be a writer if you don't open yourself up to what is out there?"

"I've experienced more of the world before you were even born Cupcake! We live in New York; it's the fucking United Nations just walking down the street. You want culture and cuisine; the streets are lined with it. Every corner there's another take out joint, or a Chinese cleaner. I don't need to get on a plane to see what I can see on any given New York corner."

"Come on, we never go out! I would love just to go to the movies. Aren't there things you want out of life? There is so much to gain by seeing how other people live. Traveling is inspirational. Why, I would settle for crossing a bridge and going to Connecticut! Even, **that** sounds exciting at the moment!" I insist.

"Well then, why don't you see if your rich professor sugar daddy will take you back? Then the two of you could see the world like a couple of fat American pigs and be inspired!" He throws the towel on the counter and curses me in Italian stomping off to the studio, slamming the door behind him. He turns the TV up very loud, until Norman bangs on the ceiling.

Alfie comes out and heads to the living room jumping up and down like a three year old. "I have the right to exist in my own apartment. You're an old man who needs to get laid. Get a life! Don't take it out on us!" he slams the door again six times for dramatic effect, knocking a picture off the wall. The glass shatters. He ignores it and returns to the studio.

I ignore him and finish cleaning up the kitchen. "He is such a child, how could I ever have a baby when I already have a child?" I ask the Gucci Sisters.

I hear my mother's voice in my head… "You don't need a man-child…make better choices Nina!"

I take the garbage into the hall and throw the trash down the chute. Cockroaches scurry from the light, that makes my skin crawl.

"Merry Christmas," I wish them, closing the door as they return to their midnight feast. I shake my head and double-lock the door. My dress is wet so I strip down to my black slip. I wrap a knit throw around me. There is a joint left on the table. I light it and put on a Joni Mitchell CD on low. My head spins as I curl up on the couch. I drank too much tonight. I'll regret it tomorrow but for now, it feels good.

Joni sings of a love so bitter yet so sweet, like wine. She could drink a case and still come back for more, still be on her feet. She knew the man had devils and demands and was prepared to bleed. Prepared to bleed to just be with him. Could this really be love or an acute addiction?

Alfie comes out of the studio; he has a softer look in his eyes. He takes my hand and leads me to the brass bed. Fighting has aroused him. I give in to his touch, addicted once again. It is the last time we sleep together.

Madame Mona Payne
Cordially invites you and your guest
To a Black & White Masquerade
New Year's Eve Party

Place: The Apartment of Leona and Derrick Storm
McAlpin Hotel Penthouse
34th Street & 6th Avenue/Broadway
Time: 10pm - until

R.S.V.P.
Mistress Payne

CHAPTER 19 – BLACK AND WHITE PARTY

As I was complaining of never going anywhere, what comes in the mail, but an invitation to a party! It had the wrong apartment number so it was late in getting to us.

I had heard stories about Mona Payne's parties mentioned often, since Alfie rejoined the theater workshop. The Storms, I was told, made their fortune in the porno film industry; and were quite successful. They were bicoastal and bisexual. While in N.Y. they lived in the penthouse of the famous McAlpin Hotel in Herald Square.

Leona and Derrick Storm had money and could finance Alfie's play 'Off Broadway'. The play starred Mona. Alfie hated being social but insisted that we were going so that Mona could introduce 'us'.

"You better get a cocktail dress. Something sexy. Not any of the butch stuff you usually wear."

"If I'm too butch, go by yourself then. You know, I ride the subways at night, so sorry if I don't dress like a hooker!" Mona, porn, and that upsetting butch comment, set off all my insecurities. "I'm not interested in a party with your new friends."

"This year has sucked! Finally I have a chance to connect with some real backers and, I want to walk in with a woman I am proud of, not some hag who rides the subways. I am growing tired of this." He said coldly.

"Butch has now turned into a hag! You think **you** are tired of this? What ever this is…" I circle my arms in the air like a lunatic, "**this** is about to all come to an end." I vented, hating him at this moment.

"Are you having your period again? Is **that** where this is coming from? Can't you take a pill, Nina?" He asks spitefully.

"I'd take a pill, but **someone** has emptied all the bottles in the bathroom for their own recreational fun." Cramps cut into my stomach and I sit down in pain. He knew my schedule better then I did.

"Please come with me." He backed down and tries to use his most seductive voice. "I need you by my side. You will see, if we can get a backer, our money problems will come to an end. You owe me this opportunity even if you leave me in a month." How I could hate him and still love him was confusing. I took a bath and surrendered to the cramps.

The New Year's festivities started on the stairs heading down to the subway. Everyone was dressed up and in a spirited mood heading into the city. New Year's excitement was in the air too, as we crammed into the subway cars, standing room only. Uniformed cops were everywhere moving the drunken people along. In our best black and white get-ups we packed in with hundreds of people heading into the city for the party of the year. The car emptied at 42nd Street, Times Square, but we stayed on one more stop to 34th Street, Herald Square.

With the money Sophia gave us for the holidays, we went to the Salvation Army. I bought a little black dress and shoes that I had to practice walking on. The dress was a little too big, too low in the front and a bit too short. Alfie said, "That's the one." To cover my excessive cleavage I wore strands of fake pearls. It was a compromise from the large silk scarf I wanted to wear, that Alfie ripped off my neck. Had I become too butch, after all?

Alfie bought a white tux jacket with an imitation black hankie in the pocket. He wore black jeans and a black turtleneck. He slicked his hair back into a ponytail. He looked like a young James Bond, or some international playboy. He cleaned up well and I remembered why I was attracted to him in the first place.

"You look delicious," he said as we found a place to stand by the exit doors between cars. The train jolted and we were thrown together. I could feel his arousal as he pushed into me. Still there was this attraction between us that was hard to ignore. He kept his hand over mine the entire subway ride. "Stay next to me all night." He whispered as he moved a strand of hair out of my face and looked down my coat. "You are lovely tonight, please stop fidgeting. I love you, you know."

Dressed like a call girl, I wondered a bit who I was this New Years Eve. What happened to my femininity? I had become hardened, tougher and yes butch. I had spent years hiding my new feminine body under layers of clothes. Even though I had lost all this weight, I didn't really feel attractive. I dressed down to ride the subways. I hid my feminine side to do my art. I felt I had needed to be the man in this relationship, take care of both of us out of necessity. Alone with Alfie I used to be a woman. Alone with him I could be sexual, venerable, dominated. Balancing on these heels, I was transformed on the outside to what I felt on the inside. For tonight, there would be no combat gear. I was a woman, wearing a sexy dress heading to a party on New Years Eve. Without my Indian Jones disguise, I was naked. It scared the hell out of me.

I Just Adore a Penthouse View

Mona Payne was a very large woman dressed in long black patent leather boots and a short pleated plaid skirt, white shirt and red tie. Her hair was in pigtails with matching plaid bows. She had a whip in one hand and a little dog in the other. When she bent over you could see these ruffled bloomers, kind of S&M meets naughty schoolgirl. Alfie loved it. Mona met us in the hall dressed in a short maid's uniform with garters, where there was a coat-check girl hanging coats on a rack. Alfie lingered, as Mona brought me into the apartment, it was huge with a wall of windows.

"Don't you just adore a penthouse view? Come in my pets, so glad you could make it, let me introduce you around." There was a sea of people already there and it had a breathtaking view uptown. In the distance, you could see the spotlights circling in the air over Times Square. There was a giant rear projector TV that showed live coverage of the festivities. Thousands of people were just blocks away partying in the winter cold. On the inner wall was a neon sculpture I recognized as one of my teacher's, Diego.

Looking around the apartment, I noticed that the men all looked alike, balding, with those cheesy mustaches and black turtle neck sweaters under their suit jackets. They wore gold chains around their necks and large pinky rings and watches too. All were slimy looking as far as I was concerned.

The women were very glitzy with short dresses or hot pants, killer boots, fake nails, and big hair teased to a great volume. They stared out from dark eye shadow and fake eyelashes, cherry red lips and bad skin covered by tons of pancake makeup. There were boobs, really big boobs that spilled out of their dresses, onto the tables and out the doors! Hair and boobs were everywhere and it was hard not to trip over them all. As sexy as I thought I looked, I was demure in comparison.

"Leona and Derrick, this is Alfie and Nina. I have told you all about Alfie. Leona can't get up she just had liposuction and needs to wear a tight corset until she heals from the surgery. Leona was as thin as a rail and by no means needed to have had liposuction. Mona hands me the dog to hold.

"She likes the pain, don't you Darling?" continuing to take us around. There were way too many people to remember all their names. I started to feel like I was in a Rocky Horror Picture Show and that I was Janis surrounded by transvestites, and bizarre aliens all here to party from some other planet. Alfie was right, I am suburban and did not have a good feeling about this.

"I don't think we are in Kansas any more Toto." I say to the dog that licks my face.

Mona continues to introduce us around. "King," Mona taps a huge guy on the shoulder, "I'm in charge of black and blue and King James here is providing the white for our evening festivities. She strokes his leg with her whip.

"Yes, Mistress" he growls back like a lion and scratches the air. He has long fingernails painted white except for the pinkies, which are black.

"Darling, be a good cat and fix my friends up with a 'White Christmas'. Look out for him Nina, he hasn't been declawed." Mona purrs and skips away to meet newcomers.

King James knocks on a door and someone who is directing the traffic lets us through and down a small hallway covered in various pictures of erotic films. Here and there I recognize Leona

186

bent over a prop or with some guy's cock in her face trying to smile for the camera.

The dressing room has a small vanity table and mirror with a few pink fuzzy chairs. A few people leave as we enter. There on the table the mirror shows remnants of white powder dust and a rolled up twenty. James pours out a heap of powder and proceeded to cut it up into lines with a razor blade.

I look around the dressing room. It is filled with shelves of shoes, at least a hundred of them all neatly arranged. There is a wall of mirrors that hide the closets. The opposite wall is covered in purple psychedelic wallpaper. Everything else in the room is pink and furry.

As Alfie takes the first hit, he snorts a line up his nose as if he were a vacuum cleaner. I watch as he heads into the next line.

James flirts with me. "Leona likes shoes, and men, in that order, shoes then men. Derrick says she would fuck anything for a new pair of shoes." James says matter of fact, "What's your currency?"

"My what?" I say stupidly, not understanding the question.

"So do you partake in Mona's theatrics? Are you in the industry?" He smiles with a gold tooth that catches the light. He looks down my dress. I pull up my dress, which only makes it shorter. It does not really fit me. "Those are real aren't they?" he asks about my breasts.

Alfie answers, "Yes they are real. Nice too. They're mine, and she is with me. I know Mona from the Underground Theatre Group. Mona is my current leading lady and we are working on a script."

"Oh, a newbie. We like those most of all." Again he says it as he gives me a once over and snorts up a fingernail full of white powder. He offers me a hit from the table.

"I hear Mona will be entertaining tonight." Alfie says as he offers me the rolled up twenty. "Here you go Cupcake take a turn."

James continued to look at me as if my dress was see-through and I was only wearing underwear. I take my turn, clearly not an expert. I laugh and blow half my line on to the table. Alfie shoots me a look that could kill. James is more forgiving, "Cupcake, I like that. Are you sweet like frosting? I can only imagine? I love biting into cupcakes and finding a creamy center... Like those Hostess snack cakes what are they called, Devil Dogs, Twinkies?

Hmmm Cupcake..." he purrs and strokes his braided beard with that same pinkie nail extended.

At any other time, this would have annoyed Alfie. Instead, he just ignored the comment and helped himself to what I had scattered on the table. He licked his finger and then the table. As long as this guy was flirting with his girl, he could snort all his drugs! I take another turn. The psychedelic wallpaper starts moving in and expanding. I head back into the party.

"Come Darling, sit with me a spell." Mona called from the couch and moves the small dog to her lap. At her feet was a man with a dog collar; she petted both. "Well I guess you are wondering how someone gets to be a Dominatrix," she asked, though I really wasn't wondering.

"My real name in Monica Patten. My father was a Colonel in the army and we traveled around all the time. No not that Patten. I grew up in Japan where the women are so subservient. Everything about them was docile from the way they wrapped their bodies in layers of fabric, and deformed their feet in order to have only a tinier footprint. My father kept Geishas, my mother was said to be his favorite. He could not marry her for he had a wife in the States. She killed herself before I was three; his servants raised me.

On weekends, my father would have Geishas come to entertain his friends. I liked to watch them prepare for the evening. They taught me the art of makeup and how to please a man. I loved their inner beauty and devotion to their art. I wanted to be like my father, a man who had many women each for different functions."

I could see the Asian influence in her eyes and makeup now that she mentioned it.

"I lived in Amsterdam for a few years. In Amsterdam, there is a red light district where the women are on display in storefront windows, available for a price. I liked the concept that sex could be for sale out in the open. Makes things so simple that way."

"Yes I heard that," I said wondering why she was telling me her life story. Everyone else on the couch was interested.

"Just put it right out in the open, and tell me your price." Leona said heavily sedated on some kind of painkiller. I realized that she was a lot older than she looked at first, or maybe it was the consequence of her lifestyle.

"Leona is in porno films. She is one of the best!" Leona's smile was full of pain. "Don't smile dear, it hurts even me." Mona says lovingly. "Derrick here is in investment banking, he's a real dick," she says in my ear. "The place looks great, guys," she says as they both try to smile and sip their drinks through straws, their faces still frozen and swollen from some procedure.

Mona turned back towards to me and continues, "When I was older, I went to school in Paris to study acting. I hear you studied art at Parsons. Paris has a decadent underbelly. I wasn't a very good actress and dropped out of school. However, I did get into the underground theaters and loved to watch the dancers pump and grind in their garters and lace, so I joined a Burlesque Theatre group. I may not have the most beautiful body, but I can definitely pump and grind and I **do** like to dress up and role-play. The only thing was I didn't want to be the subservient one. I wanted to play the male role! Dominating men into submission is so rewarding and it pays well too, Darling." By now a crowd had gathered in the apartment and it was getting very noisy. It was almost midnight.

"I have some very rich clients, high powered executives who need a way to release all their stress. All fun and games, right Leona?" She nods. "I do hope you will stay for my show, I think we will have a performance after midnight." She was very disarming and friendly, as we curled up on the couch and talked like we were old friends just catching up. Alfie was busy making King James his new best friend and disappearing into the dressing room with every new arrival. - So much for networking with the backers.

I was quite high from my hit and just trying to keep it all together. I was thirsty but couldn't drink, hungry but couldn't swallow. I felt like I was having an out-of-body experience. I ate chocolate mints, to ease my nervousness. I could feel the chocolate and the mint flavors each running through my body. I just kept eating to feel the sensation of the candy on my tongue, and then racing through my body like hot wheels on a track.

Yes, Alfie is the star of our theater group, but I am sure I don't have to tell you that. He is a very talented man. He is easy on the eyes, too. I am sure you know a man like that has many admirers, but he stays true to you. A man like that is hard to hold onto, doesn't conform to anyone's rules. I like that, he is his own person." Mona says, "You must be doing something right if he has picked you to be his lady. He calls you Cupcake, that is sweet, no pun intended." She winked. I really hated that name and everyone here was using it.

"I don't know, we are very different and lately we fight about everything, even the dishes." She cuts me off.

"Dishes! A man like that doesn't do dishes! A man like that only wants to be worshiped. He is a star!" she says way too theatrically, and the dog falls off her lap. I am sure he was laughing too hard!

"If not in his own head," I whisper, and we laugh. "Yes, that is true. He does need his own personal slave. I just don't know if that will be me. I can't afford him and he is high maintenance. Lord, I have tried. He says what does not kill you will make you stronger. I struggle to keep moving my art forward as he keeps pulling me back. I am an artist with creative desires, yet it is always about **him**." I am surprised at my own candor and figure it must be the drugs mixing with the chocolate mints. I am high.

"See I knew I liked you, the moment we met. You would make a fine Dominatrix, and you don't want to be subservient like these overstuffed balloon dolls walking around here. You got guts. Alfie told me about your subway adventures. That seems incredible. Don't stop till you get what you want. I never do." She caresses my leg with her whip. I blush and spill wine on my dress.

Alfie joins us on the couch. His eyes are all bugged and crazy, like the psychedelic purple wallpaper.

"Darling, you are stoned, good. I have been enjoying your little cupcake! She is delicious," she says as she licks her red lips and looks me over. I tug on my dress, too low, too short.

"I need to get my slaves ready. Talk to you later." She again rubs her whip across my leg and over Alfie's pants, he gets a hard on as she walks away. I can tell there is something between them that is way too familiar.

Alfie corners Derrick and pitches his new project starring Mona as a troubled housewife longing to free herself from her inhibitions. She finds a lover and plots to kill her spouse to get what she ultimately wants, money and sex. Derrick sees it as a porno film and I am not sure if that is what Alfie originally had in mind. He agrees completely. I find the whole thing uncomfortable. This was not at all what Alfie told me he was working on. I start to think that Mona could afford Alfie better than me and I am sure, keep him entertained. Why she even had slaves to do all the chores.

I despise him and see more clearly our separate paths. I think that our upcoming eviction will force the issue. It will be a means to an end. I need to be free of him once and for all. Break this bond that pulls me down. I am strong, and loving him has only made me weak and desperate. Suddenly I get it and know I need to move on.

I head to the kitchen for a drink feeling more awake then I had in years.

"Have a spiral cookie." King James said coming up right behind me so close I could feel his breath on my neck.
I take a bite and chew and chew and chew, unable to swallow.

"They are made with black hash and snow," he tells me as I finally swallow. Great, just what I don't need, **more** drugs! I wash it down with water.

"Cupcake, I had hoped to get you alone. You seem a bit out of place here, can I get you some more blow? You didn't have much, your boyfriend had enough for several people."

"I'm not surprised. No thanks, I'm good." I decide to leave the brownies alone as well. They had now left a sticky taste in my mouth. I open a bottle of Perrier to wash down the sick feeling in my stomach. The maid comes in to get another tray of something fishy. She bends down to reveal black lace panties. The King is amused. I wonder what she is getting paid for this gig.

"I bet you are his muse. A man could be inspired with you by his side." He smiled with that gold tooth and ran his figure up my arm.

My skin crawled with goose bumps. He frightened me, as did everyone else at this party. I had lost my sense of balance and my instincts said get your coat and run like hell.

"Take my card. If ever you need anything coke, crack, cock. I take the card a bit reluctantly. Mona had said he was the biggest kingpin in Manhattan. I assumed that meant dealer, and that really frightened me to have his card on me.

By midnight the city came alive with people yelling out the windows to people yelling on the streets. The maid served Champagne on a silver tray with fat strawberries covered in yet more dark chocolate. Blocks away, the ball dropped on Times Square. You could hear thousands counting down and cheering wildly at the stroke of midnight. Kingpin kissed me with tongue and hugged me close to his chest. "I love real breasts, nothing worse then hugging a women with rocks on her chest."

I looked around and Alfie and Mona where nowhere in sight.

When Alfie did kiss me, he tasted terrible. Feeling sick, I wanted to leave but Alfie insisted we were staying for Mona's show.

The lights dimmed and the music shifted as Mona paraded her leather-clad pets, around the room. Dressed as a masculine circus trainer with a top hat and a mustache she paraded two men dressed in bondage on leashes as they are led around the room. Upon her command and the crack of her whip they performed sexual acts on each other. The crowd seemed to enjoy it. I wanted to get out of there in the worst way but sat frozen in my seat just waiting for it all to end. Mona was good with the whip. Alfie put my hand in his lap he was as hard as a rock. It didn't turn me on.

Everyone around the room was watching the performance except for King James who was watching me licking his lips. The evening was so surreal, and these people were making me sick.

At around two in the morning we head out the door, Alfie fills my purse with hash brownies, black and white cookies, and our pockets with bottles of Perrier. I don't remember how we got home but I was stoned all the next day.

CHAPTER 20 - FIESTA BREAKDOWN

THE ENDS JUSTIFY THE MEANS... OR DO THEY... read the title of the book Alfie tossed aside at the library.

January's cold wraps around us as we walk the long walk home. We had spent the day at the library hunting for jobs in the trade papers. I had a few leads to fax my resume to. On the way out of the library, we run into the landlord's son who advises us that if we don't have the rent, we should just vacate the property.

Alfie was offended with his nerve. "Who the hell is he to talk to us that way? This ignorant bloodhound, what would he have if his father didn't provide it for him?"

"Maybe we should seriously consider his advice to just vacate the premises." I said to Alfie who wanted to fight. It was a long walk home. I tried to reason with him. "In a week we would owe two and a half months rent. I had agreed to the judgment to pay in full or leave. The landlord's lawyer argued that in 30 days we would be behind with another month's rent. He was right and the Judge knew this. In reality we had 30 days to move until the locks would be changed and eviction proceedings would move forward and a Sheriff would put us on the street."

Alfie wanted to stay and fight. Go back to court and buy more time. I didn't want to fight anymore, I was tired of fighting the world; I had had enough.

One by one the landlord had evicted most of the tenants and was busy gutting the vacated apartments. A sign outside the building advertised luxury apartments for sale.

We gathered a load of boxes from the liquor store and started piling up things to sell. For $25 dollars we rented a table at the local flea market and sold off our extra stuff. Through the years, as the tenants were effected, we gathered their discarded things. Cook books, religious statues, sheet music, pictures, vases, costumes, and holiday decorations. Many of these things were already in boxes marked flea market. Whenever we found people's stuff on the street we took things we needed or liked. Other people's stuff found their way into our life, lived with us for a while and now would find new homes. Alfie thought this was a lot like relationships that come and go. He felt it was a great story line for his next play.

As the boxes filled, and the apartment emptied, I kept telling myself that it was all just stuff. I could always get more stuff. Alfie refused to sell the Gucci Sisters, they were 'his ladies' he couldn't part with them. Lack of money made me desperate. I sold off everything that we could carry in two car trips. We made a few hundred dollars after paying for the table and some Chinese takeout. I hid the rest away.

When my freelance check came in, I cashed it with the greengrocer and paid off most of our local creditors. I hid the rest of the money away. I knew if I didn't, Alfie and his mother would just go through it. I had a choice, to pay the landlord and still be behind or move. Alfie wanted to stay. He kept saying that he loved me and that we couldn't just walk away from that.

"No one walks away from true love! You cannot be that heartless Nina!" My heart was broken and I was torn between my deep feeling for him and a desire to live a life where every day wasn't such a struggle.

He knew that even if we were evicted we would still have time before the Sheriff would change the locks. We could push this out another three months. If need be, we could leave the fire escape window open and shimmy down from the roof if they did change the locks. I didn't find that comforting at all. It was time to move on.

My mom offered me to come back home and stay in my old room. I hated the idea of giving up my own space, but it was time to give up Alfie. We had been through so much, could this really be the end? I kept thinking about going home. I was exhausted. I needed to regroup. I couldn't afford to stay here any longer and I clearly couldn't count on Alfie. Maybe the summer in small town wouldn't be so bad. Take the bus to the beach; take the train to the city. I could find a job; pay off my creditors, back taxes and student loans. I could start again, close the door on this chapter of my life.

I also kept thinking about the New Year's Eve party and wondering what Alfie and I really had in common any more? He wanted to live a drug-induced life dedicated to the pursuit of sexual stimulus and star in a porno film. He wanted no responsibilities as he balanced his life on a wire. Where did I fit in with all of that?

What did I want? I wanted a man who was a partner and not a liability. I wanted to look forward to a day and not just endure it. I wanted a man who had my back and not just what was between my legs. Maybe I **did** want some of the 'white bread' dream, a house, 2.5 kids and a dog. Or did I? I was confused, but I wanted out.

Liquidation Sale

The day after the liquidation sale, I took my address book and headed to the pay phone by the train station where I could call my contacts and look for work. I called my friend at Gant to let her know I had graduated and was available for any freelance opportunities. She told me of a job opening in the company and that she would recommend me. She set up an interview for the following week. I needed to bring a portfolio that showed how I could merchandise a collection. I had one week to get this together. Most of my studio was already in boxes.

Since our date in court, I was so depressed. I had been so proud of my first apartment. I walked through the door now and it was naked, and all the silly collectable things were gone. All the personality was stripped bare. Alfie was naked too and wanted to fool around, but I refused his advances. He got dressed, hustled me for some cash and went out. I washed all the dishes.

I look around nostalgic for the feelings I had once had in living here in this cozy oasis from the world, our sexual sanctuary. I loved him then, but I was no longer in love with him. We had been through too much. I had sacrificed too much to be by his side. I remembered our first date and my cat, which now seemed so long ago. I climb out on the fire escape and see kittens in the alley that look just like Hobo. It is cold again, so I head inside.

I look in the mirror; my face is sunken, with dark shadows under my eyes. I have lost a lot of weight and need a belt to hold up my pants, which I could shimmy to the floor without unbuttoning. OK, the skinny part was the only good thing, I guess. The years had taken a toll, bad diet, too much smoke, lack of sunshine, and lack of joy. Day to day anxiety created deep lines on my forehead. I had aged badly over the years. I took out some makeup and tried to hide the dark circles under my eyes with Mary Kay concealer.

I heard my mother in my head teaching me how to apply a highlight shadow under the eyebrows. I was a little girl then and she made me up with pink lips and red cheeks. What did I do to that little girl? I applied lipstick and smacked my lips together.

I pulled a bunch of outfits out of the closet till I found something that didn't look too old or too large. I settled on a black skirt and jacket with a colorful scarf. I hang these in the bathroom and spray them with water to get the wrinkles out. I had sold the iron.

I managed fine until Alfie moved in. In spite of him, I did graduate from school. I had determination then. I had ventured into the subways and built a collection of murals. That was brave, but now I was so unsure of myself. What if this was the love of my life and I was throwing it away due to lack of money? Was it that simple, was I missing something? Was I being selfish or was I right?

In the beginning, it was romantic to be cut off from the rest of the world. This loft was our hideout until we had to hide out from it. There was great lust in the beginning, and great sex. I had a purpose fighting to get my degree. Now the reality was I was thousands of dollars behind in paying student loans, back taxes and facing an eviction. The only good thing was that the phone was disconnected, which stopped the credit card officer from Citibank calling on a daily basis. Mr. Johnson could bring me to tears. He was a sadist who called every other day to harass me to pay a credit card bill that was in default. I hated him and Citibank; being without a phone was a good thing.

Alfie was happy to spend my money but all the debts that piled up were in my name. I am angry with Alfie for never taking on any responsibility. If he loves me as he says he does, then how can he let our lives be so on the bottom? How could he leave me to face our financial challenges alone? His addictions are always served first and everything else is left to falter. We are always on the fence ready to fall and the pit below just keeps getting deeper. I begin to realize that Alfie likes it this way. He goes out of his way at times to make a situation more difficult and then curses the gods that he has such bad luck.

It is what his mother has taught him, her ways to survive. Indulge in the things you want and borrow from Peter to pay Paul. Life was a drama, a struggle to be lived large. Like one of his plays, he is the star struggling with the demons and sexual tension hidden in all the shadows. His acts are staged in self-inflicted poverty and choreographed in a dance of addiction and denial. I realize I am just a player, an interchangeable actress in for a few scenes and then I will be written out. I am not strong enough to continue to the closing act; his script is killing me.

Alfie believes that a door will magically open to his success and riches will follow. He feels his addictions aid his talent and if you took them away he would have nothing. I argue his addictions get in the way of his life and keeping up with them take away from his talents and his time. He always says I should just wait, that the end would justify the means. Except this **is** our end and it has no justice, it has exhausted all the means.

When we are together, all we do is argue. Alfie insists that he loves me, that hard times are just a test of character and that all is fine. Life is just throwing us a curve! He now agrees that we should just leave and find another apartment, a better apartment.

"You must have faith, you must believe." He could have been a preacher giving a sermon on the mount. I imagine him on a stage with the Gucci sisters singing behind him as he preaches.

"Ye of little faith, how will thee be received in the kingdom of my heaven? Repent all your evil thoughts and come with me to salvation. Follow me and I will lead us into the Holy Land. We will endure, if only thee believed. How foolish ye of little faith will feel when I reach the Valley of the Gods? Will you be standing beside me in the Kingdom of Heaven or be in the crowd of peasants looking on foolishly, when I rise to glory? When I have made a fortune as the next Neil Simon, and when I entertain David Letterman with my witty banter. How foolish you will feel then. Watching from your small TV in your small living room somewhere in Smallville."

My mind separates from my body and my spirit rises above. I view the room, the situation and the conversation from a new height. From this vantage point I can better see the scope of the situation, it has all become so surreal.

"That which does not kill you makes you stronger," his sermon continues in my ears though my mind has stopped listening. I am floating above the room out of my body and it becomes clearer.

With a newfound calm, I change the direction of his pontificating. "What does love mean to you?" I ask softly. He does not hear me so I say it again louder. "What does love mean to you?"

"What are you talking about?" he asks newly annoyed.

"If you love me, as you say you do, how can you just watch as I suffer, with our lifestyle and your choices? If you love me, as you say you do, how can you be so blind to the pain I am in?"

"Oh Nina, you can be so melodramatic. Can't you see we were meant to be together? No one will ever love you like I do," is his angry response. "This is just 'a **place**', I've been evicted from many. Life goes on." He says way too casually.

Breathe in – breathe out. My mind wants to explode. "Is this what I can expect to look forward to, more evictions, past due bills, and disconnect notices? A line of Mr. Johnson's calling for the money we owe? Fine dining and botulism courtesy of the dented cans from some flea market? Sunday night phone calls filled with the saga of your mother's losing lotto remorse?"

He looks at me strangely as I continue.

"You never told me you had been evicted before. Is that what happened with the last place? It was... wasn't it? Is this just normal operations for you?" I say sternly.

"Hey, we are artists. Artists struggle for their art. It is just what it is. You should get used to this; it is what we 'so called artists' do… Nina. Don't take it so personally."

"Personally? Personally? This is my life too, you know! It is not all about you! This is not what I envisioned. You are **really** something! You need to step it up. How can you just throw it all in the wind and see where it lands? You talk love but cannot really give that of yourself. You love yourself, most of all. Nothing will ever change with you, Alfie. Nothing!" I start to shake, exasperated at these revelations.

"I have plans Nina, big plans. If you can't hold on, then that is your loss. I am going places. With Mona's connection I can audition for a part in the Storms" new video. I have a plan. I need to get some head-shots, which you can take. Make some glossies and Mona can shop these around. Now I know you are sitting on money from the flea market. We should get some pot and help cut the edge off the situation. I was thinking, if you give me the money, I could head to the track and see if we can double it." He was crazy if he thought I would hand over what little we had.

Calmly, slowly I say, "You want money for head-shots, money for pot and money for horses? Where in all of that is a place to live and food on the table?" My blood pressure explodes.

I am having an out of body experience, and was no longer sitting at the table, but high above looking down. My physical body seems to be reasoning with a mad man! I laugh at the stupidity of it all.

"Just because you stopped smoking doesn't mean that I should. I have done it before, you know". I cut him off before he finishes.

"You have stopped smoking before?" I inquire.

"No! I've gone up to Atlantic City and made the rent. I'm an excellent blackjack player. If you didn't always stop me Cupcake we would be better off. I have the ability to double that money if you would just let me." The fact that he was serious was so sad; I continue to laugh at him. This pisses him off!

I refuse to give him money. We fight into the morning hours, slamming doors, and yelling, off and on.

"Why should I be comfortable with my man doing other women on camera to make a buck? Why don't you just stand on street corners and charge a fee for a quickie? Isn't it just filmed prostitution? Do you really want to subject yourself to catching the AIDS virus? We've lost friends to this virus!" I desperately implore.

"It is not as if we have been sleeping together Nina! There is money to be made here! If you think small, you will always **be small**. For one, it is sex between consensual adults. Two, **everyone** gets tested. I can make nice money in a short amount of time. I have assets, Darling. I have what it takes to be the next Ron Jeremy." I didn't know who that was, and frankly didn't care. "You need to work on your provincial attitude! I, I, I do you know how to even think about anything but I?" Silence fills the room. I can't believe what he is saying and start to laugh uncontrollably. "There is a lot of money out there to be made. You saw the people at that party… I want a piece of that. Aren't you always complaining about money? Well here is an opportunity to make some really good cash! Mona says there could be work for you too…" I cut him off.

"Mona says, Mona says... Really Alfie, go live with Mona, she understands what you want better then I do. She can afford you. What she will do with you, I don't know. I reached for a cigarette, but put it back as I no longer want to smoke. "No, I no longer want to cloud my mind. There are too many things to deal with to just numb the pain and pretend all that we are going through does not exist. That's been our path for years and it has brought us to this negative place."

"It was that party Nina, ever since New Year's Eve. That party woke me up. I started to see things so much clearer." He inhales his cigarette deeply. "You're just going through withdrawals, for God's sakes smoke something Nina! I can't stand being with you like this. Take one of my mother's Valium. Why, you are all full of rage and you know, you have some serious issues with your anger - much like your mother." He laughs and reaches into his pocket for a vial of pills that he throws at me.

"No, I don't want that. You are right I do have issues and I am angry and it is all because of you." I throw the bottle of pills back at him. We fall silent for a moment. He takes a few pills at once. "Look, I no longer want to be sedated to get through life. I need to be clear about this and about you." I pace back and forth and reach for a cigarette anyway. "You want so much more than I am capable of giving, plus I want so much more than you can give. It is not me who is self involved - **it is you**! You are a narcissist!"

This pisses him off and he flicks lit matchsticks at me that burn on contact.

"Stop that!" I jump out of the way.

"Look you're exhausted. Let's go down to the diner and get some breakfast. Then stop off and get something to smoke. We're moving on Nina, it's just an eviction. Just hold on and everything will be ok. I promise. I feel it, money is around the corner."

"You promise, I have heard that before! Alfie, I am hungry and I've never had to face an eviction. I don't care to hang around and wait this out. We are moving on, but not together. This isn't a love affair this is an endurance test! I give up! Really Alfie, I love you, but I can't be in love with a man who chooses to be stoned all the time, or a man who sees his salvation and future in making porno films. Good luck, with all of that! Write me out of this script and get your shit out of here!" I say defiantly.

"You're a castrating bitch, Nina! I am finishing two scripts and have the potential of making nice money as an actor. Can't you realize the pressure I am under? Why can't you support me! How can you throw away what we have just because we have hit some hard times? You are a cunt! No wonder I don't want to fuck you anymore. Look at you; you are pathetic! Your skinny body has grown ugly to me." He punched the bathroom door in frustration creating a hole.

I go to the kitchen for a glass of brown water. I add some Tang and drink it down with a Valium. The drink is symbolic of our relationship, brown water covered with orange artificial flavoring and color. It tastes like rust but it is **his words** I find harder to swallow.

He continues, "You can be such a bitch Nina. There was a time that you were as sweet as sugar, my Cupcake. Now you are bitter and well frankly I have no interest in you. Still I was willing to stay with you because I understand commitment. I understand what love is." His words fall on me like rocks pounding away at my headache.

My emotions are all out of whack like my hormones. My nerves are as tight as a clock spring. My period is late, but I can tell it is coming. I am about to be evicted. I feel emotionally out of control. Yet I know I am right, and that my emotions and feelings are not due to my hormones. It is time to make all of this go away.

In the kitchen cabinet, I see my fiesta dishes, colorful and happy stacked up in a row. I couldn't sell them at the flea market. They were once a symbol of my new apartment, now they are all that is left. When I bought these dishes, I had wanted Alfie. I thought of that night setting the table and petting the cat that climbed up on the chair to see what I had done. I should have listened to that cat... This was a symbol of my independence, my coming of age. Night after night year after year these dishes sat empty as I went hungry. What kind of independence was that?

The Fiestaware in blue, and mauve, yellow and sage; one by one, I smash the dishes to the floor. First two green dishes, then the red cup with a chip, then I reach for the blue bowl. I had liked that blue bowl and put it back. One by one, I smash dishes to the ground, colorful hunks of ceramic blend on the floor like a mosaic. One by one they shatter into little pieces. They make the sound that I can no longer make.

Alfie tackles me to the floor and as my tears flow we roll onto the smashed dishes. "How can you say that to me?" I am shaking in anger. "I don't deserve that. If I have grown ugly to you then you have made me desperate and ugly." I bite his arm to make him let go and he slaps me hard!

"You bit me - are you insane? You have really lost it Nina. You need some professional help. Really I underestimated you, I thought you had more character then that, I was wrong!" Alfie quickly throws some clothes in a bag. "I can't believe I have been faithful to a woman who is willing to throw away love. Like you will ever find anyone to love you like I love you!"

Shaking, I try to speak. "It is I who have overestimated you. This struggle you choose to live every day, it has killed what love we may have had for each other. You can't care for me for you can't see beyond your own reflection. It's only about you. I am slowly dying here and you just keep walking over my body." It was quiet for a moment. "I have loved you with all my heart. I have been addicted to you, like a drug you have been under my skin, but now it is over."

"Fine, I'm going to Mona's! Now that is a **real** woman. She knows how to take care of a man." With that, the door slams and he is gone.

I curl up in a ball on the kitchen floor surrounded by colorful pieces of broken pottery. Tears roll down my face. I am sure the whole building was awake after all of that.

I wash the blood off my hands. Guess it was better than having killed him. I looked around and knew that this was it. Still shaking, I gathered the broken pieces into a bag. I am about to throw the bag away but instead I stuff it into an empty box. I will take the broken pieces and make something out of them, someday. With a marker, I label the box FIESTA BREAKDOWN and write down my feelings on a scrap of paper.

Standing soaked by summer rains,
You're in my heart and in my veins,
I've traveled far away from you,
But you followed me in all I do.

I found you locked behind a cage,
A wild animal full of turmoil and rage,
I chose your path and lived a wild,
Unleashed my passions and inner child.

Life as a struggle was all you knew,
Your struggle broke my heart in two.

Saturated by summer rains,
Sweet the destitute the exquisite pain,
Drenched by love that had gone astray,
I've traveled far to get away from you,
You no longer haunt me in all I do.

CHAPTER 21 – WINNING NUMBERS

Alfie is gone;
and I am not
upset about it.

I pack what is left of my things. The weekend is lonely but productive. On Monday, I plan to pay off the phone and electric bills and arrange for final shut off. Termination they call it. Termination I call it.

Sunday night 10:05 like clockwork, Alfie's mother calls after the weekly winning numbers are televised. Although her numbers came to her in a dream, her God did not feel it was her time. As the last disappointing ball drops, she dials the phone.

"Ciao Bella. There is noting but pasta and budder," she sobs into the phone. "I need a fifty to get me through the week. I will pay u's back. Let me talk to my Alfonso."

"I'm sorry your Alfonso is no longer here. I mean... he has been gone for days. We are being evicted and don't agree on how to move forward. I am afraid we are breaking up." I say in between her sobs. She seems to have heard and sobers up quickly.

"No, no, no, my Alfonso he loves you Bella, he will come back to you. You two are meant to be together I feel it in my heart. It is true love. I see it in his eyes, in yours." She hesitates, "you are like a daughter to me. I know he truly loves you." She pauses to light a cigarette. "Men they come and go, like dogs they are sometimes. They bark a lot, need to sniff around and pee on some trees. You look the other way. He is much like his father. You will see he loves you and will come back."

I laugh, "it isn't another tree, I mean woman, it is well, we are just too different. I do not want him back." I say followed by more silence as I listen to Sophia deeply inhale and exhale her smoke, just like her son does.

"I have loved Alfie. I did my best… but your son is not easy to live with. He makes life so very difficult. I tried Sophia, but I can't live like this any more. Your son needs a lot of attention, a lot of maintenance. If you know what I mean."

"Yes, maintenance, I know. Italian men have big egos. It starts in their pants." She says rather bluntly. "He wants what he wants when he wants. In that way, he is a lot like me that way."

"Yes." We both laugh. As we were being honest, I continue. "Alfie has addictions, Sophia, I know you understand that. His addictions come first; he sees nothing wrong with that. It takes everything to keep these addictions going. It is not just what he gets from you. He has other needs that are well insatiable. I'm not even sure I come in second place with him? I can no longer live on the edge."

"Yes, like the father, the drink came first until it killed him." She took another long drag from her cigarette. I wondered if now was not such a great time to give up cigarettes as well, as a relationship. Maybe I should get some cigarettes to pull me though all of this.

As we continued to talk like friends, I realized she understood exactly what I was saying. It was the best conversation we ever had woman-to woman. When we say our goodbyes I know I will never talk to her again and I will miss her sense of humor. It was as though she was my ally in the storm.

"I know my son is difficult man, hard to live with. I want to thank you for taking care of him over the years." She inhaled deeply. "So what will you do Bella?"

"I'm out of here in a week, moving back in with my mom. I will need to find a job, pay back some of this debt." I couldn't believe I was saying all of this. It was finally so real.

"You will do fine Bella. You are smart girl, I am sorry to lose you. Alfonso will be sorry to lose you; I know this. I wish you much luck. Ciao Bella." Sophia said sadly as we hung up.

I didn't want him back. I had said that out loud to his mother. I had been covering for him for years, carrying him for years, now it was over. He was no longer my responsibility. I felt lost and found, all at the same time! It was if I was let out of a prison, unchained, and now I was uncertain of which way to turn next.

Part of me was scared and the other part was determined to let go and start anew. With some money, I treated myself to dinner at the Jewish Deli. Potato pancakes with homemade applesauce, cabbage stuffed with rice, and a black and white cookie. The elderly man behind the counter added extra gravy to my dish and winked at me as his wife watched in horror. I bought myself a bottle of wine from the Tuscan region and a pack of Parliament cigarettes. I played the radio and enjoyed my meal in the remaining Fiestaware blue bowl. I ate everything until I was stuffed, then burped loudly quite pleased with myself.

With half a bottle of wine left, I head into the studio.

Portfolio Review

In the corner of the room, I find the portfolio that Ian gave to me and dusted it off. His card still in the inside pocket reads:

> *'Here is something to hold all your future artistic*
> *achievements.*
> *Always be creative, Love Ian.'*

Ian had been generous with gifts that encouraged my art and career. I learned so much traveling with him. For the two years we lived together, I never had to worry about paying the bills. I remembered how Ian longed to be a true artist but was unwilling to give up creature comforts. Checks from Mama brought fine restaurants and summer vacations. It came with such a price. When Mama passed away he took his inheritance and left New York. I heard he went to the South of France, bought a piece of property and settled there to paint and sail the Mediterranean Sea. He had always wanted to take me to the South of France, to see the beauty of the light that had attracted the Impressionist painters like Monet, Cezanne, and Van Gogh. Just thinking of him with his mobiles in the breeze, made me smile. He was a gift I had not been ready for.

Alfie was the complete opposite. He never cared for his creature comforts, never took care of life's day-to-day necessities. He felt that to struggle added to his life. His addictions gave him an insight to be a better writer. His addictions and denial kept him on a constant run. Catching up to a crisis instead of dealing with things in advance was nothing short of exhaustion. This is what he learned from his mother.

Both men loved and hated their mothers, were shaped by their mothers. Must make a note, I reached for a pad and pencil.

Next Relationship:

1- How a man treats his mother is how he will treat you.
Find someone who loves and respects his mother and he will treat you well.

I came across the notebook of the sketches I created in Italy, based on the farmhouse and the orchards that stretched to the horizon, like patchwork quilts. It was my summer of mosaics where my true love of mosaic art began. In the notebook was a picture I painted of the Tuscan road leading to the farmhouse. The road and farmland were painted in brush stroke textures in the style of Van Gogh. On a bench, were three artists, in front of their easels, painting the medieval hill town of San Gimignano. How inspiring they were.

I found ticket stubs from the boat that took us gambling in Venice. I remembered all the very rich people who looked miserable as they gambled away their money. Much like the people at the Black and White party. I guess sex isn't everything and money can't buy happiness. Clearly some money, and some sex together, a guy with a job; that would be nice!

2- Surround yourself with people who inspire you.
Avoid empty souls who seek drama.

I turn on the radio and pour some more wine. I'll drink to that. The radio plays a haunting ballad by Chris Isaak, about an obsessive love, called 'Wicked Game'. Mournfully he tells of a world on fire and no one could save him but his one desire. He sings of foolish games people play, and how dreams can go astray. In the song, he never wants to fall in love again.

"What a wicked game to play, to make me feel this way."

I can't help but cry at the pain and heartache falling in love can bring. The song touches me deeply. Maybe it is not the falling in love but the falling out of love?

I search through my bins and find some rejected paintings I did when I started working on the Levi's account. Working with

207

Martin had gotten me through college. As much as it was a struggle to keep up with his demands it did give me the flexibility to go back to school. Yes, I **did** drive him crazy those two years when I was in school. It was insane to think I could freelance and go to school at the same time. It was the most exhausting thing I ever did, next to this relationship, but I did it!

The chorus moans *"No I don't want to fall in love..."* As I write, cry, and remember.

3- Make fair sacrifices, be realistic and true to you.

Martin was furious with me, "Nina, I expect more from you, these are useless to me. The blue for this season leans to the green side. More turquoise less ultramarine! What you have done here is practically navy! Navy is not what I am after this season. You need to redo these." He could be such a queen at times - but he was right, I had run out of cerulean and tried twice to mix a blue by combining old blue paints. Martin had given me the work back and made me redo these overnight. I bought a tub of the cerulean blue that created the correct color in minutes. I masked off the other colors and sprayed the new color in its place; for the stripes this worked but the plaids needed to be done over. I worked all-night to correct the samples.

When I came home after handing in the work, I remember Alfie and I had a fight. We had a little money and I wanted to give half to the electric company to satisfy a payment agreement and get some food. He wanted to head to Off Track Betting to place a bet on some horse named Sugarcane. I won that fight but our fights took their toll as he always had more stamina then me.

These rejected paintings looked fine, even with the navy blue. Some things become such issues at the time, but in retrospect seem like nothing.

Two years later, I heard that Martin had died of complication of pneumonia that we are now calling AIDS. His ashes were scattered at his summerhouse on Fire Island surrounded by his friends. I remember that weekend, wanting to go, but not having the gas for the car or the fare for the ferry, to get across to the island.

So what difference did a blue really make in the big scheme of things?

I taped the painted textiles with double-stick tape and arrange them on a piece of mounting paper. Everything old looks new again and nothing lasts forever.

4- Life is short, live each day as if it were your last.

I dig further into a cabinet and find some paintings of tropical textiles. Palm trees and sailboats under full moons with an island rendered in an ocean of blues, in a Pointillist style. I had also created these for Levi's. I remembered being in a 7-11 store and the man in front of me had on a shirt with this design. I think he thought I was nuts when I got so excited about his shirt. It was the first time I had seen my work being worn on anyone. Alfie thought I was flirting with him and we had gotten into another huge fight.

5- Avoid unreasonable jealousy, it is a sign of insecurity.

I get out some tubes of paint and sketch out palm branches on the upper corner of the paper so that the motives extend to the mounting paper. I find a few old magazines on travel. God, how I want to travel again, I frantically cut out pictures of turtles, pelicans and surfers, add these to the opposite lower corner of the page, creating a collage.

6- Travel again, and find a relationship with common goals to share the world.

Next, I pulled some paisley patterns that I painted for Ralph Lauren. I remembered the culture of the Ralph Lauren office and how out of place I felt in that environment with everyone emerged in the Ralph Lauren style. Life is funny. If I didn't get delayed by meeting Ralph, if I hadn't stopped for almond-filled croissants, I wouldn't have run into Alfie that day on the street. I wondered at the strange turns life can take. Is it fate or a strange coincidence? A wicked game perhaps? Are we in control or is it predestined?

I tape a photo of a sailboat to the lower right corner of the tropical page. If it were not for that storm on the Ionian Sea, would I have jump-started my life on such a new course? Could I have stayed comfortable living with Ian?

7- Go with the flow but steer the boat when you can.

I take a break; head into the kitchen, there is a black and white cookie for dessert. Cake and cookies were my addiction. Being fat was my shield against the world. I thought I had found someone who truly loved me for me. I let myself get close and through our lifestyle (if you want to call it that) I lost almost 50 pounds. My body never looked so good. I had once thought that if I shed the weight I would feel beautiful and that would make me happy. I realized as I looked in the mirror, it isn't what's on the outside that makes you beautiful it is what is on the inside. When I was no longer overweight Alfie lost interest. What kind of love is that? I started to laugh at the irony.

8- Beauty is from within, no one can give you that or take it away.

In a large envelope I found more Ralph Lauren stuff, cuttings from the traditional tartan plaids that were used on a collection of pottery. I had a brochure of the collection that the designer was nice enough to have sent me. I mounted all of these on another sheet with fashion pictures that included a bulldog with a tartan bow.

I also found cuttings of pinstripe dress shirt stripes that were from my first job. I remember the trips to the copy room and being excited to see Alfie, when we first met, when he seemed so exotic. At that time, my desire for him consumed me like an addiction. I cut up the paintings and overlapped them to hide the spots where there were mistakes. I was good at hiding mistakes. With Alfie, my life had become a constant fight to hide the bad parts and just show the world that we were happy and in love. I was once in love but that had changed into destitution and desperation.

9- Find someone to help through the hardships and celebrate the good times.

I came across the photographs from my exhibition at Parsons. My subway signs were like friendly faces - Wall Street, Canal Street, and 5th – 6th Avenue. This was my true passion, my true love. I remembered the physical exhaustion of Canal Street. I looked upon the life-size mural taped to the wall above my studio. There were accomplishments made these past few years, it wasn't all that bad. I used the photographs and made a collage. I could talk about my upcoming exhibit.

In the midst of all this chaos, I had stopped working or thinking of the subway exhibit. It was winter, too cold to work underground. The drama of being evicted took over all my creative energy. I was too exhausted from the winter to feel any inner strength. I had one more sign I wanted to create for the exhibit. Fighting to save this apartment had made me forget that this was still in my future.

10- Challenge your self to be more then you can be. Find someone who can do the same.

I turn the pages of the magazine and there is a family, everyone happy as they play with the family dog. I tape the picture to the box with the pieces of broken Fiestaware. Maybe a future dream, but not for now; there are too many broken pieces that will need to come together.

11- Deeply fall in love with the right man and build a life together.

I turned the page of the magazine, *'Time for Change'* - the article read *'A woman changes every seven years',* I settled down to read, more than ready for a change.

12- Be true to yourself. When things aren't working, it is time for a change.

CHAPTER 22 - THE MOVING WALKWAY

Down the escalator of the International Terminal, the moving walkway carries passengers through a maze of tunnels. Sounds vibrate in the air like the tones on a xylophone. With each new note, the neon tubes along the walls alternate with a rainbow of colors, red, yellow, green, blue, violet - red, yellow, green, blue, violet.

A pre-recorded voice lets everyone know...

"The moving walkway is about to end.
The moving walkway is about to end."

Along the way, are posters of fabulous places for adventure: The Great Wall of China, the splendor of the Taj Mahal in India, the Eiffel Tower in Paris and the majestic pyramids of Egypt. I try to take them all in, but just as one moving walkway ends, another begins. The posters and moving walkways come and go quickly. I am led endlessly down a tunnel passing more posters of Greek temples, Roman ruins and the skyline of New York City. I keep walking. I am wheeling a carry-on bag dressed in a suit with heels that tap, tap, tap, between the moving walkways. I march faster to keep up with the rhythm and flashing neon lights, red, yellow, green, blue, violet - red, yellow, green, blue, violet.

"The moving walkway is about to end.
The moving walkway is about to end."

I follow along the path not sure where I am headed, but the colors and musical tones guide the way.

Morning's Train Whistle Blows

Colors turn to grey. In the distance, is the sound of a train whistle heading west, getting louder and bringing with it the morning sun. The whistle blows again as the first train of the day platforms in the sleepy town. I open my eyes to find a kitten curled up next to me in bed, purring.

Every day is a new beginning to breathe deep and to give thanks. I breathe in deeply and shake away my 'moving walkway dream'.

"Good morning Fez," as my kitten with sleepy eyes purrs louder. We both stretch not quite ready to get up. Sun pours through the windows, a hanging prism fragments the light into tiny specs of color that dance, creating a rainbow on the wall. The room is filled with hanging plants that also stretch toward the warmth of the morning light. The kitten runs to the sitting area jumping upon the white wicker love seat. He crawls up the brightly colored paisley pillows to get a view outside. To the east, a gold colored wall in the apartment glimmers and reflects the morning light.

It is my old room, my childhood apartment, updated. I had moved back home with mom across from the train tracks above Guy and Diane's Diner. Never can go home again - at least that's what they say!

When I first came home, I just crashed, mentally and physically exhausted and I spent a week in bed. Mom brought me fashion magazines and classic movie videos with Doris Day and Debbie Reynolds. Guy and Diane sent up my favorite Greek dishes, eggplant, chicken cutlets and Caesar salad - hold the anchovies!

Mom said color changes everything. She brought paint chips from the hardware store with plans of painting my room in bright colors. She made me get out of bed to choose colors. She brought me a box of lipstick samples, 25 tiny tubes to try on.

"With a new lipstick anything is possible," she said, "find a new one and create a new you."

"A lot like men." I said.

"Yes, but the right one is everything." She had a point.

Together we painted my room in tangerine and gold, with lots of turquoise accents. I realized my love of colors came from her. At the Valley Stream flea market we found the wicker furniture that we spray-painted white. We bought a bolt of turquoise paisley fabric from the 1950s and some new plates. With grandma's old sewing machine we created pillows and curtains. A few bottles of wine later, I had a new apartment.

"Colors make everything right again," mom said as she sewed a hem. "You need summer colors around you."

Mom was so happy that I was Alfie-free that she promised to never say I told you so, which I greatly appreciated. True to her word, she never did.

She took me to her salon for a makeover that included a real haircut with a perm and highlights. "You'll go on that interview looking like a million bucks." So I did!

As the first train left the platform and headed to the city, I pushed the ball of warm kitten fluff aside and made coffee to start the day. The kitchen windows are filled with African violets bursting with tiny purple and pink flowers. I mist them with a spray bottle. Fez curls around my legs letting me know he is hungry. I feed him and continue to water the many hanging plants placed up high so the kitten fluff cannot get to them.

A Vegas Wedding

On the table is a photo taken in Vegas of Mom and Fredrick and an Elvis impersonator on their wedding day.

Mom won a top sales award from Mary Kay, which included a trip to Vegas. Mom and Fred decided it was as good as anytime to get married.

We all flew down and had a great weekend. I lounged by the pool soaking up the Vegas sun and fruity rum drinks. Mom received her award at a company dinner with Fredrick proudly at her side. Fredrick liked blackjack, mom the roulette wheel; I had no money to waste. The IRS took what I could put together and settled years of past due taxes. What I had available went to a wedding gift. Fredrick paid for my ticket so I was here for the ride.

I walked around just watching the excitement and the people hypnotized by the slot machines. After a few rum and cokes I headed out to get some air and see what was happening on the street.

The air hit me like running into a wall. Dry and hot, one forgets when inside, in the nice oxygen induced air-conditioning that we are in the middle of a desert. I buy water from a vendor with green hair and arms covered in tattoos. He was from N.Y. too. The streets are a carnival of neon lights and sounds. Convertible cars run up and down the strip with tanned windblown people waving to their admiring fans as they race between bars. A group stumbles past me singing at the top of their lungs a song no one remembers the words to. It makes it all that much funnier. There are guys burnt like lobsters carrying tall plastic tubes filled with warm beer. Clearly, they have had many of these and are burnt out.

Twins walk by on stilts wearing matching red and white striped pants, oversized bow ties and top hats. One tips his hat to me and hands me a card advertising a late night masquerade. Groups of girls carrying their killer heels, wave down a limo as all spill inside. Gamble here, eat here, see and be seen here, says the blinking lights.

I duck into a few casinos before heading back to my hotel for another rum and coke. I hate casinos and meander to the elevator. In my room I pig-out on the overpriced peanuts and drink all the bottles of water. Saturday Night Live is on the TV. At least some things remain the same. Outside the night is full of action up and down the strip. My room is so high I don't hear any of the street noise. Loneliness has its merits. I fall asleep as the credits roll.

Hung-over, Sunday morning comes way too soon. I make my way to the lobby down a long corridor that sways like we are on a ship. The carpet is designed with oversized geometrics (like the designs I created with my Spirograph toy when I was a kid). I try to follow the design but the pattern only makes me dizzy. Even the elevator has flashing lights to announce the resort's evening attractions. More lights, music and dizzying carpet lead me through a maze of endless slot machines.

Scattered throughout are remnants of humans still playing slots from the night before. Bells ring as a group of silver-haired seniors in pastel polyester pantsuits, jump up and down and scream in excitement. The casino is a place where among the bells and lights are lonely people unaware of the new day outside.

I stumble through the aisles, hating this place, until I find food. I get an overpriced strong black coffee and a bagel with cream cheese. It costs me $12.00, and tastes like mud leftover from the night before. I hail a cab, which takes me to The Viva Las Vegas Wedding Chapel. Fredrick splurged for the 'Doo Wop Dinner Package' that proclaimed:

We Make Your Las Vegas Wedding
Dreams Come True!
At Viva Las Vegas Wedding Chapel,
 - we want your day to be picture perfect.
We strive to make your Las Vegas Wedding
 - memorable and stress-free.
We'll guide you through our many traditional wedding options
to help you to create a wedding that is uniquely yours!

Fredrick was proud; dressed like a gangster in a grey pinstriped suit. Mom was dressed as a flapper; a vision in beads that shimmered in the light. Equally as dazzling were her rhinestone chandelier earrings. She had on a hat with a peacock feather hanging over her eye. Her eyes were made up like Cleopatra, with dark eyeliner turned up at the sides bringing out the cat-like side of her. She was lovely, and truly happy balancing on her little royal blue stiletto heels - a vision of color!

There were a dozen of us. Mom invited some friends from Mary Kay who were in Vegas, women I had not seen in years. Fredrick's younger brother Mike and his wife sat next to me.

Elvis sang two songs and performed the ceremony with many a snarl and dramatic gestures. He was funny, stupid, but funny. There was a Doo Wop Lunch, a rose presentation, and garter unveiling. Elvis sang a few verses of **Love Me Tender** as Mom and Fredrick danced and posed for the 10 complimentary photo poses.

My framed photo is of Mom and Fredrick proudly showing off their official Elvis Certificate from the Doo Wop, Viva Las Vegas Wedding Chapel. She was lovely and never looked happier.

Mom kept saying it was all so sudden. For ten years they dated, waiting until the time was right, said Frederick. Seemed my moving back home made the timing right. Fredrick bought a little house by the highway and together they were fixing it up and planting a garden. I bought them a Cupid statue for their garden.

Mom was now busy, so on weekends I fixed up my apartment and slowly transformed it into, a textile paradise. In the living room I find the kitten on top of the coffee table. The table, (something cheap I found at a yard sale), is covered by a mosaic that was created from the broken pieces of Fiestaware. On top of the table is the last surviving blue Fiesta bowl that holds my current shade of lipstick *Uptown Girl* and the keys to my new life.

I take my kitten and a cup of coffee to the second bedroom, my Art Studio. The drawing table and a bookcase from the old apartment, now fills up a corner of the room. There is one Coke sign that I saved that hangs over the table. It reads, *"Things Go Better With Coke"*. On a long folding table are photographs of New York City grouped by neighborhoods, the beginnings of my next project.

In the corner is the Indiana Jones' **Raiders of the Lost Arc** promotional Harrison Ford cardboard cutout.

"Good morning Harrison, ready for another adventure?" I ask him this every day.

Harrison is a man of few words. I like that about him.

" I have a presentation today." I tell him. "What do you think, the blue dress or the long skirt?" I wait. "It needs to be French… OK, the long skirt it is."

God bless Harrison Ford. He continues to give me courage on my life crusade. Harrison, my roommate, my companion, my therapist, and my drinking buddy. Harrison can keep a secret as he drinks you under the table. I love that about him.

"Life is an adventure, kid." He would tell me silently, "Living well is the best revenge."

I slide on the black skirt, add a white top and a little black belt. To a sweater I add a peacock pin. It is a good luck charm from mom's wedding. My reflection in the mirror isn't bad. I've put on some weight but just enough. After a good night's sleep, I feel rested. In the bathroom, I apply lipstick in the mirror, which reflects a photo of the Gucci sisters on the opposite wall. I wonder where they are now.

I pet Fez goodbye and grab my keys. "Stay away from the plants!" Cats can look so innocent!

Guy and Diane welcomed me home like a wayward child back from the war. It **had** been a war. Their mission was now to fatten me up, and it was **my** mission to eat healthy, and in moderation. That meant more salads less cheese pie and French fries.

On Friday, the aroma of garlic chicken comes up through the floorboards. Yum, chicken cutlet day is still my favorite. The whistle of the next morning train blows as it platforms in town. I skip down the stairs to the diner where Diane hands me a cup of coffee in a paper cup covered with Apollo and The Parthenon. Above the counter are two figurines I bought from Greece, now covered in a layers of dust. One was a naked Poseidon, God of the Sea with his mighty trident, for Guy. The other was of Diana Goddess of the Moon and Hunt; for Diane.

Guy wraps up a sandwich sprinkled with Greek salad. I put it in my backpack to take on my journey.

"You're a sweetheart." I kiss him on his now graying forehead.

"Tell me something I don't know," he kisses me back. "Knock 'em dead kid," he says as he messes up my hair a bit, as he always liked to do. Diane tries to smooth it back as we kiss each other on both cheeks. I love these people, they are just like family.

I head to the pastry shoppe for an end of workweek treat. I say good morning to the bakers finishing their evening shift. They mock the once plump bohemian girl who now wears a size 8.

"Dressing for success?" asks Roberti waving a knife with buttercream frosting at me. "Looking good!"

I ordered a sweet dream cupcake, from the window display. There is a new salesgirl, bright eyed and naive as I once was. I wondered if she has dreams of a life beyond the small town? I hope her path will be less dramatic.

"Might want to put down the awning as the sun will melt the frosting on those layer cakes." I mention. She agrees curious as to why I might know this.

Ryan waves to me from behind the Deli counter. He was now a family man with three kids, having worked his way up to the position of Manager. I wave back.

"Selling any oatmeal?" I ask.

"Saturday sp-sp-special," he yells back.

Lannie, the crossing guard walks me across the street as if I need walking. She takes my arm to whisper in my ear the latest scandalous gossip; "So, Mr. P had an affair with his secretary. Seems it had been going on for several years. When Mrs. P found a hotel bill, she kicked him out, to the curb, she did. Just told him to keep walking after 20 years together." Lannie said all of this quickly as we crossed the street.

"Poor Mrs. P," I say.

"Poor nothing, she had a good lawyer, got the house and a nice settlement. She is opening a pet boutique down the block in the old shoemakers shop. A pet boutique," Lannie laughs, "seems that woman's best friend is her dog." We laugh.

Officer Nyburg rolls by in his new police vehicle. "See ya around 6" he yells to Lannie, as he waves to me. "Don't be late." He rides on by.

"Love will make you do strange things." I say, Lannie agrees, and I wonder what secrets she hides under her red hair and her military cap.

Melvin meets up with me at the train station. "Hey, I know you, it's been a while! You went away? Are you back now?"

"Yes Melvin I am back now." We have had this same conversation for months! Every morning he meets me as if I have just returned.

"Good, glad to see ya. Glad to see ya. Yes, gonna be a hot one today, awfully warm for this time of year," he yells out so everyone can hear.

"Yes Melvin, it certainly is." I shout back as I take my place with the morning commuters on the station platform.

"Sure, gonna be a hot one today!" he says again as he turns to find a new commuter to greet. "What about those Mets? Are they going all the way this year?"

The trains whistle blows in the distance and the bells of the gates begin clanking. Every day I enter a different train car to mix things up. I promise myself that even though I have joined the masses, I will try to live a life less ordinary, and take a slightly different path. I take a seat by the window where I see Melvin heading to the candy store. In the distance I see Mrs. P directing

219

workers as they hang a purple sign above her new shop that reads La Petite Amore.

The conductor takes my ticket, and punches the number that corresponds with the day, I fold my monthly pass back into my wallet; my business card falls out.

Gant Men's Sportswear – Assistant Designer

I have yet to grow tired of reading that and I slip the card and wallet back into my purse.

The interview lasted three hours. The Merchandise Manager interviewed me and reviewed my portfolio, followed by the Senior Designer and VP of Sales. When the HR person finally got to me, I was numb. Unlike the last full time job, this time it didn't feel like a death sentence. I was excited to have landed a job at such a great company.

After everything that went down, it was time to start a healthy new chapter as an Assistant Designer. With a steady paycheck, things could begin to get paid off. Student loans will take years, but at least I was earning a paycheck after all that education! I started a passport account so I can save up to travel again.

CHAPTER 23 – EAGLE EYES

At Penn Station I catch an Uptown subway to Rockefeller Plaza. Along the way, I watch the subway signs pass me by like dear old friends, 34th Street Penn Station, 42nd Street Times Square, 54th Street Rockefeller Center.

After much delay, The Transit Museum exhibit was a great success and held over for six additional months. Opening night was exciting. Many of my friends from the past showed up, which was such fun. My family: mom, Fredrick, Guy, and Diane danced to tunes played by a pianist. There was wine and cheese and three pounds of cookies from Roberti's. My job sent flowers and some of my colleagues also stopped by. It was a wonderful night!

I remember smiling a lot and shaking hands with a number of people I didn't even know. On opening night I met Dalton Edwards, a freelance writer for the ***Brooklyn Daily Eagle***. I liked his smile. I liked his eyes, clear, honest and determined. When he handed me his business card there was a spark between us. A spark. It was difficult to talk that night, but I caught him smiling at me a number of times throughout the evening. My mother said he asked a number of people questions about me. 'A very nice young man.' She and Fred liked him immediately. Three days later he called and asked for an interview.

We met in Brooklyn at Junior's, for their 'Worlds Most Famous Cheesecake'.

Once the coffee and cake were delivered he started to ask questions and take notes in a little pad.

"So you know, it is crazy to spend so much time in the subways. Dangerous. What made you do such a thing?" We divided the cheesecake, sharing a slice of chocolate and a slice dripping with cherries.

"I don't know, what makes any artist do what they do? I fell in love with mosaics while traveling in Italy. The Italians decorated everything with mosaics. I loved how they told stories to people who couldn't read. When I couldn't travel to Europe I looked to see what traditions N.Y. had in the mosaic art of storytelling. I found what I was looking for in the underground subways. Mosaics were durable to withstand cold and heat and still hold up. After 100 years they were neglected, hidden under decades of dirt, paint and graffiti. They endured. The ones from 1904 were quite ornate and decorative. I thought if I could show people what they see everyday in a different context they might stop a bit to notice their surroundings." The cherry slipped off my fork with a plop onto the plate and rolled off the table. We laughed as we both tried to catch it. I liked him, for he was easy to talk to.

"You accomplished that, the people at the show got it. I think the size of the pieces were what amazed people the most. In the subways the murals look small in comparison. The photographs are great as well; they really showed a variety of styles. You have a good eye. People **do** neglect the simple things that are around them and rituals and habits become everyday repetitions. It's good to see things from another vantage point, like being a tourist in your own land." He 'got me' too.

"So what is next?" He asked as he took notes.

"Next, why is there a need to be a next? Can it just be finished?" I laughed because I knew already he was right, there was a 'next'.

"Things lead to things. Nothing is ever just finished." He nodded his head. It was a nice head filled with insight, logic and sense. His eyes were deep blue, reassuring and kind.

"Well, I've been fascinated with subways and stations for so long. I am now interested in what happened above ground. Once the train was built and extended, above every station is a neighborhood that developed with pockets of immigrants, culture and industry. As transportation expanded so did the city limits. I would like to document neighborhoods before the turn of the next century." I admitted.

"Like a neighborhood time capsule. I like it." He nodded. "Well I guess then you have a vision of your next quest. Told you, something leads to something." Dalton and I left the restaurant and afterwards he shared his neighborhood of Brooklyn Heights with me. We walked to the promenade along the East River at the base of the Brooklyn Bridge.

"Have you ever walked across?" he asked as we rested on a park bench looking up at the underbelly of the massive bridge.

"No, guess I have to put that on the list." I said hoping it would be something we could one day do together. "I don't know a lot about Brooklyn."

"I would love to walk the bridge with you," he said as if knowing my inner thoughts. We finished the cheesecake smiling.

After the article appeared in the paper, Dalton called and asked for a date to see a movie in the Village. I wasn't so sure if I was ready for dating, but I looked forward to seeing him all week. After the movie we went for Mexican food. We walked around Washington Square Park and listened to some comedians. We watched some break-dancers and a guy playing on saxophone to his dog in a pink tutu howling the chorus on cue. Skateboarders rolled by, with the guys and girls sporting Mohawk hairstyles. There were cement tables with chessboards on top, where crowds of people gathered around to watch the masters play against each other.

Dalton had just finished a degree from NYU in Photojournalism, where he showed me around their campus. Many people knew him and were **so** glad to see him. We talked about NYU versus Parsons and our goal to pay back student loans and the shared love of new cultures and ultimate desire to travel. Dalton was dealing with a difficult breakup as well. We had a lot in common, but agreed at this point in our lives, we were not looking to start a relationship anytime soon. There was something about him that was comfortable, yet exciting, so we agreed to just continue as friends.

Our get-togethers are New York adventures. In Chinatown, we comb the shops for treasures, passing storefronts with barrels of strange herbs, dried mushrooms, and teas. Martial Arts shop with Kung Fu robes, knives, and ninja stars of death. There are vegetable vendors, fishmongers, and we stop to take pictures of storefront windows filled with hanging ducks with their heads still on. Jasmine tea and moon cakes are purchased and for dinner, we go underground to *Hung Fat,* feasting on: fried shrimp, Mongolian orange beef and assorted appetizers with sweet dipping sauce.

My fortune reads '*All is not lost, time forgets and forgives.*' His fortune states, '*The stars are aligned, the time is right.*'

On another night we met on Lexington Avenue to experience Little India. Dalton is running late from work, so I wait for him in a salon where I have my palms painted with henna. The woman stylist and I get to talk and before Dalton shows up, my hands and arms are covered in medallions and lotus blossoms.

"I see from your palm, you have man," she says as she turns my hands over and under. "Hmm, something old has passed and something new begins. This line says long life, here it says strong will and logic. Line of heart is fragmented at first though it ends strongly with much success! Do you have boyfriend?"

"No, ahhhh yes." I am not sure how to answer this. "Yes, a new man, we are just dating."

"I see this is good," she continues, "In my culture we don't believe in dating, the tradition is, that the family picks the match. I hardly knew my husband when we married. I wanted to be a nun but my family wanted grandchildren so I gave them four." She concludes proudly.

"Four, well good thing for them you didn't become a nun." We laugh.

"Good thing for me as well," she say with a smile. "You will have two children."

"Where does it say that?" I ask curiously.

"These lines here, and over here, are the lines of travel, - wow, you will go far!" She showed me lines on both sides of my palm being careful not to disturb the drying henna artwork. I see Dalton outside and wave.

As I paid my bill and tip her for the fortune, she suggests we eat at the buffet across the street, *Curry in a Hurry*. Once our trays are filled with Samosas, Chicken Tikka Masala and fried Paratha bread we ascend upstairs to a packed seating area, filled with Indian families. The food was excellent, though we spend the night laughing at what the outcome of curry in a hurry could bring.

One Sunday, we met at *Katz's Deli* for cheese blintzes and potato pancakes covered with sour cream and applesauce. Afterwards, we walked all over the Lower Eastside of Manhattan exploring the tenement buildings that lined what was once the Jewish section of Delancy and Essex Street. We bought pickles from a street vendor, a tradition that must have gone back a hundred years. Continuing, to the South Street Seaport, we ate our pickles and watched the Dayliners circle the island. We shared stories of our families and how our great grandparents came to New York to seek their fortune with hopes of returning one day to their homeland. Their journey had become our journey.

Wherever we went I took pictures of the neighborhoods, documenting the houses, the theaters, churches, storefronts, transportation and parks. Our journey through NY neighborhoods was starting to amass quite a collection of photographs in my studio. It was our ongoing joke that soon I would have Dalton over to see my photos. We were taking our time but we were more than ready.

In the summer, Dalton went on assignment with National Geographic to travel through Europe covering the summer music festivals. His postcards from Holland, Germany and Belgium hung on my refrigerator for inspiration. When he returned we met at a brewery in Williamsburg Brooklyn. It was a short walk from the Metropolitan stop on the G train. The old world Bavarian beer garden was ornate with carved wood. We had beer and mustard covered pretzels as he shared amazing stories of music gatherings and the people he met along the way.

Dalton brought me tulip bulbs from Holland, German fruitcake with rum, and dark Belgium chocolates that melted in your mouth. He told me all about the canals of Amsterdam, the Indonesian restaurants, beers at all hours, smoke houses and the red light district. I knew I loved him when he described his visit to the Van Gough museum and the passion behind the man.

I shared my summer stories, learning my new job, the Elvis wedding in Vegas, fixing up the apartment, my new kitten Fez, and weekends at Jones Beach baking in the summer sun.

"I've missed you more then I can begin to tell you," he said as he took my hand. The following weekend, we met after work on a Friday and took the Long Island Railroad to my place. It was time to see my pictures. We spent the weekend in bed with the cat, eating Chinese food. On Sunday we walked to the bakery to get breakfast. I introduced him to many smiling faces. It was as if everyone knew my secret – I found love!

CHAPTER 24
- DAN's THE MAN

In time the sadness lifted like a fog. At times, music would bring my heart back to feelings that still needed to be put to rest. I reminded myself, that this was not the love of my life. That comforted me in my lonelier moments. Every day, every week and every month that passed I grew stronger. Time created a distance from the prison that my relationship with Alfie had become. I rejoiced in my newfound freedom.

It had been a year since we last spoke. Remembering the last encounter...

"You'll thank me one day." Alfie said, as he handed me a bag of pignoli cookies, a parting gift from his mother. He then instructed two moving men to carry out his grandfather's brass bed, and some end tables from our apartment into a 'Dan's the Man' rented moving van. The man who never had any money had two men and a van to move him. Somehow he would always get by.

"Don't forget your boxes of books and tapes." I said gesturing to the back corner of the room. The men picked these up as well, interested in the porno tapes that sat on top of the box.

"What happened to the Gucci sisters?" Alfie asked looking around at what was now a completely empty apartment.

"I sold them to the antique dealer to settle some accounts." I lied. The antique dealer, now a friend of mine, suggested I take them to his friend at the auction house. I borrowed my mother's car and brought them over in pieces, assembled them and dressed them in flamenco costumes that were discarded when the dancer and her son were evicted. Seems many of us were living on borrowed time. The Gucci sisters were stunning in their colorful attire. I took a picture to remember them by. At auction they brought in $1100. After the house cut I landed up with over $1050, a down payment to negotiate a settlement with the IRS.

"I would have liked them," he said bluntly.

"Well there were things to pay off. You left, remember... so I was left to handle things." I said in controlled anger. "You always made me handle things."

"You look good," he said looking to change the subject. I was thinking the same of him. His hair was styled, still sexy and long but cared for. He had on a new shirt and had eaten. I was wearing a hand-me-down dress from my mother and had my hair up in curls. I wanted him to want me and remember me as being beautiful. I had put on makeup and painted my toes a bright red.

Presently, as the effect was working on him, I wondered why I needed the validation. Did I really want him to want me one last time? The answer was yes, just so I could walk away.

"We could ask them to bring the bed back up... once more for old times sake?" He brushed my arm with his hand. As always, chills ran up my spine. I actually thought about it fleetingly.

"No." I said abruptly, trying to shake the spell that he so easily could put me under. "We need to be a memory." I said with a smile, pushing away his touch. He sadly agreed.

"A wonderful memory you will always be." He kissed my hand gently, not wanting to let go. "I will always love you." His lips caressed my skin.

Slowly, I removed my hand from his and backed away. Determined, I fought his charms and focused on the move. As the two men came down the stairs arms loaded.

With the remainder of his things gone, I closed the door for the last time and we walked down the stairs together. It was really over, terminated was the word used by the utility companies. Terminated was the term I used for this relationship. It sounded so completely final, people didn't ask many questions after that.

Alfie tried to put his arm around me but I backed away. Outside of the building, he took my hand and kissed it again, always the romantic. He asked one last time if I would join him, "I'll make it up to you, we'll laugh about it all then."

"I'm laughing now, ecstatic that it is over." I tried to be brave but my vulnerability still came through as my lower lip quivered. I held back my tears and took back my hand, determined to be brave until he was gone.

"I will always love you, my Cupcake. You know, love is never having to say you're sorry." I thought that was a stupid remark and almost wished that he were a man enough to say he was sorry. Sorry for all the shit he had put me thought; the hard times, the poverty, desperation and struggle.

"Just think of how much you grew as a person living with me. Think of how boring you would have been, if you had never met me," he was arrogant till the end, smiling. He made me laugh not knowing if he was philosophically deep or just stupid?

"Forgive me, if I forget to thank you. I look forward to being bored for a while, it will be a nice change of pace." His hands reach around me and under my shirt. Old habits are hard to break. I moved away, no longer wanting to let him so near.

"No, I am no longer yours." These words cut him but he brushed them aside.

Instead, he offered me a final cigarette. In his European way he lights it for me and looks deeply into my eyes. His eyes reflected no light; they were tired, stone cold, and dead. What id I ever see in this man? As I inhaled the smoke it tasted gross, stale like death on my tongue - dead as this relationship had become.

"We are terminated," I whisper.

He shakes his head in sadness. "You'll miss me," he says.

"You will miss me more," I say flippantly, as we try to laugh away our pain.

"I **will** miss you." He says back, in a whisper. "We had some laughs…"

Together we smoke in silence, remembering when we were in love and happy. We terminate our cigarettes smudging the burnt ends into the sidewalk.

"Ok, well goodbye for now," he says.

"Goodbye."

We hug each other tightly, neither one of us wanting to let go. Alfie joins the men in the 'Dan in the Man' van and he is off in a trail of smoke, gone from my life for good. I choke on the exhaust fumes hugging my bag of cookies.

I head to the Chinese restaurant and order enough food for two people. I never saw Alfie ever again.

Sometimes, when I have time to sit still, my mind thinks about him. In retrospect, it seems like some bad horror film I watched. Where the heroine runs into the cemetery to escape the danger. The audience yells, "Don't go in there," but she just keeps running and doesn't listen. I was that girl in the cemetery, but I escaped.

Harrison, Drinks and Therapy

In my new apartment, Harrison Ford and I spent many nights over Chardonnay examining why I put up with Alfie for so long. I read books to Harrison that I borrowed from the library: *The Narcissist Among Us, Understanding Addictive Personalities and their Enablers, and The Silence of Abuse.*

From all that I read, I realized Alfie was lost, lost like me. He was pampered by overprotective women and never grew up. He could be handsome, charming and eloquent, or ugly, angry and cruel. Depending on the cocktail of substances in his body you never knew which of his personalities was about. The world had let him down when he was just a boy. His scars wrapped around his frustration making him an angry man. Drugs numbed the pain, sex made him feel something, but there was never enough of either.

He was self-absorbed, a narcissist checking his reflection for its perfection. He was taught that he was a prince among men, and that it was just a matter of time till the world saw him as the star he truly was. He had talent but could not get beyond the walls he built up. His self-inflicted addictions consumed his every day. He would never find a world where he could belong…

His parting gift was a copy of the book *Naked Lunch*. " My favorite author, if you read this you will understand me better."

I read the book. William Burroughs, the author, longed to be a heroin junkie living on the streets searching for the next fix. Life was seen through a haze of illusions. Like a surreal Salvador Dali painting all oozing and melting a mix of bazar dimensions, as a time clock ticks away at your existence. I read the book and threw it away not being 'into' Surrealism.

What made me think I could have saved him? I asked myself this question a lot. I felt the same pain of being abandoned and rejected as a child. I too had lost my father and needed to somehow figure it out on my own. Maybe I thought if I could right his wrong I would somehow right my own?

The last I heard of Alfie, he was working on an Off-Broadway musical called *Sour Balls and Pickles*. It was a workshop idea he and Mona had on fetishes, and she had found some backers to help set it up. I saw the ads in the Village Voice for the Off-Broadway production that ran for two weeks and was badly panned. Alfie never made it into porno films but his brass bed was featured in a video called *Brass and Ass*.

By summer, the headline of the *New York Post* featured Derrick Storm and his wife being arrested for insider trading. The trial was extremely scandalous and he was also connected with illegal prostitution and judicial corruption. All his assets were seized. On the top of the list was the penthouse apartment at the McAlpin Towers and his lucrative porno business. To avoid the scandal, Mona left the country and headed to be with her father in Japan. The last I heard of Alfie, he was living with his mother and the brass bed in a basement apartment in Jackson Heights.

CHAPTER 25 - INSPIRATION BOARD

That, which does not kill you,
makes you stronger...

After life with Alfie, I don't stress the small stuff and everyday I am grateful that my life has possibilities. I count my blessings choosing which things matter most to me. I feel that for sometime, I had been dead. I had died of a cancer that required all my energy to overcome. I had died, and was born again with all my senses acutely aware of the beauty of my surroundings. Harrison Ford reminds me every day that life is an adventure and I am determined to live it to the fullest. For this I am most thankful.

At my new job, the office space had been recently remodeled to be an open workspace, allowing for collaboration between design departments. The Inspiration Room was at the center of the building open to many corridors and offices that glowed with natural light coming through huge windows. The round room was the collaboration and inspiration area where we would have meetings.

At the Korean market I bought a bouquet of sunflowers that I placed in a vase at the center of the round table. On the inspiration walls I had hung several postcards of Van Gogh paintings of sunflowers and the French fields at harvest layered in colorful brush strokes.

I liked to come in early and enjoy the place before it became busy. This morning everyone was in by 8:30 a.m. preparing for the meeting. The morning was spent sharing new concepts for the Summer Collection, which was to be inspired by 'All Things French'. I shared my stories of my train ride through France and the fields of sunflowers. I compared the textures in the paintings to the flowers on the table and everyone enjoyed my presentation. I talked about how artists like Van Gogh, Cezanne, Picasso and Matisse went to the South of France in search of the light, a light that reflected off the Mediterranean Sea intensifying all colors.

I was assigned to the Men's Swimwear Collection. On the segment of the wall that was dedicated to swimwear, were scraps of ideas: sailing boats, yachts, maps of the Mediterranean Sea, sea creatures and mermaids, and my Van Gogh postcards.

During the meeting, our senior merchandiser, Jack, encouraged collaboration, which made for an exciting meeting. He was an excellent leader and we all worked hard to meet his approval.

"Great job everyone." Jack said as he contemplated, deep in thought, his fingers touching each other, as if in prayer. "Brian, you will cover the New York / French influence. What is French in our pop culture? What is on display in our city museums? Melissa, I would like to you to research how we have interpreted French style in fashion? Leslie and Nina, you two seem to have an understanding of the brand and the scope of this season. I like your energy. I need to go to the corporate office overseas. Why don't you meet me in Paris?"

I swallowed hard, 'why don't you meet me in Paris?' was not a question you hear every day. My heart began to race and I hoped I wasn't blushing.

"Yes we can shop the market for inspiration. I will sit down with my calendar this afternoon and give you both the dates by the end of the day. Nina, do you have a current passport?"

"I... no, it has expired." I say mindlessly lost in a Parisian dream.

"Well then you should expedite your passport immediately. There is a passport office right at Rockefeller Plaza - go over there at lunchtime. - Expense it." It was set, just like that!

A Dish Best Served Cold

As I stood at the passport office filling out the forms, I kept saying it over and over in my head. 'Why don't you meet me in Paris'. I was being sent to Paris.

Filling out forms and standing in line took most of the lunch hour. I had less than 15 minutes left. Quickly, I ate my chicken sandwich in the shade of the skyscrapers of Rockefeller Plaza. I watched the masses of people wandering around in the last of the autumn warmth. There were busloads of tourists taking pictures. It was several years since my first job, wandering around Midtown on my lunch hours. Several years later, I was a new woman with an opportunity to travel to Paris. I couldn't wait to tell Dalton. I couldn't wait to tell my mother, she had always wanted to travel to Paris. I would need some new clothes.

Walking around Rockefeller Center I realized that in a few weeks the fountain would turn into an ice skating rink then, the tree would be put up to welcome the Christmas season. Winter would be here soon and I looked forward to seeing the window decorations and watching the skaters under the colored lights of the Christmas tree. I looked forward to sharing that with Dalton. I looked forward to many things.

There were so many wonderful things that Dalton and I shared in common. One was our wanderlust, a desire to travel and experience new cultures. After his return from Europe, he submitted a proposal with National Geographic to cover the World Music Festival next spring in Morocco. By then, I would have some vacation time and some money put aside. He said that I

234

could be his camerawoman and that the magazine would cover expenses. The trip would begin in Fez to cover the music festival. From there we could take a trip to visit the mosaics in the ancient city of Volubilis. Then we would take a train to the ancient city of Marrakesh. It was my dream trip.

Among the stores in the Plaza was a travel bookstore. I went in and bought a book on Paris that had an excellent street map and a book on Morocco past, present, future.

I took-out an iced coffee at Dean and DeLuca and headed back to the office.

I passed the Gucci store and admired the new mannequins dressed in leather for fall. Like my Gucci sisters, they were statuesque and beautiful but different. They were silver, streamlined, their features less realistic - more abstract, ready for a new season. How far I had come since that Holiday eviction and liquidation sale of all my possessions. ...It just seemed like a bad dream...

Seasons change; it was time to move on.

Crossing through the lobby, I say "Hello" to the guard at the front desk and take an elevator to the third floor. I use a special key pass to open the electronic doors to the office. My desk has a window with a small view that overlooks the traffic on 5th Avenue. From the corner of the window if you stretch, you can see the statue of Atlas holding up the world upon his shoulders. My burden was now lifted and I was ready for new quests to begin.

I sip my iced coffee, as I spend the afternoon preparing tech files for production and cutting up samples with color chips for the mill.

The bells of Saint Patrick's Cathedral chime three times. When I reach for my bag, next to my Mary Kay cosmetics and my tour books of Paris and Morocco, I discover the Roberti's Pastry Shoppe bag! It is Friday, three o'clock - time for my weekly treat, a dream cupcake. I open the book on Morocco and turn to the chapter on *The Souks of Marrakech*. I take a bite and daydream!

A life well lived is the best revenge.
  Revenge like dessert, is a dish best served cold!

Made in the USA
Lexington, KY
25 February 2017